Jack's Back

Michael Adrian Cote

AuthorHouse™
1663 Liberty Drive
Bloomington, IN 47403
www.authorhouse.com
Phone: 1-800-839-8640

Published by AuthorHouse 12/19/2014

ISBN: 978-1-4969-5652-1 (sc)
ISBN: 978-1-4969-5651-4 (e)

Library of Congress Control Number: 2014921345

To my friend Renee Shenesky
Who inspired me to finish
this book. Thank you for your
friendship, your honesty and
above all, your encouragement.

THE DEVILS MEAN STREAK

The devils got a mean streak
And he's knocking on your door
But don't let the devil in
Cause he's rotten to the core

Hell trick you into believing
That the wrong you do is right
And make you take the wrap
While he stays outta sight

Hell pretend he's your friend
Then stab you in the back
And laugh his evil laugh
Right after the attack

The devils got a mean streak
So don't let the devil in
Cause with the devil on your side
You know you'll never win

Paula Claire Roberts

Jack's back

Charles Van Helsang was banished from the ranks of his fellow scientists. He was a very introverted man and did not have many friends at all. It's been rumored throughout the hierarchy of his colleagues for many years that the good doctor was actually incapable of making any lasting relationships, especially on a personal level, and despite repeated attempts to befriend him. No one could penetrate that solid indestructible brick wall he so adamantly kept erected.

They thought of him as somewhat eccentric and brilliant. No one ever knew he had a special hidden agenda. Charles Van Helsang secretly continued his forbidding experiments with a vengeance. He devoted many hours arranging, organizing and configuring his new home-based laboratory. It had all the latest electronic equipment. Video surveillance cameras were installed all along the perimeter of his property. There were motion detectors and sensors so delicate that when tuned properly can detect the movements of the tiniest field mouse. This network of security made Charles feel very, very comfortable. No one can approach his home now without him noticing, the state of the art security system was outstanding. Like in the building in which he used to work, he now has somber solitude in his home.

Charles Van Helsang is clearly a man ahead of his time. Although he had to make a recent location change, he did not stop making public appearances. He had to keep up relatively minor schedule for public speaking engagements. Every so often he would have to speak on his accomplishments with his most current work to date. He was a very shrewd man. He made sure his private investors were pleased and intrigued with the research he was engaged in. Whatever questions that were directed to Charles from his supporters were immediately answered with a dialog and portrayal of a poetic narrator. Charles was still privately funded for his medical research for infectious disease treatments, along with cancer research and cures. Charles already had won critical acclaim for more than one discovery of treatment for blood infections, and the annihilation of two separate cancers which infect the deepest regions of the human mind. In addition to his unprecedented discoveries he also wrote articles and gave lectures at prestigious Universities, such as Harvard and

Yale. All public interaction unnerves Doctor Charles Van Helsang, but he also knew it was essential and absolutely necessary to ensure his private funding. Charles did not have to like it but he also knew it was benevolent to his prolonged influx of cold hard currency.

Born in New England Charles Van Helsang is the great grandson of the well-publicized and renowned Doctor Michael Van Helsang. A great pioneer in his field! Doctor Michael Van Helsang was the most famous Doctor/Scientist England has ever known. He was a very tall man standing six feet and three inches tall. He had an athletic build with bleach white hair and a thick handle bar mustache to match. Some say he was very charismatic, especially when it came to the ladies. An unusual ladies man considering the long hours of work he maintained at such a demanding profession. What no one ever knew was that Michael had a secret only he himself knew of, a frighteningly dark secret.

Charles Van Helsangs childhood was stricken with poverty. There was hardly enough money for food, in fact sometimes there was just enough food for him and nothing at all for his parents. His mother cried often because of the struggles Charles had in school maintaining his grades; he took a lot of time off from school to work in the fields in order to be of help to provide food for the table. Things went on like this, seemed like a life time and that was only until his father accidentally discovered his grandfather's lost will of rights. Upon reading the will and unknowing to anyone, Charles's family inherits his grandfather's estate with a very large sum of money being held at the State National Bank as we speak. From that very moment Charles's parents never went without ever again, and that include Charles. Charles's grades in school improved tremendously as he ended junior high school. His high school days were even more enlightening to his parents' surprise. He was a grade A student and he quickly found out he had his father's strength and agility as he excelled in a number of sports including; baseball, football, track and field and even wrestling. His favorite sport of them all was football, the quarterback position. As Charles did understandably poor in grammar school he excelled in high school graduating top of his class and was the schools proud valedictorian. His family couldn't be more proud. He only wishes his real parents were still alive to see it. Charles was an only child, his mother died while giving birth to him so he never did get a chance to get to know her but he always felt her, her spirit that is! His father passed a year before Charles entered high school. Charles became a loner after his dad passed away and his aunt Peggy raised him ever since. She was a very kind and gentle lady and told him endless stories about his mother. His mom and she were best friends in fact; it was Aunt Peggy who introduced his mother to his father. So you see there was no way anyone else would be raising little Charles because Aunt Peggy felt highly obligated to him. It was simply out of the question to even ponder the thought. Aunt Peggy was so proud of Charles. Charles had not only received an academic scholarship for maintaining an impressive 4.0 grade point average he also received an athletic scholarship in football. Charles was an excellent athlete as well as a fine young gentleman. Aunt Peggy was beaming with pride that afternoon when Charles nervously opened a letter from Yale University; she knew it was a day to remember. Charles was so excited and thrilled; he could hardly believe this was happening to him.

Charles went on to study Nano Technology and also excelled in Biology. He went on to become one of Yale Universities' elite members. His studies were meticulously entwined; live organisms created at the atomic level possessing incredible intelligence. They actually communicate with Microcomputers back and forth with each other. His college years were a mirror image of his high school years when it came to making friends or communicating on any personal level. Charles was very quiet and really had no true friends. The closest people to him outside of Aunt Peggy were his college professors, his Biology Professor and his Science Professor especially. Though he played football and was a star quarterback, he always declined party invitations after games. His excuse time and again was that he had too much work to do in Biology. Charles worked endlessly on microscopic organisms. His dreams were of being a pioneer in a forbidding scientific research. Charles was secretly interested in; cloning.

Charles lives outside of New England, north east of the United States in a very old Historic Town. It's a very old house in Stockbridge Massachusetts. Its miles away from the nearest town and any neighbors were far and few between. His nearest neighbor was three miles south east from his home. Charles equipped a moderate laboratory on the second floor of his home directly above the enormous elaborate library where he could always find his aunt enjoying a good book. Charles Aunt Peggy remained on the first floor while Charles resides on the second floor within ear shot of the lab. The house was of an enormous Victorian style, it was very warm and comfortable. There were eight fire places, one in each of the bedrooms with which made cozy warm winter nights. Not a night went by in the winter when there wasn't a crackling fire, a cup of tea and a soft light in a comfortable reclining chair, and Aunt Peggy cuddled up in it totally absorbed in a book. The library is also used as an office. It was Charles's great grandfather's favorite room in the entire house. Aunt Peggy told him endless stories of how his great grandfather used to entertain guests and how the evenings ended with everyone retreating into the library for drinks and cigars. Associates and friends traveled long distances and with the New England chill in the air, a night cap was just the thing to keep warm during the ride home.

Charles Van Helsang dedicated most of his time experimenting with cloning and crossbreeding. His agricultural work was also astounding and Charles was very proud of his accomplishments with this work. Charles created numerous new breeds of plants and vegetation which intern drastically improved certain medicinal treatments pertaining to cancer. Cloning and crossbreeding isn't exactly an invented procedure. It's been happening for centuries by plants and vegetation's on their own with a little help from Mother Nature of course. They pollinate each other to create new species all the time. Nature has adapted to its ever changing environment which is exactly what we as humans should always do when ever scientists discover a new treatment. Sometimes this work is so controversial and is met with adamant protesters against it. They are quickly and proficiently explained to that this is essential work for the future cures and eradication of life threatening and life altering diseases. Not only are cloning and crossbreeding experiments advancing medicinal treatment and therapy's alike, they are also inventing new plant and flower species for visual pleasures. In the lab are some of the most unusual and exotic flowers man has yet to see.

Charles Van Helsangs work was and is very controversial. His colleagues made no conscience effort to diminish their own feelings and comments towards Charles's research. They said that Charles's thoughts ran wild at times thinking everyone was out to get him. It was never like this before; he just couldn't understand why people looked down upon him. He thinks he knows! It all seemed to have started when he took the sudden turn or detour, as you will, and started a taboo research. A forbidding practice thought by his now estranged colleagues.

Even though Charles Van Helsang is a very distinguished scientist revered throughout not only the United States but almost the entire world. He ignored repeated attempts to be persuaded from this barbaric impulse to experiment with animals, so he moved his research to his home and continued his research in secrecy.

No one is going to interfere with his dream, his life's work. His cloning experiments will flourish one day, and he'll prove to the world that he was a man clearly ahead of his time.

Years went by and although Charles has many disastrous results crossbreeding he continued his research, he was relentless. Aunt Peggy no longer lived with him as she became more and more dependent on people to help her get around, so Charles sadly opted for a very comfortable and classy retirement home. If she had to go he made sure she was well taken care of. Charles moved his Aunt, his mother's sister to a very beautiful and well maintained convalescent home. It was and is a picturesque country setting North West of their home in Stockbridge. An elegant residence built for comfort deep in the Adirondack Mountains of New York. The grounds keeper lived on the property with his family. He worked full time year round which attuned why the plush landscape was revered throughout the surrounding communities. Mr. Parker, the grounds keeper was offered numerous jobs and had many opportunities with much greater pay to leave the Adirondacks and work for someone else, but he just couldn't see it happening. Mr. Parker was born and raised here with deep roots. There was no way or any amount of money which could attempt him and his family to leave their warm comfortable home.

Charles methodically documented his research and experiments, a very tiresome and tedious task in which he had very little pleasure especially when his latest results have much to be desired. In the beginning of his scientific home endeavor he had many failed experiments with his cloning. He began these experiments with mice. It was indeed very depressing from time to time. The mice were very deformed all the time. They had missing limbs and some were deformed beyond recognition. Feet were missing and twisted and mangled in some cases, some of them had no toes; some of their eyes were misshapen and missing entirely. The same thing happens to their ears. Their fur was somewhat matted, short, long, and every now and then there was no fur at all. They say scientists are very patient people, they are persistent but they are also, human. Sometimes disappointment plays a depressing part of life so whenever Charles felt he was heading in this direction which wasn't very often; he would take a drive into the next town and stop in one of his favorite pubs. It was called the Golden Cage. Charles would sit at the bar and have a few drinks, chat with the bartender and wait for his friend to show up. Barbara was a very beautiful red head, she didn't ask questions, she just knew. She was not an employee of the Golden Cage but she did use it as what someone would say a home based office away from home. Barbara was a lady of the night and she made no qualms about her chosen profession.

Barbara was the only person who could distract Charles of his daily grind of experiments, and what pleased him most was neither of them had to speak a word to each other. Eye contact spoke volumes. Barbara was a pleasant get away from his routine. Not only were there miss-shapes with mice, there were other species that Charles had problems with too. Charles thought he might have different results if he tried his experiments with birds. Maybe the structure of their DNA would prove to be more adaptable. After another painstaking year to a year and a half, this once new theory didn't fare any better than the mice. The birds developed with the same type of maimed deformities. Some birds had no beaks; some had missing wings and mangled wings, no legs, and one experiment yielded a featherless bird. All in all he theorized that it was a grotesque display. Still, Charles was relentless and it sometimes drove him deeper and deeper into his work. Every miscalculation was meticulously documented. His obsession grew to extreme proportions. Whenever he went into his kitchen for a bite to eat he couldn't help but think of his Aunt Peggy and quickly was relieved that she no longer resided in the same house, only out of fear of what she might say about his lack of hygiene and his severe weight loss. He knows she would chastise him about his personal neglect, in an elegant forthright manner of course. As he thought of her, he smiled.

One night when Charles was fast asleep in a chair in his laboratory, he was dreaming of winning a Nobel Prize. He had successfully cloned a human being in his dream. There's no limit to what a cloned human being would mean throughout the entire scientific world. People will have new hope for all kinds of possibilities. When it is known that certain couples could not have children, cloning will make that possible. Cloning will bring new research for all types of ailments and cancers. Of course he would be richly famous beyond his wildest dreams. The military would definitely be an interested party. However this experiment was still a dream. Charles was awakened by a strange sound. I must have been dreaming, he mused. Then that same noise erupted again. It was his security system; someone was entering through his driveway. He looked at his computer screen; it was the delivery truck that he was expecting. It just so happened to be a day early.

Charles was eager to meet with this delivery man for he was anxiously waiting for some new supplies that he believed would be the missing element to his immediate experiments.

Charles Van Helsang was feverishly intent on becoming the most famous scientist in history, and this delivery could quite possibly be the last piece to the puzzle. As a matter of fact, Charles was ninety five percent sure that this is the defining key. After receiving the package he stops by the kitchen for a quick sandwich and a bottle of fine scotch to bring up to the lab. Charles starts to sweat as he slowly approaches his lab; he has this overwhelming feeling of apprehension. It's quite uncomfortable. This is it he said to himself. This is the day I create history! Charles new calculations will soon be put to the test today. It took six long hours to put this whole test together and his patience is running thin and this discernible test will start in mere seconds.

There's no possible way in the world to comprehend the full magnitude this very possible break through tonight. My god he muses, I'm a nervous wreck. I wonder if this is how an expectant father feels on the day of his wife's delivery. The most minute of details won't be visible for at least ten days from now; the suspense is driving me mad. A mixture of enzymes, protein and another unnamed liquid substance derived from a chromosome of human DNA. This particular substance is believed to be the key ingredient all placed in a clear glass flask, carefully placed atop of a circular contraption that moves around and around. The machine is small and is kind of reminiscent of an old phonograph, or maybe a record player like the one Aunt Peggy use to have down in her bedroom. Obviously it was some type of mixing device used in the medical field. Known only to himself, his intent was not only to successfully clone these mice but to also go on to something unheard of in the medical world; to create life without the assistance of a female. I will go on to clone the most intelligent human being on the planet! It will end up the most renowned discovery of mankind. It's no wonder Charles Van Helsang was an outcast from his colleagues. A movie buff would even venture to say he was, and is a mad scientist and that this kind of stuff only happens in the movies. This is precisely why he has an elaborate security system. His work is considered top secret as far as he is concerned.

Everything has been going as planned, it's been nine days and the first signs of life are looking very positive and just a few more days now and I will be ninety percent sure of the outcome. These mice will go down in history.

In the coming weeks a miracle ensues. Two perfectly formed mice were slowly developing in the laboratory.

His work was in its homestretch. Charles inscribes into his journal; my destiny is yet to come. Though I have nearly completed this important stage in cloning these tiny creatures, I must not allow myself to get anxious. I will, have a son! But only and I stress only when I'm completely satisfied that I have completely isolated every single aspect without question pertaining to this ground breaking research.

One night when Charles was fast asleep he was dreaming of someday having own family. It was a pleasant day, he was playing catch with his son and he looked like he was very happy. While Charles was dreaming about his future he awoke abruptly with an intriguing idea. I think I just figured out what was missing. Charles immediately went into his laboratory and started mixing and measuring. He was ecstatic as he swiftly moved along, he was visibly glowing.

It's been a few months now and all his crossbreeding experiments are starting to come to fruition. The next dry run will clear up all past doubts. Three weeks from now under microscope, I will see the physiological changes that I've been longing for.

Journal entry; I don't know if it's a miracle or if it is indeed a grotesque miss use of science. In either case it is a significant breakthrough in my own research, and I can't help but feel entranced and blissfully happy. A celebration is in order. Charles had Barbara on his mind. Tomorrow night I am going to the Golden Cage; I'm going to mingle, drink and dance, it's going to be a wonderful night.

This is a defining moment in my life and I'm making the most of it tonight, and so what that I can't share the news with someone right now. I'm climbing out of my shell tonight and I'm solemnly marking this day as my historical merry occasion.

The night went a planned. Barbara was very receptive and they both danced the night away. They laughed and played and had a terrific time, and it didn't end until they awoke together the next morning.

The crossbreeding experiment was successful and on one very late night an escape was in progress. As Charles was fast asleep he had forgotten to lock the cage of his "prize mice "It was his first breakthrough, they weren't just ordinary mice. They were special and now they had escaped. There were two of them each unique and first of their kind. One of them was crossbred with a dog and its companion was crossbred with a cat. They were much more intelligent than any normal mouse, and finding them will more than likely pose a tiresome search. So instead of looking for them Charles had planted some food and special traps for them not to get hurt, and he did this throughout the entire second floor of his home. After all, Charles attention is specifically focused on his immediate future. Charles lifelong dream is imminent; it'll be any day now.

Charles Van Helsang put together a ground breaking comprehensive scientific cocktail (as it were) formulated to induce super intelligence. It is and already was his intention to intertwine this formula with the DNA of his great grandfather Michael Van Helsang.

In his time Michael Van Helsang was a well-known, respected and wealthy prominent doctor. He was a pioneer in the medical field, more precisely surgery. He loved helping people and held himself with the utmost dignity. He was a relatively quiet man when away from his office, and he cared little for publicity. He always believed that reporters hurt people more than just inform people. He himself was in the business of helping people so you can see why he had little use for reporters.

People say that he was a striking figure. Very tall, over six feet three inches. His eyes were blue and very large. He had a solid square jaw bone and a streamline nose. A handsome man by most peoples observations, especially Aunt Peggy's.

Aunt Peggy use to confess to me that she actually had a childhood crush on him, even though he was much older than she was. I miss Aunt Peggy; I must make plans to visit with her soon. Everyone seemed to love Doctor Michael Van Helsang. Little did Charles know or anyone else for that matter, that the wonderful Doctor Michael Van Helsang had an unmistakable evil side in which he took to his own grave.

A miracle ensued in the coming months. A perfect baby boy started forming in the confines of the laboratory, a test tube baby. It's a creation of human life without any help or assistance from a female. "Now who is the mad scientist" This will be known as the greatest scientific creation in history.

Carlton Van Helsang came into this world without a mother, something Charles neglected to think of. He was so focused on the work itself and all the experiments with the time it took just to order supplies was exhausting, never mind having to think of a mother for the child. Someone needs to help me take care of this amazing baby boy; I cannot raise an infant alone! Panic starts to set in. What am I to do?

Charles remembers stories his Aunt Peggy use to tell him. Stories she had read to him, when he himself was a young child. Charles decides to advertise for a nanny. It was something that Aunt Peggy had told him when he was small. He remembers a story of hers that took place when she was a small child and how her friend's mother had passed away from an awful plague at the young age of thirty two. Her friend's father worked really hard every day for long hours so he couldn't give her the attention she needed, so he set out looking for a nanny, after all it was a common experience in England, which so happens is where she was living at the time. There was nanny's taking care of children all the time, even with both parents living. Charles must come up with a convincing story of why this child is motherless and most importantly why he wants to keep this child with him.

Charles is frustrated. He placed an ad in the local newspaper days ago and no one's come yet, there hasn't even been a single phone call. Charles thinks of the woman he knows from the Golden Cage Café, although she was a street person, a commoner at most. She was very beautiful, and Charles couldn't help but wonder how much beauty she held onto in the inside. He always got along pleasantly when he was with her. It didn't bother him that she was a lady of the night, which was how she survived in this world.

Maybe I can seduce her into caring for Carlton, yeah, maybe, get her off the streets. I'll entice her with every essential that she could ever want or need. She would have a beautiful home to live in, her own private bedroom with a private bath. I'll buy her a wardrobe fit for a queen. She'll never have to worry about food or medicine and I'll also include a sizable amount of cash at her disposal, with of course a daily limit; I'm not crazy. How can Barbara refuse me?

On the other hand, maybe it would be best if I hired someone else, someone with experience, and someone responsible with hands on experience with tiny infants. After all, Carlton is the most amazing baby on god's green earth and I just cannot allow an inexperienced person looking after him. The person I hire must have an up to date resume with exceptional references. I want every single one of Cartons needs and wants met with enthusiasm and then some. I think I'll personally visit the employment agency and lay down in writing as well as verbally all my requirements and desires in what I expect for my son. No mistakes this way. I must have the best possible honest woman available.

After three long weeks of expectant waiting, a lady named Gertrude Steele has finally come calling on the want ad. This lady had an aristocratic background and was found by the employment agency. This particular employment agency was a well-established company.

There were three people who did the main research and background checks. This lady was highly recommended. Her credentials were flawless and even better; she lived alone! She had no family so it was easy for her to relocate, she can even move into the same home of her potential employer and with her specialty being in infants, it was a marvelous idea. How else can a person be there twenty four seven, that's just what it has to be when it comes to caring for a tiny infant, especially this baby. This was Gertrude's final statement in which Charles was convinced to hire Mrs. Gertrude Steele as his son's nanny. He's absolutely convinced that little Carlton will be well taken care of. What a tremendous burden lifted from his shoulders. Now he can selfishly focus his attention back into his work. Gertrude is expected to arrive with all of her belongings in about two days. Gertrude Steele was a no nonsense get the job done woman, and her credentials were flawless.

Charles made up an elaborate story of why he was alone and he also explained how consumed he was in his work. He voluntarily showed Gertrude his college diplomas and his credentials as a scientist; she was impressed and happy to be employed by such a respected gentleman. He further explained how time consuming his work was and how he must not be disturbed for minor problems, he's only to be disturbed in cases of emergency. He also made it clear that he has no understanding at all when it comes to children, and I'm sure I'll have a question or two from time to time regarding my son Carlton. Though I haven't the time or the patience for children I would absolutely, positively, never allow anything to happen to my son, I just wanted to make myself clear.

Carlton is such a tiny baby and it didn't take long to find out that he was a colicky baby. He was always crying. Gertrude was up all night for most of the first few months. She had brought Carton to see the town Doctor, but it was to no avail. No one could figure out why this special little baby was always crying.

Carlton's nanny, Gertrude Steele wasn't the prettiest flower in the bunch. Charles sometimes wondered if her behavior had been influenced somewhat by her own looks, she was a strong willed woman!

Gertrude was a heavy set woman and she looked to be close to her fifties, women never tell their true age, she did say she was forty two years old. She has a portly round face, small black piercing eyes reminding me of my Old Catholic school teacher that I had in the fourth grade, she always frightened me and the other children in the classroom. She did have a solid square jaw and her jet black hair was always tied up in some type or form of a French braid. It always seemed to look that her face was being stretched backwards. She seemed much shorter than five feet six inches. Just a mere glance of this impressive woman warranted respect. Gertrude Steele was true to her name.

In the first few weeks of her employment Charles had made it a point to get to know her somewhat. (This was difficult for him; he was not a very good social person). They sat together for dinner a couple of times per week in effort to build a friendly relationship. Like many people whom had skeletons in their closets, Gertrude Steele was no exception. She was raised on the streets of London England, left to fend for herself at the tender age of eleven years old. Both of her parents were killed in the war. Her father was killed in the front lines and her mother was killed from random enemy gun fire, her mother was a nurse in the war and was killed right outside of the medical tent. Gertrude eventually ended up in an orphanage. So many kids in one building meant that she never had enough to eat, her clothes were always hand me downs except when Christmas came. The nuns from Notre Dame church use to visit at Christmas with brand new outfits, socks, undergarments, candy; Christmas was a wonderful time all the same. The nuns would stay the whole day and late into the night telling stories of Christmas's pasts. They smiled and sang songs; it was the very best day of the year for all of us, the next day it was over. In some years it seemed like Christmas never came because it was always over so darn fast.

Even though it was hard getting food to eat, Gertrude remained a plump, okay, a heavy set little girl. She was continually picked on and she learned at a very young age that kids were mean and cruel and they didn't care about the things they said. If a new child came in and was a little different than the rest of them,

They were subjected to all kinds of mental ridicule and often physical abuse. So Gertrude had to learn quickly in how to defend herself and it didn't take her very long because in another year she had gotten much bigger and she taught herself how to make mean faces with a piece of a broken mirror that was stuck on the bathroom wall above the dirty sink.

The teachers were no different; they picked on the kids too. Gertrude was very smart for her age and picked up on this quickly and realized this is why the children acted the way they act, to some degree anyway.

As Gertrude and I dinned together, I found it strange, but I also understood her. I could understand where she was coming from in her life so far. She never showed emotion while in my presence; she was cold hearted and seemed to lack compassion. I only hoped that she didn't put up the same walls while Carlton was with her. I'm worrying too much, her references were amiable. Her voice seemed constricted at times, it was somewhat mono tone, her arrogance protruded that the world owed her something and in the short time that I've gotten to know her with respect to how she grew up as a child, and it was completely understandable in my personal view. She was after all very good at her job.

It's a strange emotion that's been coming over me lately. I never thought that I would have such strong feelings for another person. My son Carlton has awoken me to these new feelings. I sometimes have an overwhelming sensation of dejavu'. It brings me back to when I was a child in how my father cared for me (it's funny how the life cycle works) I'll never forget that my son is not exactly an ordinary child either.

While Gertrude took care of Carlton, and Charles was completely satisfied that his son was indeed in good hands, he retreated back into his laboratory. Charles at this point in time demanded solitude while he continued his work on remedies and cures for a variety of sicknesses and diseases at his home built laboratory. He made it clear that it was in everyone's best interest to stay away from his lab.

He didn't want anyone to get sick from his research. There were a number of infectious organisms that Charles was working on. Charles made it a point to up-grade his precautionary measures, there's no way he could allow something to happen to his son, especially if it was something do to his negligence.

The government was still expecting results and why wouldn't they. They are still privately funding Charles for his research in the medical field. Charles was grateful for that for his funding on his cloning and crossbreeding experiments were starting to dwindle. Just in the nick of time Charles thought. If Charles Van Helsang ever went public with his son at this time it would be disastrous.

Charles Van Helsang no longer experiments with cloning, why take chances he with the government he thought. His lifelong vision had given him Carlton. He did it and no one can dispute it. He now feels there's no more need to continue in this human research, this chapter in his life is now closed.

Gertrude is now solely responsible for raising Carlton, and it surely wasn't easy to deal with. Although he was rarely sick, he cried an awful lot. The Doctors didn't know why and couldn't figure it out; once again they had contributed it to him just being hungry. Once he began to walk and had a little more control of his balance his father Charles would take brief moments from his lab to play with Carlton and just plain interact with his son, rare occurrences, indeed. Charles still finds it difficult interacting with people, he even shows his unsteadiness when he's with Carlton. Charles is a very introverted man and it's intimidating to many people. He does put forth an effort to familiarize himself with Carlton; secretly it's an emotional strain on him. Sometimes Gertrude wonders if he actually loves his son or not, it's really not her place to make verbally such outrageous comments.

So she just keeps them to herself. More and more than not lately, Charles's time with Carlton is based on Gertrude's need to leave the house for shopping and or appointments. Gertrude is secretly and quietly starting to dislike the neglect that Charles portrays towards his son, she thinks he spends way too much time in his lab. What's really going on here; she ponders to herself.

Carlton is now a little over three years old and one weekend after the fourth of July in the middle of the night, after 2:00 am on Sunday night to be exact Carlton was at the foot of his dad's bed in his cute Scooby doo pajamas crying hysterically, sniffling and shaking. He says in such a panic stricken voice; can I sleep with you daddy. Charles quickly realized that Carlton must have had what his Doctors perceived as another nightmare. This is starting to cause serious concerns for Charles.

Charles, for the life of him could not figure out what possibly went wrong with his dream come true, his life's work. He worked feverishly trying to figure out why his son has these awful nightmares, he even lost some weight, he has hardly left his lab for months. Carlton's nanny was becoming concerned; things around the Van Helsang household were really strange lately.

Charles is frustrated as hell; he's at the point where his concentration and his focus are in desperate need of repair. He hasn't the faintest idea why those dreadful nightmares keep invading Carlton's nights. He's determined to unlock this mystery because he's afraid that if there's any kind of internal maladies, it would be problematic in all kinds of ways, especially if he ever had to go public with this extraordinary experiment.

What the doctor really needs right now is a night out on the town away, far away from his work. He's been cooped up much too long. A night of dancing and drinking is something he hasn't done in over a year. Maybe he'll even meet someone tonight and get lucky. After a few drinks in him he'll be more inclined into having a conversation with someone on whatever topic comes to mind. Charles did have somebody in mind. He was thinking, I'll just drive down to the dark part of the city and see if I can just find her, and if she's not around I'll wait twenty minutes or so and then I'll just head back to the Golden Cage Café. Charles wanted more than a drink tonight, he wanted her! After all, he was a man, and a Man had needs, and she was a working girl. It was a perfect arrangement for him, no problems, no demands, and no responsibilities. No stress, it was perfect; just what the Doctor ordered.

Charles walked into the bar with purpose; it was actually his favorite place outside of his lab. It was a place that she frequented, she was accepted here. She was a very beautiful woman despite her dirty, ugly occupation. Charles already had three drinks, scotch and soda was his usual drink and he was conversing with a poorly kept middle age woman, making sure to keep one eye on the door so that he wouldn't miss her come in to the place. The next thing you know, the door of the Golden Cage Café opened. Charles always remembered his manners and he politely, though excitedly excused himself from this lonely, depressing, homely, kind, lady. All heads turned! It was Barbara! And she looked fabulous; a grand entrance was just her style. The bar was packed and she even knew the pretty heavy bosomed girl who was dancing in the gold cage completely naked above the bar, and did a double take of her. Charles just stared at her a moment, he was momentarily mesmerized. She stood perfectly still for just a moment. She was wearing the sexiest red dress, no doubt in the whole county. Feeling a bit tipsy already, Charles had no problem in saying hello to the lady.

Hi Charlie, how are you honey, it's been a long time. Could you be interested in buying a lady a drink? That's always been his 'que' with her. Charles could only smile. He wanted to soak in her beauty, it was a Kodak moment. He cocked an eyebrow and said; whiskey or wine baby. No one, even in a million years would ever believe that this was the reclusive Charles Van Helsang. Unknown to anyone, he does have an interesting, bold dark side.

Barbara was thinking to herself as he approached her; an easy night, I'm so glad, turns out that Barbara was exhausted from a very busy afternoon. Besides a Doctor's appointment she had to walk six miles to three different clients, it's a wonder she made it to the club at all. Barbara only missed one Saturday night in the past thirteen months. One time she was practically on her death bed due to a bout with pneumonia that had lasted for over three weeks. Still, that didn't stop her from showing up.

Charles and Barbara had a wonderful night as they danced and laughed until they closed the place down. After closing they drove through town on the edge of a lake to the only diner within miles. She had a very light late breakfast which consisted of one English muffin, a spoonful of home fries and a pouched egg. Charles on the other hand had a grand slam breakfast; two eggs, sausage, bacon, home fries and banana pancakes. Barbara was amazed at Charles's appetite and made polite fun of him. She said to him; be careful big boy and gave him a flirtatious smile, whatever do you mean Babs, you know exactly what I mean! This night is far from over mister.

Charles brought Barbara home with him and all along the way they touched hands and told jokes. She has this undeniable, overpowering sex appeal that absolutely no man can ignore. When it comes to men, Barbara was always a little bit naïve; she's always been easily manipulated. The only down fall about her that he was aware of was that she is addicted to drugs and alcohol. This terrible addiction had a strong hold on her thinking. She was unable to make sound decisions from time to time. None of that mattered to Charles because of the intense sexual attraction that offsets his better judgment.

Barbara always liked Charles. She always thought to herself that he was her favorite, he always treated her with respect and she liked that he was kind and gentle, and it didn't hurt that he had money too. Even though Barbara could have any man she wanted, secretly she wanted what she had never gotten; and that was love. Her parents told her on more than one occasion that she would never have a long lasting, loving relationship with anyone so long as you are still using and abusing drugs and alcohol. Her parents once lived the life; they were right!

Charles went back to his lonely existence, experimenting with new procedures. A couple of years have passed and Carlton is still having bad dreams. He's a good boy and he's bright. He's almost six years old and he's been anticipating going to school. Gertrude did an excellent job of raising Carlton. He has very good manners, he doesn't wine when he doesn't get his way and he never refuses to help when asked to do something. On another subject, I've noticed Gertrude has been more and more possessive and a bit too nosey. She's been snooping and asking about Carlton. It's been going on for a long time now. I think it's time to make a changing of the guard. Since Carlton will be attending school soon. I feel it's is now time to make new future arrangements.

It's time to go to school now Carlton, let's go! Get up! Charles gave Gertrude the day off, and he already talked to his son about her leaving soon. He made up a story that she has a sick relative and had to take care of her similar to the way she took care of you.

Can I have French toast today? Dad, what! For breakfast dad, can I have French toast please? Gertrude use to make it for me, oh, sure you can. While Charles makes breakfast he asks his son: Are you nervous about school, it's okay if you are ya know. No, I'm not scared at all, I can't wait to go. I am going to Miss Gertrude though. Well don't worry too much; before you know it you'll be making a bunch of new friends, do you really think so, of course I do. I was your age once, you know it's going to be a whole lot of fun, watch and see.

Charles asked Barbara to marry him, after all it was becoming harder and harder for him to keep going to the Golden Cage Café. At the same time Gertrude needed to go, her intrusions were becoming a nuisance.

Charles and Barbara had prearrangement. Charles needed a baby sitter and Barbara needed stability in her life, a place to live without all the whispers. She's been really depressed lately. Her neighbors use to be discreet and very private. They all knew Barbara. They knew who she was and what she did for a living, and for a long time they didn't seem to care. So she thought. In the past couple year's people started snickering towards her, even the neighborhood children started to make rude comments towards her, and we all know kids can be downright cruel and to the point in fact.

Too many people knew what she did for a living and at first it didn't seem to matter much, but they started hearing and seeing other things that weren't going to wash very well with the rest of the community. Her drug addiction had escalated and if you couldn't see it then you were legally blind. Her physical appearance as well as her demeanor were drastically changing and not for the better. Barbara needed a big change; she needed shelter and more money to Maintain her addiction. It worked, she thought to herself. For the last year or so she had coaxed Charles and now he asked her to marry him; what would my parents think? Though it wasn't out of love, she didn't care. She knew she had to take care of Carlton, and thought it would be easy because he's almost grown, yeah right! He's what? Six years old! Drug addiction has an awkward way with people's minds; in fact she knew she was getting the better end of this deal.

It didn't matter that she had very little education; Charles was and still is mesmerized by her beauty. She still is very beautiful, and besides that, he still wanted Gertrude gone. Barbara's education was attained in the streets; she was a scholar of the gutter. She left school at age twelve. She could not read nor write and had a very limited vocabulary. She likes to think that she survives on her beauty. Needing or wanting something, she only had to flutter her eyes and smile. When she glances in someone's direction they become simply entranced by her beauty, and she knew it.

Barbara had long wavy blonde hair with natural red high lights. She always tried to look nice on the outside. She had deep set beautiful big round blue eyes with a mischievous twinkle. High accentuated cheek bones which molded perfectly with her heart shaped jaw line. To top it all off, she has a dazzling bleach white smile with surprisingly straight teeth.

Barbara accepted his proposal and Charles couldn't be happier. Charles believes that Gertrude inflicted mental and emotional abuse on his son Carlton. He didn't know for sure and he couldn't prove anything, either. He was just glad she was leaving and being replaced by Barbara

The first night that Barbara moved in was a little awkward. Carlton never met Barbara, he was anticipating this moment for a couple weeks because his dad had explained to him that he had met her a long time ago and now they are getting married. All three of them got dressed up and went out to dinner together. Secretly to Barbara earlier, Charles insisted that they go to Carlton's favorite restaurant. They figured it might be a little less stressful for him. After all he is still a young boy and the only other person other than his dad in his life, was his nanny. So it's a very big transition for him at this age.

Barbara and Charles wanted to make a good impression with Carlton since it's their first dinner together, so they both agreed that a familiar place will ease whatever tension that there might be as far as Carlton was concerned. It wasn't Charles's intentions but they all ended up going to Burger King. It was in fact kind of amusing as they pulled into the parking lot they both smiled at each other while Carlton sat buckled up in the back seat of the car. They exited the car and as they did Charles told his son that; next time we all go out, it's Barbara's turn to pick the restaurant. He was smiling and he agreed as he led the way he looked at Barbara and she caught him by surprise. She winked at him. Carlton turned beet red. Carlton was happy and all seemed well. Barbara had an elegant dress on with spaghetti straps and Charles had on one of his black suits that he wore whenever he had to give a lecture. They were stylishly dressed in a burger joint, but the important thing is, is that Carlton is comfortable since he is playing a significant part in the unfolding of the night. They laughed and each of them told a joke or two. There was a large woman with hair combs in her hair sitting directly across from Carlton and his new step mom. She had four children with her and anyone can see that they were all her children, each one of them looked exactly like her, what a powerful resemblance to her. Each one of her children had a different kind of hamburger in front of them. One of her kids stuck two French fries up his nose and another one stuck French fries in his ears and the lady's two little girls covered their eyes with pickles. They were all yelling and screaming. Their mother didn't seem embarrassed at all; she was more concerned with the consumption of her own meal. She looked hungry and paid no mind to her children as she ceremoniously kept stuffing French fries, onion rings and not one, but two whoppers into her amazingly small mouth.

Barbara and Carlton are getting along nicely, he took to her immediately. Charles had an inclination that under the right circumstances they just might get along splendidly after all. He had secretly found out about her, she had a less than stellar back ground as far as her education was concerned, but that all didn't matter to Charles because she was taking Gertrude's place and she is much more pleasing to the eyes and hopefully not as precocious. After they had finished eating their burgers, Barbara asked Carlton if he had any more room in that belly of his because she knows of this really cool ice cream parlor with homemade ice cream. Before she said the words "ice cream" it looked as if he was going to say that he had no room. When she said "ice cream" he burped and laughed as most young children do, then his eyes lit up like a Christmas tree. Ice cream! Yes please! Can we dad? Please! It was Carlton's night out, so of course Charles said yes. It was a very pleasant evening after all. They all went home after they had their fill of ice cream, watched a little television then Carlton went to bed. He gave Barbara a little kiss on the cheek that surprised her momentarily, and he gave his dad a hand shake because boys don't kiss their dads at this age, he's too big for that he thought, good night. Charles and Barbara were exhausted and both retired to bed about an hour after Carlton went to bed.

Barbara's childhood was full of mental and emotional abuse as well as a constant flow of physical abuse. It was a routine, in Barbara's house and it was all she ever knew. It was like this ever since she can remember. In her eyes this was normal, she knew nothing else; isn't this how all people live?

It was her sick drug addicted parents who introduced her to this lowly life style of drugs, violence and sexual abuse. Not only did her parents partake in abusing her sexually they also allowed perfect strangers to participate in humiliating sex acts with her.

Barbara will never forget the first time. When most people, especially young people grow up and learn from their parents about the birds and the bees, the conversation seems awkward and somewhat uncomfortable, there's no curiosity factor as far as a child is concerned and years later you find that your parents did the best they could to enlighten you. Most people see how difficult it must have been because now it's their turn to explain to their own kids. Well, in Barbara's house, it wasn't at all, pleasant. No, leave it to beaver house hold there. Her parents told her after she seen them take money from some strange smelly man, that she had to go with him into the basement, and that he was going to make a woman out of her. Little does she know that he's going to rape her! She was only thirteen years old. He did not beat her or hurt her physically except when he actually had the intercourse with her; he realized that she was a virgin because of her bleeding and how she yelped when he penetrated her. He had gotten nervous and quickly finished in what he set out to do, grabbed his clothes and left. This is how Barbara lost her virginity. It was scary and humiliating especially for a thirteen year old naïve little girl. There was no boyfriend, no holding hands, and no dates for a movie when the boys would try to sneak a brushing glance of a booby when they would try to put their arms around the back of the seat. It was a nasty, smelly, fat slob, that raped her in the moldy dusty basement on a torn and stained couch. Trash was everywhere, drug paraphernalia askew, and beer bottles all over, it smelled like urine and garbage, a frightening experience to say the least.

Barbara's parents took advantage of her solely to maintain their own addictions to drugs and alcohol, they cared of nothing else. Barbara's screams and cries were never heard. They fell on her parents deaf ears, as long as her parents were getting money from someone to be alone with her for a few minutes. It was like that old Richard Pryor and Gene Wilder movie; hear no evil see no evil.

Without realizing, she too, was badly addicted to illegal street drugs. She started learning and excepting that drugs and alcohol made her happy, and she liked being happy because everything else around her was so awful and sad. She was just a kid and didn't understand the long term ramifications. She did quickly grasp on to the fact that all her problems and fears went away while she was drunk or high on drugs. Barbara didn't understand that her fears and her problems were just temporarily put on a shelf, and that she was just masking the problem. Drug addiction is a unique disease, there's no cure for drug addiction. It's something that will be with her, all her life. A lifelong battle.

As Barbara got older, she became more and more dependent on drugs, her tolerance increased with time, just the same as any other person whom is addicted to drugs. You need more and more just to maintain the same level of alertness, and to ward off the pain that takes hold in the addicts' bones and joints. Along with her addiction, she had a severe depression problem. She's a very lonely child.

Still, Barbara had gotten older in spite of her addiction, and it really didn't hurt her beauty. She had the good looks of a model, in fact, she was quite beautiful. No one could tell what was beneath her masterful disguise. She did become a very angry and spiteful person in her twenties. She was domineering and street wise, thanks to her sick parents. The world owed Barbara, and Barbara was making withdrawals.

Barbara's parents died together from a drug overdose after the authorities had accumulated a significant amount of evidence against them ranging from drug trafficking, child porn and prostitution, burglary, gun charges and assault and battery with intent to maim. If convicted they would have to spend the rest of their miserable lives behind bars. Instead of facing all these charges they made a secret pact with each other, something along the line of their wedding vows; until death do us part, and committed suicide together. They were found lying in bed together holding hands. They had been there for approximately eleven or twelve days, that's what the coroner's report had read. There was a note addressed to Barbara, they had managed to scribble down some words and all it said was; were sorry Barbara. They were buried by the state without a funeral. No grave stone, just a number, and it was too good, as far as Barbara was concerned.

Barbara lives rent free in a rooming house, a courtesy says her landlord. A classic slumlord. She does not have a job because she has no work experience. She does favors for him, to him, to be more precise, she has sex with him and in return, she has a place to live.

Now with her parents out of the picture, Barbara could do what she wants now. She can fuck who she chooses to and she can get high when she wants to, not when they allowed her. She's now on her own and she has just herself to support. More money for me she thought.

Every now and then she would dream of having a normal relationship with someone and as she got older she tried to clean up her act more than once. She started believing things about herself, that no one wanted a freaked out, dumb drug addict, no matter how beautiful she was. Her last relationship ended abruptly, he was a nice man with his own business, and he was attractive and smart, and also rude. He told her when he left her; people need to beautiful on the inside more so than on the outside. She became depressed again and impatient. She couldn't figure out men for a long time, so when Charles approached her with his proposition she was so overwhelmed. They got married by a justice of the peace in Las Vegas. She now is a step mom! She needs a drink. There was no honey moon or reception, no party. It was strictly, business. They were already lovers, and that suited them just fine.

Barbara was completely, utterly self-centered. She never even took care of a hamster. She could hardly take care of herself, let alone somebody's brat. She secretly thought that this new responsibility was going to be just awful. She's thinking that she's a bad influence. She actually hates children and all of their annoyances. They always disrupt the daily routines of adults. Even though she doesn't even have a routine, she feels particularly uncomfortable. Barbra's desperate, and she tries to take drastic measures. How can you do what you want with a damn kid hovering all about?

Months have passed and it's already becoming monotonous as well as tedious. Charles is never around; he's always in his lab. He's abandoned his son to me, and its frustrating s hell.

Barbara decides to get some privacy, especially after Carlton had scared the hell out of her last night. Carlton screamed in the middle of the night. Barbara was in a sound sleep. It was another night mare. It was as frightening to Barbara as well as Carlton, to say the least. It was starting to affect her during the daylight hours as well. So Barbara decides to punish Carlton. She locks him in the basement. She had enough; it's been over a year, almost two years. Carlton is about eight or nine years old now and she can't get any privacy, and on top of it all she thinks he's got some psychological issues. She talks Charles into having Carlton she psychologist or a psychiatrist. Why does he need a shrink? He's just a boy. Charles is unsure. It's undeniably a selfish feeling trying to escape or evade the fact that something might have went wrong in the lab when Carlton was conceived. His desperate and painstaking attempts to find the source of the problem just keeps eluding him, it's been years now, and it's been taking a toll on his health

It's the first dinner in over two years since Charles and Barbara had dinner together outside of the house. It took over an hour to drive through town and into the suburbs on the other side of the county. It was raining cat and dogs, the rain was so fast and furious at times that they had to stop twice because of poor visibility. They drove in silence. they weren't exactly that close any more, they really never were that close anyway for that matter, but ever since Charles locked himself up in his lab to try and figure out what might have went wrong with his experiment, Barbara and he drifted further and further apart.

They made it to the restaurant in one piece. It was a quaint, quiet Portuguese place. It was pretty much empty except for one couple sitting by the fireplace. The bad weather is the blame for slow business tonight the maître d' explained, but it sat just fine with Barbara and Charles, they weren't exactly outgoing these days. Barbara orders the house special, but first I would like an appetizer of; stuffed mushroom caps please. And for Charles it was a tasty steak and shrimp dinner. They both had a cup of Portuguese kale soup to go along with their meals. They ordered drinks and Charles just blurts out; I finally agree with you on a psychiatrist for Carlton. After a great deal of thought, I think it to be in his best interest. He comes to his own conclusion that his son, his invention, was just an average child. He doesn't and he hasn't shown any signs of mental superiority. Charles thought to himself; another failing aspect of the experiment. He had such high hopes that his son will grow up to become quite simply, a genius. Someone revered throughout the world, even.

Charles falls into a deep depression and unconsciously withdraws even deeper into himself. His work needs drastic attention, a personal and private excuse, to fall even deeper in despair. Isolation is always been the biggest problem with depression, and what's really sad is the fact that Charles knows this.

The mood softened up a little after they sat down by the warm crackling fire. They had another drink and briefly talked about Carlton's immediate future, and to get to the bottom of these persistent nightmares he keeps having.

Carlton's stepmoms addiction has grown in leaps and bounds over the years, and she's become an angry, spiteful woman. She locks Carlton in the basement every day until an hour or so before Charles shows up in the kitchen. Lately for the past year, Charles has been coming out for dinner at precisely the same time, it's kind of eerie in a way, likes it's an appointment. She wonders if he's even doing anything in the lab. She never hears a sound coming from there, nothing scraping the floor or even falling off of a table.

Carlton is absolutely terrified of the basement. This house once belonged to his great grandfather, Michael Van Helsang. It's a very old house; it's cold and has a stale musky smell to it. There's a dirt floor and there are some cracks in the foundation. When he had brought, or snuck a candle down there with him one day he saw there was only one enclosed room. It has wooden walls and it was almost empty. There are no windows anywhere. There was a small pile of junk in one corner, old furniture and a couple tools and just stuff that has accumulated over the years. The shadows scared the hell out of Carlton, there are no lights and it's damp and moldy. He sits in a corner huddled down low and blows out the light. He cries softly and wonders why she's so mean, why does she puts me down here.

Carlton is so young to have to endure such cruelty. Why, he asks himself, why? What have I done to her? He's still too young to realize that some people are just plain mean, and can't help but being cruel. Most of these people are products of their own environment, they don't know any other way. They can't see themselves doing anything wrong unless it's been pointed out to them, and then they don't understand anyway. Carlton suddenly realizes that he's not alone down here in the basement, his breathing gets shallow, he's scared, and he's straining to listen. His eyes are wide open and unblinking. There it is again! Another squeal and he hears tiny noises, possibly mice?

Maybe a stray bird? Or maybe something else? It could even be a big rat, like in the movie; Big Ben. Please, don't let it be a monster. It's cold and dark in the basement. Carlton huddles in the corner and doesn't dare move, out of fright. The seat of his pants is beginning to get wet because of the damp floor. His matches already got wet from being in his back pocket. He doesn't make a sound. He thinks he seen something scatter across the floor not more than five feet in front of him. But his vision just hasn't adjusted yet and he thinks maybe his imagination is just getting the best of him.

There a straight staircase with thirteen steps leading down to this dungeon of a basement, and at the very bottom there's an old wooden riser; it's actually the last step. A half-moon shaped platform that's looks a little out of place there. Maybe that's how these old houses were built because of the dirt floors. Sometimes Carlton sits at the bottom of the steps and wonders if there is such a thing as the boogey man? He's better off not being in the open and decides to stay away from the platform, because its right smack in the middle of the room.

Little do Carlton's father and stepmother know? He's a lot smarter than he appears. The next time he goes down into the basement, he'll be prepared.

He hides a few candles and matches on his person and takes a flash light and a blanket to help with the damp floor. He even manages to smuggle a Sony Walkman radio cassette player with his favorite cassette; Elvis Presley. He turns it on and the song playing was; don't be cruel, and thinks of his step mother immediately. Carlton loves his Elvis Presley music.

Another day in the basement, Carlton looks around for a stick or something that he can use to defend himself, that's if he feels he needs to. There might be rats down here; he sits in a corner and starts reading a book by candle light. The book in one hand and a broken broom handle in the other hand

Carlton's basement treatments go on for a couple of years. Not even his psychiatrist knows of this, he's managed to keep this a secret so far. One day while quietly sitting on his blanket eating a piece of cake that had brought down with him, he finally spots his basement tormenter. It's a mouse, two of them. Something about these mice seems peculiar; they look like that they're enjoying themselves as if they were playing with each other. They don't even seem to be intimidated by me or the candle light. Carlton gets a closer look one day at his only companions down here, in what he now calls; hell. He's been feeding them for a long time now and they've been coming closer and closer to him. Carlton tricks one of them with a piece of swish cheese that it couldn't resist, and now it's only about three feet away. Carlton is unsure of what to make of it, he's not even sure it's a mouse. He backs off a little and whatever it is sits upright on its hind legs and just looks over at Carlton while eating his small piece of swish cheese. It looks as though the mouse has a deformed head. It's not deformed though! It just doesn't belong on a mouse. Carlton thinks that the candle light is playing tricks on his eyes. Maybe I've been in the dark too long? I am kind of pale. He hears someone upstairs, footsteps. He quickly extinguishes the candles, but not before he gathers up his meager belongings and puts them into the empty room at the end of the basement.

The next day, Carlton is exiled to the basement again, by none other than his comatose, wicked stepmother. Over the years, Carlton has developed a very distasteful disliking to Barbara. He knows that she's a drug addict and he's bared witness to all types of men, coming and going from his home, and at all hours of the night. They weren't exactly in the upper echelon of society either! Some of them were drug dealers, but most of them were what prostitutes called; tricks. Carlton heard her moaning and giggling from time to time when she didn't realize that he was lurking around. Carlton's always been very observant, and one time he embarrassingly caught her performing oral sex to someone other than his father. The man was very tall and had greasy jet black hair slicked straight back. All his clothes were still on except for his pants, they were bunched around his ankles. When she stood up after he painfully moaned, he handed her some money. That wasn't the first time that Carlton had spied on Barbara. Carlton's wonders to himself; does his dad know about her bizarre dealings, and if he doesn't, he's not planning to disclose any of this information. Anyway, adults don't always, and more than not, believe children's tales. He gets punished enough and won't take that chance.

Without a doubt Carlton sees different heads on these mice, he's dumbfounded. What in the world is this? No way! It can't be! It's a mouse! Or maybe it's not. Maybe it's a freak deformity, bad genetics. One of them looks like it has a tiny dog face, and the other looks to have a tiny cat face, with whiskers and all. Carlton starts to wonder if he's been locked up down here too long. A large cockroach ran past and it momentarily broke his gaze. Am I hallucinating? He investigates further in the next couple of days. He willingly heads down into the basement careful not to distract his stepmother from her business. She doesn't even know he's gone. Carlton captures his mice, that is, he thinks their mice. He has them trained to eat out of his own hand and he furthers his expectations by teaching one of them a trick. One of them learned how to sit up on its hind legs. It's really quite a silly spectacle to witness. Carlton now has another secret. Since he spends so much time down here in the basement he's sure not to compromise his new friendship, even if it's only two freakish mice. They seem harmless enough and they keep him from longing for the company that he's always desired. He's intelligent and wise enough not to divulge this information about the mice to anyone, he doesn't want to be publicly ridiculed. Who would believe him anyway, a mouse with a head that resembles a dog and it does tricks like; sitting and rolling over. Yeah right, I can see it now. They'll send me straight to the Looney bin for sure.

It looks like the mice have made themselves a home right under the stairs. I wondered where they went to, when I wasn't here. Carlton investigates; the curiosity is gnawing at him. He saw both of them scamper more than once in that direction, at first he didn't think anything of it. It was always dark and he thought that they were just scared and running from him to hide. There's a tiny hole in the side if the platform, hardly noticeable, you would only see it if you were intentionally looking for it. Like a cat, the curiosity is getting the best of him, so he gets a closer look with his flashlight. No longer is Carlton afraid of the basement. He's explored the whole room and has decided to build himself a club-house, in the empty wooden room at the far end of the cellar, but right now he's checking out the hiding place that the two mice had constructed.

Unknown to Cartons dad, Cartons mind has developed at a rapid rate. Although Charles has dismissed the hopes of his son becoming extremely intelligent, he still works in the lab feverishly at trying to solve the mistake that he might have made. There really is no problem, but Sir Charles does not know this. His son just needed to grow up a little more and further develop as a young boy. As the old saying goes; good things come to those who wait.

Carlton has a sanctuary now! There are lights, there's blankets, books, a small chair, cushions from an old couch. There's a portable television set especially equipped with a new pair of Sony headphones. Carlton installed his own phone jack or head set jack onto the television so that he could use his headphones from his new Walkman radio to listen to the T.V. in perfect solitude. He doesn't want anyone upstairs to hear a single thing. Barbara might think that he's having a good time or something like that, and as long as his mean stepmother still thinks that she's punishing him and he's out of her hair, then everything will be just fine as far as Carlton is concerned.

For a long time now Carlton discovers or better yet, realizes that he has an uncanny ability to disassemble and repair all kinds of electronics, electric devices, and appliances. Everything from old radios and television sets, electric can openers, electric clocks and some of the most modern household items including advanced equipment such as computer video games, and personal computers.

Carlton sums up his ability to be a gift from the Lord. Maybe it is some type of divine intervention. Lord knows he has never had any type of schooling or formal training in any of these sophisticated areas or professions. Lately he's also noticed that school is becoming somewhat boring. He gets through his classes in a fraction of the time that it takes the rest of his classmates. His teacher Mrs. Marques has been impressed with him for a long time now. She is a very kind woman standing about five feet two inches, she has big puppy dog brown eyes, shoulder length black hair with a nice wave to it, and she does not wear makeup except for a small amount of lipstick. She really doesn't need makeup because she has a natural beauty bout her. She has high cheek bones and a heart shaped face and her most appealing attribute is her smile. She has such a natural smile, all the children in the school absolutely loves her. Mrs. Marques gives Carlton extra school work almost every day because he always completes his class room work before all of his classmates. Some of the kids at school pick on him out of jealousy, he's the teacher's pet, they say. You think you're so smart, you're just a book worm and nobody likes a book worm, that's why you have no friends, ha ha.

In one of Carlton's meetings, a session with his psychiatrist, he tells his shrink that he doesn't care very much for school. It's starting to become very boring. Although Carlton is shy and reclusive he manages to correct mistakes that his teachers make every now and then. He doesn't say much more about anything else except for his night mares. He wouldn't dare say anything about his mice, and definitely nothing at all about the basement, although he did in fact mention he built a clubhouse recently. Doctor Fischer thought that was an interesting undertaking, maybe even amusing to him as he thinks of a club house, actually a tree house that he and his childhood friends had built down by the railroad tracks many years ago. Carlton put up foam walls all around the room, he used a staple gun to finish it and then he put up old drapes he had found in the attic, they were of a dark paisley pattern. He had looked up sound proofing at the library in school and read that foam pads make excellent sound proofing, and what was really nice was that the foam was very economical, he could afford to pay for it out of his allowance money he gets from his father every week.

One day Carlton was listening to some music and reading a chemistry book from school at the same time when he decided to get up and stretch. He had opened his club house door and saw his two new companions scurrying across the dirt floor towards the staircase. While Carlton was nosing around the staircase with his flashlight, he peeked into a hole, a hole in the wood that he assumed that the mice had made.

Carlton stumbles upon a secret panel on the side of the platform where the two mice reside. There's a small metal handle there, he pulls it with his fingers trap door opens. He's excited and scared all at the same time; his eyes are wide open and unblinking. He looks quickly up the stairs hoping no one heard anything. His heart is now pounding out of his chest, what is this? A secret passage maybe? Carlton hesitates, he wants to explore but its dark and he's a little frightened. The trap door, once removed, reveals a steep stairwell made out of stone. He shines his flashlight and notices that the stairwell is actually roughly carved out of the land/property and it goes deeply into the ground. I can hear mice squeaking down in there, sounds like an echo. Carlton is beaming with curiosity now. He remembers a distant time when Aunt Peggy had told him that this house indeed holds many secrets; he had thought at the time that she was just teasing him. Now, he's wondering if she really was telling him the truth because his intense imagination has just kicked up a notch. He chooses not to go down the stairs at this time because he wants to be more prepared, so he closes the trap door and he walks back to his sanctuary to think up some kind of plan of attack.

The next day, Carlton brings one of his baseball bats with him into the murky basement. He was listening to an Elvis Presley tape on his new Sony Walkman. He enters his private room and notices above the doorway the sign that he had put up with the three initials carved into a pine wood board, it read; VIP. Carlton needed some time to build up his courage; he lit two candles and sat down on the old sofa cushions. He now thinks that he's ready to explore. Carlton descends the stairs after releasing the lever to the trap door. It's extremely dark down there and he grips the baseball bat so tight that his fingers turned white. He turns on his flashlight and notices that there's just as many stairs here as there is above the basement, and there's even a stronger musty smell, he thinks it's probably because he's going deeper into the ground. Carlton's adrenaline is pumping feverishly and all his sensors are acutely heightened. He lights a candle at the bottom of the steps then proceeds cautiously down the narrow tunnel. There are spider webs everywhere. The tunnel is only about six feet high and three feet wide, the ceiling is made of some sort of metal and there are metal supports along the walls. He wonders if this all could cave in on him, and if it did no one would know. Now some paranoia starts kicking in. He notices that the tunnel comes to an end, at least from this distance it seems to come to an end. There's a large thick wooden door at the end of the tunnel. It's locked with an old fashioned padlock and a thick chain. I never have seen such a humongous padlock in my entire life. The keyhole is almost an inch in diameter. What in the world is behind this door? Do I really want to know? He's daydreaming now, maybe it's some kind of a monster or maybe it's a treasure. He holds onto his thoughts as he clutches his bat. Someone is coming, OH NO. He shuts off the flashlight and then he notices the dim light from the candle. He's scared now, and he's wondering, who can it be? It's quiet now! He hears the noise again. To his surprised relief, it turns out only to be those dammed mice. There squeaks seem to be magnified in this narrow tunnel. Immediately after this scare, Carlton leaves the tunnel and goes back to his sanctuary. I need something to pick that lock.

Carlton comes home from school the next day and discovers that he's home alone. No one is here! So he sneaks around like most young boys do. He checks out his stepmothers' room, no one here. He proceeds down the quiet hall to his dads' room and he steps in. He's investigating, snooping really. He finds a big combination safe in the closet, it's huge. We must be rich he muses. He starts getting nervous so he leaves the room, though he's never seen his dad angry, he was sure not to tempt fate.

Carlton realizes this could be his best chance to break open the lock on the door in the basements secret tunnel. If in fact he needs to make noise he is now sure that no one was home to hear it. He takes a few extra candles with him this time and lights all of them once he is down in the tunnel. He closes the trap door behind him and proceeds to break open the lock with his trusty baseball bat leaning against the side of the door. He starts perspiring, and then all of a sudden, it's open! He grabs the baseball bat and realizes his heart is pounding so hard that he can hear it. He slowly opens the door and shines his flashlight and notices what looks like an old fashioned light switch. It's set in a wall plate with two buttons on top of each other. He pushes the one that is protruding outwardly, the one with a little white circle on it and instantly the room lit up. Simultaneously one of the lights arched from the electricity and blew out and glass fell from the ceiling. Carlton was astonished. It looks like an old fashioned laboratory right out of an old movie. This will be Carlton's secret for sure. No one must know of its' whereabouts. Carlton is awe stricken; everything is covered in dust and cobwebs. It seems like he entered a time warp, and went back in time. He finagled his way around the small room noticing all of the old fashioned equipment, there's a bunch of thick glass flasks everywhere loaded with dust. Some of them are discolored at the bottom due to some sort of dried up liquids at one point in time. On top of a table, there's something that looks to be an old ink flask with a dried up quill next to it. Carlton picked up the feather and it crumbled in his hand. There's what looks like the world's first toilet bowl in a far corner of the room. He laughed as he looked at the hole in the middle of a wooden chair, how do you flush, ha, more laughter. Carlton is so excited as he quickly checks everything out. There's a solid floor here and it looks like some type of rock or brick and it's relatively flat with no lumps or cracks in it. He finds it kind of strange because in the main basement up the stairs, the entire floor is dirt.

Carlton thinks to himself as he closes the door. This is where I will start my own invention! It's perfect here. There's electricity and breathable air because of the ingenious air ducts that were located on the far wall of the room next to the make shift bathroom. He goes back to the club house and turns on the television set. Plugs his head phones into the TV and proceeds to watch one of his favorite science fiction shows; Star Trek. Spot is his favorite character on the show. Carlton was always intrigued with the transport machine, he wondered to himself when he was much younger whether or not if the machine was real or not. Of course, when he was a mere small child that is what he thought. Anyway, he loves it whenever they say; Beam Me up Scotty. Carlton goes upstairs now and grabs his coat then he heads outside and gets his bike from around the back of the house. Still thinking of the Transport Machine he travels down the bumpy road on his bike to his only school buddy's' house, Johnny.

Charles somehow finds out that Carlton has been sneaking around the house, disrespecting his, and Barbara's privacy, and poking through their personal belongings. Although Charles is aware of his son rummaging through the house, he decides not to mention it; after all he didn't steal anything. He's just being a boy. He remembers when he was a boy and did the same foolish things once or twice, okay maybe more than once or twice. Charles has finally given up hope that his son would grow up to be some kind of genius. Whenever they got together which was less frequent lately, and with the reports from Carlton's psychiatrist he sadly and reluctantly determined that Carlton was just a normal kid, just like every other kid. There was never anything special, no signs, and nothing extraordinary. The Doctors reports stated that he was a very polite boy, typical for his age. He said he thought school was boring and has only one friend in school, a good friend. The Doctor is still working diligently to decipher the nightmare problem. He said; it's puzzling because of his inability to remember anything that could possibly trigger these dreams. He comes from a good background and does not watch scary movies on television. At first I had just thought that the boy had a vivid imagination and I quickly assessed that, that's not the case because of his physiological changes as he did talk about them. His eyes grew wide, his pupils dilated; I could see them from across the room. He shook with what didn't look like fear but rather excitement. It intrigued me and I looked forward to more consultations with him. I am surely eager to unravel this mystery, and I give you my word! I will inform you of any and all positive developments at once!

Little did Carlton's father know? Carlton was indeed, coming into his own. Carlton realized a long time ago why his dad pushed him so hard, he only wanted him to be better than the rest. He pushed and he pressed school work, he even went as far as giving him extra work, and quizzes in chemistry.

Carlton didn't need extra school work, what he wanted, he didn't get. He wanted; love, and affection. When he learned that his dad was incapable of giving any of it freely, he did what a lot of kids do, at that age. He rebelled. He did it by deliberately sabotaging his school work and doing poorly on his S A T's. Not only did Carlton not want his father to find out that he actually aced his SAT's in a fraction of the time that it took anyone else in his entire school. Carlton has major plans for his new laboratory, and he didn't want to attract any kind of attention to himself what so ever. In the academic sense that is.

After finding his great grandfathers laboratory, Carlton starts cleaning it up very discreetly and quietly. Carlton seems to excel at just about anything that he sets his mind to do.

Now, Carlton's dream is to invent the first of its kind; a transport machine, similar to what he's seen on television, like in the movie "The Fly" and Carlton's favorite TV show; Star Trek. The Star ship Enterprise with Spock and Captain Kirk. Carlton doesn't have any of his own money, not real money anyway so he learns how to improvise by becoming a very clever thief. He needs to refurbish his secret laboratory and has two major obstacles. One obstacle was getting the equipment that he needed and the second obstacle was getting it all by his wicked drug addicted Step mother.

With ease, Carlton instantly becomes a professional thief thru the help of the internet. A person can learn anything that they desire via the computer internet. Carlton thought at first that it would be difficult getting his lab furbished without being questioned by either his father or his wicked Step mother. So Carlton studied the internet for a while to get a better prospective on everything that he needed, this is something that he accomplished very quickly and in the privacy in his club house. He knew his dad wouldn't be a problem at all, since he's always locked up in his own world upstairs in his own laboratory. He sometimes didn't even see his father's face for three to five days at a time. Then when he did it was usually a brief conversation, asking about school or maybe telling him that it's time for us to make an overdue visit to see Aunt Peggy. He has noticed lately that his dad is looking rather thin. Carlton wonders if he is sick or not. Then quick as it came, he dismisses it. He works hard and sometimes he misses meals, he's too smart to starve himself. He's okay! Carlton's step mother was an entirely different story. She doesn't become active until late in the day when the sun sets. They say; the freaks come out at night! Carlton's starting to understand the underlining reasoning; Turns out that getting by her was in fact the easiest obstacle in Carlton's plan. A little dope goes a long way to get a drug addict in a comatose state. He researched all of his new ideas on the internet and he used the computers at the local library. He accidently came across some very useful information on a web site dedicated to drug addiction. Someone said in a chat room to someone else; "I guess they were scheming or something "That's only if you use your own computer for personal stuff, it could be traced, don't you know this? But how can you be traced if you use someone else's computer? Carlton immediately remembered the school library had computers that were linked into the internet and wondered if the local public libraries were the same. So that's when he asked the question in the chat room. Do the public libraries have computers with access to the internet? And low and behold, he got an answer. Whoa, dude, that's what I've been trying to tell ya. Use the public library's computers if you're up to something that might get you into a mess. So as Carlton searched the web for equipment that he will need and also stumbled onto some useful information about drugs. What it takes to make people sleep specifically. Every time he logged off the computer he made sure to erase everything that he did on it, and kept a mental log. His memory is very impressive. Not only did drugging his now wonderful crack head dope fiend stepmother keep her quiet, it also kept her out of his hair for a while. It was the perfect solution to his minor dilemma, now whenever he needed to get something by her; he made sure to immobilize her completely. Always paying attention, not to induce an overdose. That wouldn't be good at all, in fact it would be a minor catastrophe, and it could possibly lead to an uncomfortable and embarrassing predicament with all of this stolen equipment. Carlton's thoughts about her were; what a crazy bitch.

Its Carlton's laboratory now! He takes his time refurbishing it with all of the latest technology of today. He has plenty of time so he told himself; you never can be too careful! Actually his obsession with the internet in finding all of his information is exactly where he came across this phrase, it's a quote that he will eventually come to live by. He just doesn't know it yet. It took Carlton a little over a year to accumulate every complicated electronic device known to man. His dedication was admirable. He just placed the last of his computers in his lab and then decided to take a quick cat nap back in his old club house. He turned on his Sony Walkman and put in an Eagles tape and fell fast asleep. Lassie and Felix were playing on the floor right besides Carlton. The nap didn't last very long as he abruptly screamed and almost jumped out of his sneakers. Lassie and Felix scampered across the floor into a tiny hole at the bottom of a wall, screeching.

Carlton's heart was pumping furiously and his breathing is noticeably irregular. The very instant that he opened up his eyes he momentarily did not know where he was. He quivered then his sensors slowly returned to him. He was relieved that

The club house is sound proof! The nightmares are progressively getting worse. He can almost smell the air, it's so real! It's like I'm right there in the middle of it. He doesn't understand why he gets those terrible dreams and neither does his psychiatrist. Carlton's childhood was so depressive and secretly abusing, only himself and his psychiatrist is actually aware of his inner most thoughts and desires. Carlton longed for love and affection. He sometimes watched television movies of wonderful families all getting alone so splendidly having fun and wishing he could be part of it. He read many books escaping into the world of books is more like it, there was always a book with a new family and new adventures. If he thinks about it for too long he instantly dismisses it as not real, this is reality, here and now!

During Carlton's school days he has only one friend, it was a strange and peculiar way that they had first connected. They were both perceived as loners, though totally opposite in the academic sense they still managed to become friends. Seems like what it might have been is some mysteriously secret longing for acceptance and love. Both of them absolutely loved their lives in seclusion although they sometimes became frustrated and agitated from the loneliness. They both wished that they were worldlier, enough so that they could understand more of why people can be as cruel to one another and then just brush it all off as just; reckless abandonment. Periodically they have eyed each other creating a subconscious bond through their own individual psyche, unknowing to them at the time. They were in the beginning stages of becoming friends, yet they haven't even spoken a word to each other.

One day after class some kids were looking for some entertainment at the expense of others happened to be picking on this small kid who looked sick to his stomach. He was very pale when Carlton got a closer look at him, then he recognized who was being tormented. It was Jonathon Hunt. Jonathon was a genuine albino complete with fiery red eyes. Unknowing to Jonathon at the time, they were destined into becoming very good friends, in fact they will become best friends.

Children can be so cruel. They sometimes assembled in packs or gangs too young to understand the long term ramifications associated with street gangs. In school they all gathered together at recess, lunch time and also after classes. They consistently harassed and intimidated the lonely Albino boy just because he was different than they were. He was an easy target. Carlton finally befriended this ghostly white kid, same one with the strange looking eyes. His skin was almost translucent; you can practically see his blood pumping through his veins.

It was already a miserable day. It was dark and wet outside and the weather man on T V said that it will most likely be this way for a couple of more days to come. On and off showers cloudy and windy. Carlton was not a tough kid, not by any means, and he definitely wasn't a trouble maker like most of the other kids that hung out together after school. All of whom are secretly scared and ashamed of their own homes. Quite a few of these children come from abusive families and broken homes. They tend to lash out in school mimicking scenarios associated with their own home lives. Carlton fought his battles with words. He is much more verbally articulated than even his own school teachers. He always did his absolute best when it came to avoiding fist fights. Not that he couldn't handle himself, if the moment suddenly arises; Carlton is very athletic and agile. He couldn't explain it right now in his life but he somehow knew that fist fighting was just totally wrong and nothing good ever comes from it.

What Carlton and Jonathon have in common is the mere fact that each of them had thought and believed that they were outcasts. They didn't fit into today's society, two pieces of a different jigsaw puzzle.

Carlton quickly stepped in the middle of these rowdy kids in hopes in stopping them from tormenting Jonathon. Although he was vastly outnumbered, it didn't seem to matter to him. Carlton was determined to state his piece. It seemed to be working; they were all surprised and started to stare down at their own feet in dismay, then they slowly started to disperse. Carlton could not believe what he was seeing, he was taken aback. Could he be that influential, he thought to himself? He heard someone call out his name and turned around to see one of his school teachers approaching. He quickly surmises this must be the real reason that those kids quietly dispersed and chuckled to himself, so much for being influential. Ha ha, the jokes on me. Can I help you Mr. Tracy.

After the gloomy day, Jonathon and Carlton quickly became friends. They respected and appreciated each other and started to spend a great deal of time together. Carlton started to help his new friend Jon with his school work. He is his tutor now and teases Jon about it from time to time, but never in public. Carlton is very wise for his age. They decided to go fishing together today and you can find them every Saturday in the game room at the local mall.

They were both addicted to pinball machines. It was a refreshing change from isolation at School although there were many kids at school they were still alone, at least they were together and at this point in time that was everything to them.

Carlton and Jonathan didn't see each other during summer school breaks, but they still stay in touch by correspondence via emails and the occasional letter. Jonathan's parents went away every summer. They were both schoolteachers and like the students they too had the summers off. They kind of felt bad for their son John because of his best friend not being able to come along with them. They did ask him and Carlton. He politely refused, he lied and said he and his dad had major plans this summer, but maybe I can go for a week in August, we'll see. Yes do, that would be very nice for Jonathan. Jonathan's parents were very impressed with their son's friends, they thought very highly of call and they knew he was a good influence of their son and both of them hope Carlton come visit in August.

While Carlton was downstairs working on his invention he glances up at a computer screen, the one he's got linked to his hidden video cameras in the basement and also to his dads surveillance equipment, a buzzer sounded and he seen someone coming into the driveway. He realized it was his dad and he wasn't alone, he's with his stepmother. They are home early. It's rare these days that both them are seen in public they both lived very separate lives. Carlton Never did understand their relationship. They have nothing whatsoever in common with each other, except, maybe sex. Of course that must be it. Carlton witnessed Barbara firsthand, performing sex acts with strangers in their own house, at first he was too young to understand and laughed at himself now as he remembers, he used to think someone was getting hurt with all the moaning and small cries. Prostitution and drugs is a lifestyle which is almost impossible to stop completely. It's a lifetime struggle and many people falter and lose the battle and end up dying before their time. Sometimes he thinks and wonders to himself while in his now private room in the basement how and why they got together in the first place. My father must know what she does and if he does not know why he continues to allow her to keep on doing it. It might never be known, and heads upstairs to greet them, a really awkward gesture he thinks but proceeds anyway. Charles approaches his son as Barbara heads upstairs to their own room. Charles asks him to come with him next weekend to visit his great aunt Peggy, he enticed her in with the idea that she was asking for you you know. Yes, sure I'll go with you. I kind of miss her anyway. Charles thought he was going to get an excuse or something, but he was slightly surprised and he smiled. They didn't talk very much it was more awkward for Charles then it was for Carlton. Charles asked him if he was hungry and said Barbara and I brought home a doggie bag from the new Greek restaurant in town, they serve so much food a person can't possibly eat it all and it was Barbara's ideas that you might like to try some. Wow! Carlton said to himself, to surprises in one day. Did I miss a holiday or something? Yes I am a little hungry and if you are going upstairs please tell her I said thank you. I am a little tired and I overstuffed myself, I'll tell Barbara you said thank you and I think I'll retire to the library. Good night son, good night dad.

Carlton misses his friend John during summer vacations but simultaneously is relieved that he's not here to witness his crazy stepmother, his crazy stepmother's despicable behaviors that she frequently and so elaborately exhibits, not to mention her drug-induced outlandish impatience when his presence is made known (get down in the basement you miserable brat) she would say. Carlton is really starting to dislike her.

Carlton's early teen years are much more to his liking then that of his earlier childhood and staying away from his stepmother was easy back then.

Carlton no longer minds going down into the basement, he even relishes the moments when his stepmother yells at him to go down into the basement. He absolutely loves the sound proof room he built a few summers ago. A quiet place to study, and to entertain himself without any distractions at all. His own personal private retreat from the world, and don't forget his secret, his carefully camouflaged and cryptic laboratory.

To everyone and no one's surprise Carlton's recreation room in the basement is a clever and convenient cover to conceal his new passion. His great great grandfather's laboratory which is now furnished with all the latest electronic equipment for his use and his used alone. The only reference left to remind him of the old laboratory was a small framed picture of a man holding an achievement award; Carlton can only assume that it's his great great grandfather. He's never seen a picture of before but all that might change when he and his father pays a visit to see Aunt Peggy next weekend. The pitcher is strange thinks the man in the picture resembles his dad, it's quite canny and it unnerves him. Carlton does think that it's his great-great-grandfather Michael Van Hellsang.

Carlton is not quite obsessed with his original invention yet (the transport machine) but he does go over some figures from time to time and his concentrating of metabolite is the key he believes that would unlock the doors.

He's been working on a contraption of a much less magnitude and believes he'll be finished within the next week; he calls it the "freeze wave". It does the exact opposite of what a conventional microwave oven does. It actually cools solids and liquids, he hasn't thought about its use on a grandeur scale yet, like nationwide are even worldwide. He has more important business to attend to. He really does enjoy his private sanctuary room; he's kind of grown accustomed to his solace, his privacy.

Carlton spent his high school years at a school called Mount St. Charles Borden Academy located in one Woonsocket Rhode Island, it was a Catholic school. His friend Jonathan was there and it was so easy talking his father into sending him there also.

Eugene Banks was Carlton's guidance counselor as well as his friend Jonathan's guidance counselor. Carlton was too smart for his own good sometimes and that fact unnerved a lot of people. It was a big reason why his guidance counselor was constantly discouraging him behind the scenes. Carlton was constantly being told that he was a coward and a manipulator. He was distrusted by the majority of the staff all because they can't figure him out. While Carlton's friend Jonathan was humbly being molded by Brother Eugene and looked after in what seemed to be a genuine concern, Carlton was monotonously the end told by the same brutally forward person "you'll never amount to anything "you're wasting my time and this fine schools time. Carlton has everyone right where he wants them. One thing that Brother Eugene was correct in was with his initial assumption, it was the fact that Carlton could manipulate people and very easily I might add, he was a master of manipulation.

Carlton's guidance counselor always went out of his way to hurt him, and sometimes it did get to him, especially when after he was up all night studying or working on something and was tired. When his guard was down brother Eugene just might happen to be lurking around the next corridor anticipating a one-sided confrontation (you weren't allowed to talk back) this man was mean and emotionally distressing.

These are supposed to be the most impressionable years of a young person's life. High school is supposed to be fun and excitement to a kid. And so Carlton did start having a little fun himself, he and John attended an occasional dance held by the St. Anne's Catholic School for girls. It was all quite amusing, for Carlton had no rhythm at all, and his friend John poked fun at him all night he even mimicked him in the last class before the anticipated event came fold. While there teacher stepped out for a minute John asked out loud, who was going to the dance and a few hands went up and he said aloud have you seen Carlton dance yet and chuckled a few giggles and some sarcasm, then John walked down the center aisle of desks with his arms stretched out in front of him stiff legged like Frankenstein and the whole class busted out with laughter then the teacher came back in and with no punishment either, he was one of the nicer teaches and understood they were all excited about the dance, all the kids in school like Mr. Banks.

Eugene Banks couldn't help it; he was a product of his environment. His parents lived in the E St. projects, not far from one of the roughest areas in Boston Massachusetts; it was called the notorious "combat zone". Eugene Banks is considered by most a very short man in height he stood about 5'5". He was completely bald and the kids at school called him Mr. Magoo, but never to his face, as he's heard rumors? He wears thick round glasses that strained around his chubby face; he's at least 200 pounds and sweats profusely. He currently lives in Cambridge Massachusetts, and he never did forget that he came from some of the meanest streets in Boston, and it was an everyday occurrence to fight just to get into the door of the building that he lived in. Some of his pent up hostility is dreadfully exhibited through his work and right now one of his favorite victims is Carlton van Helsang. He was a very small child at the time and got picked on and beat up on a regular, just because he was small and smart, he got bullied and now he's bullying back.

Jonathan Hunt phones Carlton this evening and says hi Carlton what's up buddy, how the hell are you? Can I cool off my drinks yet? Laughter, without adding ice says John. What's so funny Casper Carlton calls him that when he is mad at him. What, you don't think I can do it huh, well you'll see. As a matter of fact old buddy it's almost finished, I just have a few more kinks to iron out. Really! Yeah! Really! Can you go out tonight? I wanted to see a movie. I'm sorry John but am really intent on getting this contraption to work and I'm sure it's going to happen real soon maybe even this week. Then we'll just have to see what brother Eugene has to say about me then, won't we. Oh all right, I guess I'll see you in class tomorrow then, okay, good night, good night John.

Carlton was actually working on his transport machine. No one knew his other invention; freeze wave was already finished for over a month now. The freeze wave instantly cools liquids without having to use any ice. It's a backwards microwave oven he says. He goes on to explain about this one drawback to ice and that it waters down whenever you're drinking. You don't have this problem with the freeze wave.

Carlton's waiting for the opportune time to unveil his new invention, "The Freeze Wave". If the time comes and it may not. If he's ever questioned about how much time he spends in the basement, he'll always have his invention the freeze wave the fall back on for an excuse to throw them off track. Carlton turned on his Walkman radio, and popped in an Elvis Presley cassette and started listening to his favorite song "love me tender"

Carlton realizes he's getting close to finishing his experiment. He unsuccessfully attempted to transport paperweight, an inanimate object and it dissipated into space and never did materialize, Carlton thought to himself, not here anyway. After a few calculations and a few changes and tweaking this and that, a month went by and he was ready try again.

He used another paperweight in this time something did happen, something extraordinary, although it wasn't a success he was overwhelmed, he was momentarily frozen in time soaking up his own excitement. The paperweight did indeed move through space and time from point A to point B. What happened was, it had melted. The atoms and molecules didn't quite come back together the way they were supposed to, or the way I intended them to. The paperweight was just a warm blob but it was a vast improvement, at least now something is visibly happening and Carlton couldn't be more empowered with an intense diligence that came over him. He was caught up in a vigorous flow of adrenaline. His dream will soon be reality. He thought of the old television series "Star Trek "and wondered if anyone behind the television magic would ever entertain the thought that a transport machine could actually materialize someday. Well, that day is not far off. He recorded his information in his journals and then happily took a break and strolled almost skipped down the tunnel to a sanctuary, his fabulous sanctuary, smiling profusely he decided to watch another rerun of his favorite television show "Star Trek" that's right, Spock goes home to the planet Vulcan.

Eventually he falls asleep and in that state of euphoria he dreams of his own breakthrough invention. He slept for hours and he awakens to another god awful nightmare, the TV had automatically shut off from a timer that he had set and when he awoke it was very eerie in the dark, it was deathly quiet.

Haunting visions and nightmares continually plagued columns mind. Carlton methodically approaches the completion of his Nobel prize-winning invention; the transporter. His doctor, Dr. Jonathan Fisher, had specifically told him to get a notebook and write down everything he can remember about the bad dreams that enter his sleep, no matter how grotesque they might be. Sooner or later we'll get to the bottom of this. He was a persistent man and somewhat arrogant. It's said that his colleagues despise him because of his repulsive straightforwardness. He was ambitious nevertheless and his demeanor left little to be desired. He exceeded his certain power and he had very little patience for people in general. He did have many achievements and was the best at what he does.

Carlton and Jonathan finally made it through high school. They graduated top of their classes, and both had very different futures ahead of them. Colin was accepted at yearly University, his father's alma mater and he could not wait to start packing. Jonathan his friend, decided to go and enlist into the Marine Corps. Jonathan grew into a good man, and as the poster says; they were looking for a few good men he wasn't trying to fool anyone about himself, he knew being an albino he probably didn't have a very long lifespan and he wanted to see part of the world and serve his country. His own father served in the Armed Forces and was proud his son followed in his footsteps. Like Carlton, John couldn't wait to start on his new would venture. In the next few months they lost touch with each other.

College life changes even the most humble of people as does the military. It's their first time away from home, two very different atmospheres with no guardians. Time to grow up and become a man. Carlton loved his college sorority house, who didn't. Being on his own with all this freedom, hardly even doing laundry, hanging around with burn out friends, all types of personalities. Eating pizza and drinking beer at midnight, listening to loud music. Aerosmith and Led Zeppelin rocking the halls in the dorm. It was truly heaven, a reprieve from the immaturity that came with high school except when the porcelain God requires its timely deposits from too much partying. Many a student kneeled down praying before her, it'll never happen again! Only to meet her again and again.

Carlton was a really good athlete in high school so he tried out for the football team his freshman year at Yale. After a few grueling weeks of practices and skirmishes he learned that he had made the team and was really happy.

The quarterback position, he was an excellent quarterback in high school, he had broken two records in his senior year, the most yardage passing and nine more touchdowns than the previous record held. After making the team he dramatically slowed down his late nights with the guys, he became all business and only played when the team had a game. Carlton's nemesis at the quarterback position was Jimmy Welch, he was a senior, his last year at Yale and he doesn't particularly care for his new competition, in fact, he hates Carlton. It's because Carlton is competing for Jimmy's quarterback position at Yale. He won't admit it, but he knows Carlton is very good (but he's just a damn freshman) Jimmy surmises. Jimmy Welch would never admit it, he's in denial, he is in fear of possibly losing his first string quarterback position to a rookie freshman and this is his last year to make a good impression for the NFL. He doesn't want to end up like Drew Bledsoe from the new England patriots football team who lost his job to an unproven Tom Brady in the 2001- 2002 NFL season. Hence forth, Tom Brady leads the patriots' team to the big dance and ends up winning Super Bowl number 36.

Jimmy Welch had major cynical plans to ensure and seal his position, and no one was going to take over for him, after all he was a senior at Yale and was no dumb snot nose freshman.

It was a cool dark rainy night, the end of September, the streets were flooded and an occasional car drove slowly by splashing a wave of dirty water onto the already slippery sidewalks. There is no one out and about; it was raining sheets pattering the Windows. Jimmy Welch disguised in a dark ski mask along with three other masked men stormed into Carlton's dorm room. Two of the intruders quickly grabbed Carlton's roommate, they were very strong, they held him down while he protested and yelled (what's going on, let me go…) A brutal beat ensued, no harm came to Carlton's roommate, and they both were gagged. Carlton's arm was twisted behind his back, his right arm, his throwing arm! It was intentionally twisted to the point of no return. It snapped making an awful sound like a baseball hitting a bat. Carlton passes out from the pain; you only hear a muffled shriek because he was gagged. His roommate was tied up with rope and clearly was not harmed. It was a message for only Carlton they thought.

Despite all the blame and controversy that followed Jimmy Welch all his remaining year at school, he remained as Yale University's first string quarterback on their ailing football team. It was a pretty dismal year for the Yale football team mainly because of Jimmy Welch. He lost all respect from the majority of his teammates as well as some of his teachers, coaches and certain professors. No proof had ever surfaced that Jimmy was responsible for the terrible beating giving to the new comer, quarterback Carlton Van Helsang. He was in everyone's thoughts and in everyone's eyes the only person who had something to gain, Carlton was just a freshman, he was brand-new to the school and was very talented at the quarterback position, and he didn't even have time to make any friends yet let alone make enemies. It was a tragedy that went unpunished. The Yale football team suffered one of their worst years in recent history, falling five games below 500%. Obviously Carlton couldn't play so he concentrated on his studies and ended up making a couple of good friends after all, one of them in particular took up more of his time than most.

Carlton's sophomore year was much better, he'd love living at the dorms. He spent a few weeks hanging out with his best friend during summer vacation. Lance Cpl. Jonathan Hunt took 2 1/2 weeks leave to spend with his family and even as importantly to him, his friend from Yale University, Carlton. Carlton spent most of the summer working on his invention putting to use some useful knowledge he derived from physics class. Carlton couldn't wait to get back to Yale. He thought to himself and strongly felt he finally had what he personally perceived a family, and he was also Yale's starting quarterback, life couldn't be better right now.

Three games into the season and yield was three wins and zero defeats. After the game is seem like not only the team celebrated but the whole school was excited. Back at the sorority house Carlton made his way through the crowd of students drinking and stuffing themselves with pizza and junk food, as he got into his room and no sooner did he sit down his phone rang. It was John! Oh, excuse me, I meant, it was Lance Cpl. Jonathan Hunt. Hey buddy, great game today, I saw it on cable TV. I'm keeping an eye on you. Hi John, it's so good to hear from you and a nice surprise I must add. Some of my jar head friends don't believe me when I told them that the quarterback from Yale University is my best friend. Looks like you're having a great season. Yes, I guess some lucky so far, it's not luck at all, I seen you play throughout our high school days, you're too modest.

The next night Carlton received a visit from one of the offense of lineman, it was big Carl, that's what we all called him. 6'4" and 280 pounds and fast as lightning. He is one of the reasons for our early winning season this year. Carl was a tight end on Yale University's football team, it was his third year, a junior and he was a quiet but popular figure on the team. Carl confessed privately to Carlton. He said, I'm so sorry Carlton. Carlton looked confused, you had a great game the other day Carl so what you talking about. You could easily tell that Carl was having difficulty expressing his mind his facial features were resonating sorrow. Carl went on to say I was blackmailed last year. What do you mean blackmailed? I was failing two of my classes, English and history and I had someone taken my exams. My dad isn't rich and he works too many hours paying for my education and if he ever found out someone else was taking my exams he would absolutely kill me. Not to mention it would break my mother's heart because dad would disown me. What does this have to do with me? Jimmy Welch knew this about me and made me go with him to your dorm room last year. I'm so sorry Carlton. Carl had tears slowly rolling down his face now. Jimmy said he only wanted to scare you because you were a young freshman and really good and he was afraid of losing his job on the team. I didn't want to be there but he would've let the cat out of the bag and I would have been disgraced. I held down your roommate if you can remember he didn't get physically hurt and it was Jimmy Welch who broke your arm. God I've been carrying this all year, it was eating me up alive. I always liked you Carlton and I still do, that's why I am telling you now. My hands were tied I hope you understand and I hope we can still be friends. Then big Carl left.

Carlton's sophomore year at Yale University was doubtfully the most fulfilling year of his life so far. Not only is he the starting quarterback having a successful year, there was a beautiful girl in his life also. His first kiss.

Glenda Walker was Carlton's new girlfriend, she was intelligent, witty, and spontaneous and she was absolutely gorgeous. Glenda was head cheerleader for the yield football team and it seemed like a fairytale matchup. Head cheerleader and star quarterback, it was something out of a romance novel. She had long wavy light brown hair flowing gracefully down her back below her waist; banana curls caressed her light cheekbones, deep dark piercing hazel eyes and a voluptuous full figure with a tiny waist line. Her smile was absolutely captivating. Glenda had teeth so white they sparkled, and why wouldn't they, have major at Yale University's dentistry. Glenda had been admiring Carlton for a long time now; she goes out of her way to make eye contact especially during the home games. After his first win she boldly walked right up to him in front of all of his teammates and congratulated him with the shy kiss on the cheek with eyes all flutter. Obviously he was totally embarrassed and his teammates did little to defuse the awkward moment. They pushed and shoved him towards her as she teasingly turned away. She glanced back to peak over her shoulder with the cute little smile as she did notice his friends teasing him why hasn't he even taken a step from the spot where she kissed him, she wondered. Carlton was still looking at her, mouth slightly ajar with the very genuine surprised look on his face, a crooked smile. She thought it was the sweetest picture and kept walking back towards the rest of her cheerleader friends who are all whispering with each other and giggling.

Weeks and months flew by. Carlton and Glenda are a well-known couple now and are admired throughout the campus. It was very difficult separating during summer vacation but they promised each other they would stay in contact and pay each other a visit.

Call Times invention is finally completed. It occurred at the end of his summer vacation two weeks before the year was to start. He successfully transported an inanimate object from point A to point B. And after numerous tries, he now can pinpoint where he wants his objects to appear. He uses XY coordinates of the earth and the magnetic poles synchronize his machine. He's experimented with locations for a whole month and he is beyond pleased with the results. His last experiment was transport picture of himself and his girl Glenda. They took this picture last month when she came to visit, a photo taken at the beautiful cliff walks in Newport Rhode Island. He has it hanging in his dorm room at school. School didn't start for a couple more weeks so he used the excuse upon entering the closed dorm that he wanted to avoid all the hustle and chaos beat the traffic jams of personal property, clothing, books, etc... Sure enough, as he unlocked his room door, there it was, without a scratch. The picture of him and Glenda, he knew it would still be there, he could help but be excited and smiled as he gazed at it.

Now it's time to go a step further. Carlton's two friends who kept constant eye on him whenever he's in the laboratory are the next test. I see and Felix are about to embark on a journey that will ultimately put them in the history books, or are they about to meet their maker? Less than a week left before Carlton's senior year at Yale University he decides he couldn't wait any longer to find out if his invention can actually send a living life form. Though Carlton isn't overly religious, he didn't recite aloud a prayer, after all these mice were his companions for a long time.

Carlton's senior year had started and his two companions are safe and sound scampering to true out the old house. Needless to say, he knew it all along. The experiment was a groundbreaking monumental success. Now his final year at Yale University. He's a big man on campus now but that didn't stop his girlfriend Glenda from cheating on him. Carlton was devastated. The breakup, it was ugly, the school press heard about it and it was all over the campus. Carlton goes into seclusion. He focuses on his transport invention. He swears on revenge! Somehow, someday both, Glenda Walker and Jimmy Welch will pay.

Over the Christmas holidays Carlton had two weeks off and to his untimely surprise his best friend Jonathan, now a Sgt. in the United States Marine Corps, had the same two weeks home on leave. It was just what the doctor ordered; his best friend really knew how to cheer them up. It was his despicably fun filled two weeks and both of them were saddened by having to return to their normal lives. The night before Carlton went back to school he reminisced about time he and Glenda spent an evening on a blanket under the stars enjoying each other's company with a couple of wine coolers. He smiled slightly as the memory of that night faded.

He remembered Glenda spotted someone in the distance walking their dog under a hazy streetlight, it was a Crisp clear night and the only sounds were crickets playing their music, so we both guessed that our voices must have carried and we watched the man with the dog as he strained to look in the direction of our voices. Glenda, always the spontaneous one with a mixture of mischief said to me let's give him something to think about or to dream about, you know, maybe even something to fantasize about tonight after he goes to sleep. I smiled and agreed with her and then out of nowhere she just started to moan and was putting on quite a show, we were quietly laughing and giggling as the dog Walker was now bending at the waist doing his best to try to see us, walking quickly up and down not taking his eyes off us for a second. It was one of our fondest memories; I couldn't help but shed a small tear snapping back to reality knowing that it will never happen again with her.

Carlton's nightmares still plagued his nights and certainly not long after his breakup with Glenda, he's been mysteriously getting visions during the day. It's the same people in his dreams and it's nerve racking he can't seem to shake these tormenting episodes. Carlton's psychiatrist Dr. Fischer keeps trying new treatments and medications and although he portrays optimism nothing seems to make a difference, the periodic impressions just keep coming. Carlton is so used to them by now and it's not even scary anymore, they're more of a nuisance at this stage than anything else. Dr. Fischer said my neural pathways might be the problem understandably it's an educated guess nonetheless; it's still an irritating problem.

Dr. Jonathan Fischer suggests another technique. He recommended Carlton to get more involved in the community, maybe become a big brother some underprivileged child, make one of those kids your project. Help them out with their school work; explain life as you went through it at their age. Take them out pool ball game or something, have some fun. Build some trust and confidence in someone who desperately needs it. You know, your daydreams started soon after your breakup with your girl and that's when you started isolating, too much time to think. Too much of anything is not good. So doing something nice for someone other than yourself just might overpower your subconscious minds ability to keep tormenting you with your dreadful nightmares. Carlton takes the sound advice and puts it in motion.

Carlton graduates from Yale University with honors. He commences a teaching career at a local college near home. He decides to take his psychiatrists advice and attempts to befriend some children at a small orphanage two towns over from where he lives. One night he comes home from the orphanage to find his dad lying on the bathroom floor. Even though Carlton and his father had slowly drifted apart over the years, he is hoping that his dad's okay Carlton can hear the sirens outside and is flushed with relief. As the paramedics rush up into the house up the stairs towards the door, Carlton's already there letting them in and guiding them to his unconscious father. A worried look engulfs his face as the paramedics demanded some room; they lifted his dad on a gurney.

Turns out that, Charles Van Helsang was very sick, and was keeping it a secret. His wife, a known drug addict was quietly taken his medication for herself. She's been using heroin and barbiturates for years, along with anything else that she gets her hands on including my father's medicine.

Barbara was sick and tired of her husband neglecting her, who could blame him, she was a rat wretch, the lifestyle she chose really took a toll on her now lost radiant beauty, she was no longer eye appealing and her demeanor was even worse, a very measurable hateful woman. She tried to rid herself of her unsuspecting husband and she couldn't, truth was she didn't even know how.

Carlton's friends, Lassie and Felix, these two mice went through the transporter numerous times now and might I add without a scratch. Carlton decides to take the plunge and try it on himself, a monumental event indeed.

At least, a complete and absolute success. Carlton couldn't be more elated. The transport machine left tingles all over his skin; he rushed towards a full length mirror up, stripped himself of his clothing and inspected his body. He made it without a scratch, not even hair was out of place on his head. At first, right after rematerializing he was a little off balance his equilibrium shifted but quickly settled. It was like hovering in air and your feet not actually touching the ground. The split-second your vision returns your mind reacts to a message insisting you're on solid ground all simultaneously. In that split second is when your actual physical balance is somewhat thwarted. (Can you say Nobel Prize).

After Carlton's father is near death experience Carlton's relentless scare tactics with Barbara was making her go mad. In her hostile confused state she was rapidly becoming mentally unbalanced, probably had to do something with my father's medications. Charles recovers and immediately sets out to converse with his son about his stepmom Barbara. Have come to a decision he said, it should have happened long ago I have decided to have Barbara committed to a home, a professional home of course. Some place private, and discreet. Carlton concurs emphasizing the privacy suggestion. Carlton tells his father to relax; I'll take care of finding the suitable place for her. Leave it to me dad. Get some rest now you've been through a great ordeal already. Carlton has already started a plan rid his father of Barbara and now his father wants her gone, it'll be much easier now. Charles also tells his son that his aunt Peggy would like to see him sometime soon.

Carlton's been getting these strange sensations and compulsions lately. They distract his thinking and he becomes frustrated, as intelligent as Carlton is, he cannot seem to pinpoint from where this unbearable affliction originates, not even his psychiatrists has been able to help him. He now considers Dr. Fischer his friend and after all these years Carlton knows the doctor has done his level best, but still Carlton can't help but think it's all useless. His mind will never be free.

A mysterious passion for killing seems to have been plaguing Carlton's mind in recent years; he's even mentioned it to Dr. Fischer only to be discarded. Dr. Fischer says that people who kill are taught at an early age to be ruthless and mean, and you my friend were raised in quite a civil household. in his dreams it does seem to be very therapeutic as she quietly surmises to himself (wishful thinking).

Carlton starts reflecting back on his own life. He remembers a great deal. He can go as far back as two years old when he was being yelled at by his nanny for not using the potty properly. Then of course he remembers when his nanny left and his new Guardian came into the picture, his wicked stepmother. He never could figure out why there was a change, he never did say anything to his father about the awful things she did it was fear for repercussions. Carlton didn't want to add fuel to a burning fire, there's no telling what she might have done to him, it was horrible enough to be mandated to the basement. He was scared of her. That's when he was six years old. She didn't scare you too much longer after that brief period when he was six years old. Carlton was a very quick learner and overcame these many fears very quickly.

Charles Aunt Peggy look forward to the big holiday of the year for her anyways, always expecting a visit from her grandnephew on Easter Sunday, Thanksgiving and Christmas, he never failed to show up on those days. She has been surprised one day recently though, it wasn't a holiday or special occasion but there in the flesh, Charles showed up unannounced and his aunt Peggy couldn't have been more pleased. Charles had chatted with her all afternoon and after he explained his ordeal they had a very pleasant afternoon. She mentioned to Charles right before he left that Carlton has been to see her in a while. He said he'll make it a point to mention it to him when he gets back home.

Labor Day was the next holiday so father and son with genuine anticipation set out for a Leisurely drive en route to see Aunt Peggy's convalescent home deep in the Adirondack Mountains. After an hour and a half of driving, Carlton pulled off the highway when he spotted the sign on the edge of the highway embankment, which said restaurants and fuel. They headed for Starbucks for some hot coffee.

Carlton's great aunt Peggy was his only living relative besides his father. She was dad's mother's sister something like that and I was thinking, maybe she deserves more attention from me. She had told me once, when your dad's real mother, my sister, she died giving birth to your father and I ended up raising him as my own. This is what she has always told me, over and over.

After refueling the old town car at the newly constructed mobile gas station, we asked the polite attendant directions to the nearest Starbucks coffee shop that we had seen on the highway sign. She was really a sweet kid. She had short blonde hair, a small pug nose and light blue eyes like a clear sky, she had dimples when she smiled and spoke with an elegant choice of words. Her name tag said Annie. She told us it's the only place she goes for her coffee even though we sell coffee here, she winked as she lowered her voice and teasingly said, don't tell my boss. She said it was a half a mile west, go left out of our parking lot and you'll see it on your left in five minutes. My dad was already heading to the car, probably thinking I was flirting or something. I said it was a pleasure to meet you Annie and thank you. You're very welcome. Goodbye now. As I stepped inside the car my dad smirked and said did you get her number?

I laughed and said, she's a little too young for me pops. He looked at me and said smiling, which way Casanova?

Aunt Peggy was a very jolly old woman. She was extremely intelligent and very witty. Her mind is as sharp as it was 50 years ago, although she's slowed down a bit physically, it hasn't stopped her from doing what she wants to do, even at her rest home. She carries an aura of determination and everything she sets out to do. No one really knows her exact age. Some people do seem to believe that she's over 100 years old; at least they assume she's pretty close to it. The people who cater to her listen to the stories she tells. They become entranced by the acute memory of days in years gone past. From time to time she reminisces when there were no paved roads at all, just beautiful meadows, fancy outfits and a person's word was as good as a written document by a team of lawyers today. She signs and smiles.

For anyone to be in Aunt Peggy's presence, you can't help but see and feel a strange maternal quality gracefully flowing from her.

This Peggy Russell was very attractive in her day, and still is quite lovely. Her skin still has a radiant shine under a thick pallet of wavy white hair, which intentionally is almost always meticulously pinned up with an old-fashioned hair comb. Only her private nurse has seen

Aunt Peggy's hair down. Her private nurse washes her snowy locks and add its full length flows over her shoulders cascading down her erect spine,. Her hair would get make a younger woman envious. She has huge bright brown eyes and still to this day has perfect vision. Her hearing isn't exactly 100% but she's too proud to get a hearing aid. Amazingly, she doesn't look a day over 70. Aunt Peggy's timeless beauty still entrances men today of all ages.

Both men, Charles and Carlton gladly abandoned their dreary routines that day. They look forward to seeing their lovely aunt and spoke of her fondly as they traveled along, and not only for the sake of an old woman's possible last wishes, but also to catch up on each other's latest experiences, trials, tribulations and more simply put, what's happening lately? They haven't seen much of each other and Carlton broke the ice by explaining his first invention the freeze wave. Although it's been finished for a few years called and is just recently applying for copyrights and trademarks.

Barbara is in one of her mind altering states again induced by a massive heroine injection, a handful of barbiturates and a bottle of vodka. Charles and Barbara are moving along I495n. It's a miserable afternoon. Barbara is hunched over in the passenger seat at least your seat belt is on, and she can't seem to help but drool all over herself. Unknowingly she's on her way to a private, exclusive, insane asylum. Charles can't wait for this ordeal to be over with.

Barbara doesn't like leaving the house anymore so she had to be tricked and encouraged by Charles into believing that there's a big party and it's not exactly a white-collar affair. Let's say, it'll be an addict's dream come true, a fantasy camp, that's its nickname! It's a little bit of a ride, it's in Andover Massachusetts, and so you can just sit back and enjoy the ride, okay honey. There was someone famous their last time and he had gotten caught with all types of psycho- tropic drugs. This peak to her curiosity and all of a sudden she opened her eyes and then closed them with a smirk on her lips. There was heroin, cocaine, antidepressants, LSD, methadone and cannabis, and that's just the tip of the iceberg, there are also gallons of booze.

Charles is driving very carefully. It'll be a while before they arrive because the weather doesn't want to be too cooperative it's actually snowing downright nasty out there right now; there is hardly time to remove all the snow it's coming down so hard. Charles doesn't leave the house much himself so naturally he's not used to driving in this kind of weather. He wants to make it there in one piece and he'll worry about getting back home later, so long as she gets her committed and out of his life forever. His doctors tell him he needs to stop stressing over every little thing, and they weren't mean in Barbara either. No one knew about her problems with drug abuse. She always was a closet drug addict.

It's so miserable outside and noisy from the plows and the street sanders that Charles didn't realize he had a flat tire. He was driving slowly and with the snow and ice on the road he couldn't tell. It was only when a pickup truck pulled out dangerously close beside him to tell him that. Then he panicked. Oh my God, he was scared and nervous and didn't know if it was a bunch of rowdy teenagers, a drunk driver, or just some lunatic. He finally rolled down his window and was glad the Lincoln had power windows, and he attempted to throw them a finger for scaring him when he noticed the cab of the pickup truck was brightly illuminated and the driver was pointing to the rear of the car in a downward motion. He was driver yellow truck with the words department of transportation, stenciled on the door. I was relieved for a moment but then again he was trying to tell me something. He pulled forward, I rolled the window up, now he's in front of me slowing down, the road narrowed and I couldn't go around him. We both stopped and I locked my doors as he exited his vehicle and proceeded to walk towards my car. He was yelling at me, and he said, you got a flat tire. I rolled the window down 2 inches and he said it again, what? I said you got a flat tire in the rear and then asked me if I wanted some help changing it.

Oh my God, I could have been killed thank you so much, what's your name son, he said Billy. My name is Charles and I don't know how to fix this, Billy said don't worry about it, do you have a spare tire? Yes, okay then I'll fix it for you. It will be the 10th flat tire that I fixed tonight. Really? Yes, down at the yard where I work we had a line of trucks coming in with the same problem; a car is much easier to work on. Charles said, how can I thank you, please don't worry about it, its part of my job. So as Billy finished, Charles insisted on giving Billy a $25 tip. He was a young man about 25 years old and he was unexpectedly surprised and at first politely refused, and Charles wasn't taking no for an answer, so he purposefully shoved the money in Billy's coat pocket and said, thank you very much and go get yourself a hot cup of coffee. Billy couldn't help but smile and said thank you sir you have a pleasant evening, no! Thank you young man! Charles drove off and thanked the Lord for his timely encounter. Barbara startles Charles, she starts yelling. You scared the hell out of me, what's wrong? Oh my God, she's now mumbling something gibberish and falling in and out of consciousness. Why are we in a parade? What Charles answered? How are you high! Do we have to wash the car as she thinks confetti's fallen and covering the car? Hey! Give me a drink! I want a drink! Soon honey, were almost there. He's put up with this behavior way too long, far longer than anyone else would have ever permitted. Charles couldn't drive too fast because of the slippery roads, although he quietly wished he could. Charles thought toward himself, how can this woman's mind be so chaotic, distorted and unmistakably tormented and always a acutely confused. It stopped snowing and simultaneously he quietly enjoyed Mother Nature's picturesque beauty as he was driving. A tranquil scene forming right outside this vehicle. It was like magic; there it was, right before his very eyes, so pure and untouched, a peaceful night. He passes by a field covered in a blanket of fresh snow, the tree limbs are hanging low from the weight and icicles are forming. It was so beautiful and then he looked at his passenger in disgust. She turned into an ice cold bitch over the years, there's no help for her left.

Charles and Barbara finally arrive at the plush Andover Memorial treatment facility. I pulled the car all the way to the front doors under the veranda. Barbara is still comatose, so far so good she hasn't opened her eyes (probably can't thought) she starts to shiver and I'm not sure if she's just cold or if she's coming down from her last fix. I never did acclimate myself to the world of drug addiction, so I couldn't know for sure, if I would have to guess, I'd say she is withdrawing. She mumbles something; can I have a blanket Charles? I'm cold. Oh well, maybe I'm wrong.

Charles thought of his New England college days, seems like such a long time ago. He remembers sitting at his desk and one early evening in particular comes to mind. He was feeding an intense tenderness, he had just finished watching a very touching movie and his heart strings were being tugged. He grabbed that some stationery from the desk drawer and intended to write his dad a letter when, as he pulled up the shade above his desk he stared out the window of his dreary dark dorm room. A blanket of fresh snow had covered entire courtyard and it was the most beautiful picture. Every branch was heavily covered with snow along with picnic benches and statues. It was untouched by anyone not even a hungry squirrel or chipmunk scurried through, an intoxicating white velvet blanket and it was imperative that he take a photograph.

I still have that picture today, a truly beautiful moment in time during the hustle and bustle of college campus life. It's been snowing here for most of the day. I'm standing by a window in the lounge and although it's elegant in its self with its firm oriental carpeting and French leather furniture with soft light from English teardrop chandeliers. I couldn't stop myself from cutting off the world, if just for a few moments to admire the beautiful site outside the lounge patio. Everything looks so serene and mystical at the same time. The sun is shining now and it's almost blinding to look directly onto the silvery sparkles as they covered every square inch of the hospital's lush lovely grounds. It's Mother Nature at its best. I love the four seasons in New England and I always will. I spent a month in the Hawaiian Islands once, it was a February and I got a sun tan, But still for some reason I longed to come home to the winter months. Excuse me, but tall gentleman walked over to me and asked, are you Mr. Van Helsang? Mr. Charles Van Helsang, why yes, can I help you? I'm Dr. Silvera; we've just admitted your wife under the conditions described in our contract. She's completely in our care now. You can see her if you like; I don't think she'll be responsive, oh. Yes, I'm afraid she put up a struggle with the staff and we had to heavily sedate her, already causing trouble. That sounds like Barbara. I apologize for her hostile behavior. Then I guess how be heading to my hotel, I had made arrangements to stay at the Sheraton, could you by chance point me in the right directions Doctor. I sure can, please call me Charles okay Charles. Just get back on I-93no. and drive approximately 6 miles and you will see it or the side of the highway, in fact you cannot miss it, there's about a half dozen signs advertise in it. Thank you very much Dr. They shook hands and Charles left the building without a second glance back. He felt the tremendous relief wash over him, then smiled for the first time that day.

While Carlton's dad was traveling with Barbara to Andover Massachusetts, Carlton heads down in the opposite direction to Boston, to the local chapter of the big Brothers foundation. Carlton's been making periodic visits there for about a year now. It was recommended by his psychiatrist and it's made a profound impact on him lately, a most humbling experience.

Carlton has always had a soft spot in his heart for unfortunate children. He absolutely despises people who intentionally inflict harm and partake in child abuse. He went through it himself as a child but not to the extremes that some of these children endured. He vowed to himself never to allow it again if he had ever come into a position or power to do so.

Carlton involves himself in other charities and organizations as well for the better welfare of children, but this is his favorite. In the heart of the city, there's a Catholic organization dedicated to teaching sports to underprivileged children. Most of the kids there come from broken families and Carlton volunteers some of his time in coaching peewee football. It's heart-wrenching to see all those beautiful sad faces with hand-me-down clothes and holes in their shoes and sneakers. It makes his day when one of them smiles. One afternoon as he crouched down to talk to them about a strategy for beating their rivals, one of them out of the blue gave him a hug. Oh how he's longed for the same thing when he was a child.

Carlton now had unlimited resources, although some people wouldn't approve of how he gets it. Whenever he runs out of money, and he did run out of money from time to time paying for Red Sox tickets, Celtics tickets, ice cream and sometimes clothing. All to provide in making the kids happy. Carlton would just make another withdrawal, a private withdrawal in the middle of the night of an unsuspecting bank or sometimes a credit union, all courtesy of his soon to be famous (transport invention). He would put on a black outfit complete with ski mask so no one could see his face, and particularly the surveillance cameras. The newspapers ran articles about the robberies and the reporters loved it, no clues, not a trace of evidence, no tampering with alarms, no breaks in doors or windows or Roofs. The black masked bandit does it again! Some people think it could be a CEO of one of the big branches, an inside job. We might never know who it is, all we do know, is that he is the cleverest thief of the century.

Charles returns home. He now can have peace of mind in his own home. First thing in the morning I must assume the task of removing every trace of her, and then it will be complete. All of a sudden he feels out of breath and is having chest pains. He attributes it to just anxiety from the last couple of days, or is it.

Charles Van Helsang suffers a massive stroke early the next evening. He had just taken a bath and put on his soft flannel bathrobe and went into the den. After he lit a small fire in the fireplace he felt a numbness creep up his left arm, his cheek was tingly and as he hurried to sit down on the sofa, it happened. It was the most excruciating pain he had ever felt, he couldn't breathe and then the room got deathly quiet as the light slowly went out.

Charles Van Helsang is paralyzed on almost his entire left side. He has no use of his left leg and he can barely move his arm. His face is grotesquely distorted. The skin on only the left side of his face is now an atrocity, it's awkwardly sagging downward and his eyes socket is stretched to the point that it looks as if his eyeball could possibly fall out. His mouth is now permanently angled downward towards the left side as if there was a fish hook and it with the lead sinker weighing it down. It's unquestionably shocking to look at.

Carlton found his Dad clutching at his chest with his right hand lying on the floor of the den. He gasped in horror, he yelled, dad! With lightning speed, Charles leaped over to him crouching down close to him to feel for a pulse in his neck. A faint relief swept over him, he also noticed that his breathing was shallow. Carlton quickly ran to the hallway where there was a telephone. He dialed 911 someone answered on the second ring, it seemed like forever, he didn't even say hello, he said, my name is Carlton van Helsang and my father just had a heart attack I think. I don't know how long he's been lying here on the floor because I just arrived at the house, please help me he's barely breathing, and he is unconscious. Give me your address Mr. Van Helsang and an ambulance will be dispatched as we speak.

What bad timing this all was. Carlton was about to tell his dad about his invention (the freeze wave) it hit the market today. Over 300 stores are carrying it, and now this terrible tragedy strikes.

A week has gone by and Charles can't speak properly anymore. His new malady has affected the nerves in his mouth and his tong pops in and out of his mouth due to the lack of muscle control, and he also has a constant flow of phlegm on the side of his chin. He is unable to speak at this point and doesn't seem to want to try.

Charles condition worsens. Five weeks pass and a team of doctors and an out of his room, a constant flow of nurses bombarding him, doing checks on all the electronic devices that's hooked up to him. He has another stroke. The doctors conclude that Charles Van Helsang has for clogged arteries and his aorta has turned to sponge, almost 8 inches of it is this way. Charles is now institutionalized. He cannot do anything on his own. He has 24 hour around-the-clock nurses. The Final Resting place, Charles knows he's dying. He manages to scribble a note on a piece of stationery for his son, it took a great amount of determination and sweat to do this simple task and a nurse had come into his room as she was alerted electronically at the nurses' station. She politely chastised him as he whispered to give this note to my son. I'll give it to Dr. Green to give to Carlton, all right! Dr. Green of the hospital staff where Charles is committed gave Carlton the note in which Charles had tirelessly had written. He wrote, I apologize for not letting you know sooner and there is a number to his personal safe at home.

I'm sorry Mr. Van Helsang, a young nurse approached Carlton yes, what is it? Is it my dad! Is he okay? Yes he's sleeping right now; there was a minor episode earlier that's been taken care of. What I wanted to let you know is that there are no visits today sir. Oh really? Yes, but Dr. Green would like to speak with you, if that's okay.

Before Carlton leaves the hospital he stops by the hospitals cafeteria for coffee. He opens the sealed envelope that Dr. Green gave him containing his father's note. A flush of desperation falls over him, thinking this is it, it's all over. God please help him. I love you dad, don't leave me yet.

Carlton pushes his coffee aside and painstakingly opens up the envelope. He has an awful time trying to read his dad's hand writing, he thinks it says, I apologize for not letting you know sooner. It looks like; it's my life's work and some numbers too. 12-30-72. Carlton's now confused. What in the world, why did he put down my birthday here? Is he delirious? What is he trying to tell me?

For the life of him he can't figure out what significance his birth date has to do with anything. Carlton assumes the painkillers and morphine has his dad hallucinating something. Dr. Green happened to begin himself a cup of coffee and approached Carlton and said; our call you to let you know when you can see him Mr. Van Helsang, and please accept my apologies about what happened earlier today. Thank you Dr.

The next day Dr. Green called Carlton and got his answering machine. Mr. Van Helsang this is Dr. Green. I'm calling you to let you know you can see your father tomorrow, he's been stabilized. Carlton drives down to see his dad He's in and out of consciousness and he tries to speak but he just cannot. He's getting frustrating and too excited. Buzzers and lights are sounding off and going off all around him. Finally after he's All red in the face and blurts out as clear as day; the safe! Then he immediately closes his eyes. Simultaneously as this happens a stampede of nurses explode into a child's room, and a very large male nurse demands that Charles leave the room immediately. What's happening? You have to leave now Sir. Charles doctors came running into the room and they all ignore Carlton, then the big nurse grabs Carlton by the elbow and again says; please Mr. Van Helsang you must leave the room and allow the doctors to do their work. You can wait right outside the room. Tears are now visible on his pale cheeks.

Back home at his father's house he sits in the kitchen with a tall glass of Tanqueray Scotch and soda waiting for the microwave to heat up some of last night's leftovers.

He drags himself over to the kitchen window and gazes out into the darkness. He faces the backyard and looks at the woods surrounding the house and remembers how he almost got himself lost when he was about 10 years old, a slight curl of his lips appeared from the memory. The microwave beeped and he abruptly snapped out of his trance.

Carlton grabs the plate of meat loaf from the microwave and burns his fingers without even caring, sits down and attempts to eat while he daydreams and reminisces back to when he was a small boy, how he ventured throughout the house from room to room then stumbling upon his dad's huge black cast iron safe. It was almost as big as he was. He remembered how he fantasized of how they might be treasure in there, maybe gold and he would be rich. The scotch has definitely induced his dreamlike state and he realizes that his supper has gotten cold.

The very next morning despite a severe hangover, Carlton revisits his dad's big safe with the hot cup of coffee in his hands. Could it be? Carlton goes back downstairs feeling a little better now, thanks to the coffee, he retrieves the note his father scribbled and went back upstairs two steps at a time. Carlton now grabs hold of the safes combination wheel; it was chrome with black lines and numbers. He thought back when he was a kid. For the heck of it he tries turning to the numbers on the note, his birthday. He grunts and smirks 12 left 30 right 72 left. Even tries to handle and it doesn't budge. He thinks maybe he went to fasten tries again, still no luck. So much for treasure! He stops and looks at the safe and then proceeds again and this time he goes the other way, 12 right 30 left 72 right. Bingo! The handle turned with ease and he was astonished. Not knowing what to expect he pauses a moment, then slowly opens the heavy door. Carlton thinks he understands now, the safe contained his father's (life's work) there are piles of files and notepads, there is even three stacks of $100 bills, and must be over $100,000 here.

The contents of his dad's safe held all of his dad's scientific data and painstaking research. On top of everything else, lying there in plain view was his dad's personal diary. Carlton slowly regresses from the room and heads downstairs with the diary. He pours himself though he shouldn't, another scotch and soda. Thinking about his earlier hangover? He methodically walks into the familiar library, puts down the drink and the diary. Lights a cozy fire in the marble fireplace and then settles himself into a comfortable reclining chair. His father's favorite chair and then begins to read the diary.

Carlton spent most of the day reading and looking over files that his father had accumulated over the years. He was intrigued with his dad's work. It was scientific research for finding cures and medicine. He's even won a Nobel Prize for a literary explanation of a cure for a particular childhood ailment that I cannot pronounce. Why has he never told me about all this? I might have followed in his footsteps. God only knows I have the intelligence. I'm sure I would've made good scientist, after all I am an inventor and no one in history has done what I have in creating a real live usable transport machine. That reminds me, I have some work to do.

Carlton puts away his father's diary and files; actually he just lays them neatly by the reclining chair. He decides to make himself some lunch and goes downstairs into the laboratory. The food dispensers are almost empty. Felix and Lassie were sleeping and now are wide awake. I haven't seen them in a while with all the commotion happening lately I simply haven't had time. Carlton filled the food dispensers and then powered up all of his electronic equipment, he also turned on some music. The Eagles greatest hits bellowed out of the stereo and he quickly lowered the volume. He then started the tedious task of reviewing his notes. Carlton has been working on a homing device for his invention. He wants to be able to activate it and immediately be transported back to his home base, which at the moment happens to be his laboratory. His invention is widely based on an electronic pulse emitted through a telecommunications minicomputer located in the transporter. Right now at this point in time he can only use the machine to transport one way, but he's progressing extremely rapidly in developing his homing device. It would have been completed he thinks if it weren't for his dad becoming ill. He has spent a great deal of time with him at the hospital and rightly so because it's the only family he has beside his great great aunt's Peggy. It won't be long now before he designs his latest peripheral in association with his invention. He'll be able to calm and go anywhere in the world on a moment's notice.

Carlton spent many a morning awakening with sore muscles, stiff neck's and severely aching limbs as daybreak comes shining through the libraries felt pity drapes. His father's papers all askew, dirty dishes on the desk and around the chair where he slept. He moseys on over to the window, brushes aside drapes, he thought he heard something. He peeks out the window and notices the mailman approaching his house. He thinks he's got a package is something. The doorbell rings. Just a minute! Hello Mr. Van Helsang I have a certified letter here for you, could you please sign this form me, sure, thank you.

Have a nice day sir, thank you; you two. Carlton closes the door and walks into the kitchen; he retrieves a butter knife from the utensil drawer and opens the envelope. There is a letter from the manufacturing company that's mass-producing the (freeze wave) and there is also a check. He wonders with wide eyes if there's been a mistake, the check is made out to him Charles van Helsang in the amount of $250,000. He's in shock and can't believe his eyes, is it real he ponders? Wow! He doesn't know what to do. Obviously he can't tell his dad right now so he phones his great aunt Peggy and tells her the good news.

Two weeks went by and Carlton completed his work on his homing device, and now it's time to miniaturize it. He wants to be able to surgically implant a tiny transmitter under the skin of his hand or forearm so that he always has instant access back home to his laboratory. Right now the homing device is the size of a Bic cigarette lighter and it could easily be lost, may be falling out of the pocket. This cannot happen he has the capability for doing this and the technology but like with anything else, he needed a starting point.

Carlton takes a break tonight from reading more of his father's work and drives into town for dinner. The baked stuffed chicken was delicious as usual at the country road house in. It was a warm cozy restaurant with a crackling fire in the center of the room, a large River stone fireplace that delighted the customers. Over the years I've heard certain acquaintances say; let's go to that restaurant with the round fireplace. A very popular place among the people who live here and the owners couldn't be more polite. After his wonderful meal Carlton headed back home to call it an early night. He got undressed, Went to the bathroom and brushed his teeth and immediately went to bed.

Carlton awakens from another spine chilling nightmare. It's still fresh in his mind so he quickly grabs at a pad of paper and a pen. He can't place the vision anywhere and nothing ever seems familiar. These intimidating dreams are brutally puzzling. He writes down what he remembers because Dr. Fischer had told him to do so. It never seems to fail, not a month that goes by without Carlton getting a visit from some kind of super unnatural force at work deeply hidden in his subconscious mind, imposing on his peaceful nights whenever he least expects it. It's disturbing as hell, God help me with this dilemma, please! At least fill me in with an understanding.

Everything around him is blood-soaked. That's always been the unrelenting theme. Different faces briefly formed in an out of focus, some have dazzling smiles and some resonate a downright panic stricken desperation.

Towards the end of the night with rain dancing on the windowsills with staccato, like tunes called to reads on. He's all of the sudden feeling faint. He discovers that his dad; Charles Van Helsang intentionally deceived the whole world.

Charles is bewildered and his face is pale, his eyes are wide in disbelief. It's almost beyond comprehension. His eyes are drastically dilated, their bulging out of his head. His face is twisted and scrunched; he groans" no" it can't be. He's now frowning looking at himself. The lines on his four head are visibly red as he yells aloud" damn" I can't believe this. I'm actually a test tube baby! Charles is not his real father; this is a heart wrenching reality. Charles Van Helsang formed Carlton in a test tube. Carlton remembers reading something about this when he was a kid, but it wasn't until the 1980s that vitro-fertilization took place with the use of tests tubes, hence I was born in 1972. Carlton wonders who his real dad could be.

What's even more significantly and unmistakably incredible is that after reading further he finds something intensely more shocking. Now he needs a stiff drink. Drinking straight from the bottle of scotch he took a long swallow and his eyes warded, then his throat and esophagus burned. He realized that he's either a monster, or he's the most incredible amazing creature on earth, or at least since God created Adam and Eve. Carlton van Helsang is a" clone" he was genetically engineered from his great great grandfathers DNA. Michael Van Helsang, a genius in his own right, he was a well-known surgeon in England.

Carlton has a dire need to confront his father right then right now. he wants to drive to the hospital but it's after midnight and he's a little under the weather also. He decides to have another scotch, a double scotch straight up. He soon realizes that he could be deemed a product of a mad scientist. Maybe his father's colleagues were right in their assumptions about him, or, maybe Charles was a scientist way ahead of his time. Would anyone ever know? Although it was an outstanding breakthrough in modern day science, it's imperative that it never be revealed. Today's society is not ready for something of this magnitude. The creation of human life, without the use of a female egg and sperm.

My father's a genius, but he should have told me. His anger is mounting and he can't help but get aggravated. Then he stops and thinks, I also have a secret, so what makes me so righteous in my own thinking and not my father. He kept this a secret to protect me. With this newly recognized revelation his anger starts to subside. He turns on the television and tunes in to see the news to get his mind or of all this new information. I'm still paying him A visit first thing in the morning.

Carlton got up early the next morning. Daylight was just starting to loom over the horizon. He hastily got dressed and couldn't wait to confront his father. He slept through the night peacefully with no bad dreams and now was energized and empowered with an array of questions. As he leaves the house he has to squint his eyes from the bright sunlight. He gets in his brand-new BMW, courtesy from the (freeze waves) first check, and then starts out towards the hospital. He doesn't even stop anywhere for breakfast and arrives at the hospital 45 minutes later. He finds his father Charles in intensive care.

Intensive care unit or not, I want some answers! It's not visit her hours yet and wonders if he should go downstairs for a cup of coffee. Quickly he decides against it, the suspense is too much. Carlton walks in the room and notices Charles hoped up to every medical device in the room, he looks like hell. The Grim Reaper must have just paid him a visit, he thought. I hope he's at least conscious. Carlton touches his arm, hey dad are you awake? He sluggishly opened his eyes. And all at once Carlton bombarded Charles with question after question. Carlton gets carried away, his frustration evident and his anger is mounting. He cannot understand anything his father is trying to tell him. After 15 minutes of discomfiture he has to leave the room, a nurse came in to remind Carlton it's not visiting time yet Sir. He goes downstairs in shock and tries to relax with a small breakfast in the hospital cafeteria. After reading the morning paper Carlton was calm again, coincidentally it's visiting time. He halfheartedly walks back to his dad's room and the nurse explains that he lapsed into a deep sleep, what do you mean? Carlton said, is it a coma and she reassured him it wasn't and it's because he is very very weak. Carlton stares down at him and said the frowns. She explains he's been through quite an ordeal and needs his rest. Carlton leaves the hospital the same way as he arrived, confused.

Late that very night temperatures dipped below zero and at exactly 8 minutes past midnight the great scientists Charles Van Helsang quietly passed away. The doctors and nurses tried desperately to revive him and could not. Carlton got the devastating news around 12:30 AM.

Carlton is utterly devastated. Just when he needed his father the most, now he's really gone. I'm all alone in the world now, harboring too many secrets. Carlton phones his longtime friend Jonathan Hunt.

Hey John what's up? Hi Carlton what a pleasant surprise, Carlton chokes up, and tears are forming. I'm, what is it Carl? I'm afraid I have bad news. What, what is it you okay. Yes, but my father passed away last night. Oh no, I'm so sorry, can I be of any help. As a matter of fact it's why I called you and am glad you asked. Do you think you could help me to take care of things? I really could use a friend right now you know. There's nothing that would keep me from taking emergency leave Carlton, I'll pack a bag today and I meet you at the airport sometime tonight. I'll take care of my reservations right now and I'll call you back with the airlines and time of arrival, okay. Thanks so much John. John said; Semper Fi good buddy and hung up the phone. Carlton was so relieved. His best friend is on his way for moral support.

A spectacular funeral ensued. As promised, Sgt. Jonathan Hunt (USMC) is at his best friends Carlton van Helsangs side in his time of need. There was a small procession as Charles was a very private and reclusive person himself. People who worked with his father in his earlier years were present and the pastors eulogy was heart wrenching. One of Charles is longtime colleague's spoke of how Charles was a quite extremely intelligent man who was ahead of his time and Sgt. Hunt smiled at Carlton.

After Charles Van Helsangs funeral, Carlton decided to get away from you all too familiar surroundings of his home, his father's home. He makes it withdrawal at 1:30 AM inside the massive volt of one of Boston's biggest banks, although he doesn't need the money he feels the need to act out in an aggressive way. He reminds himself to hurry because there's not much air in an airtight volt.

Carlton and Jonathan take a trip to an old college favorite vacation spot. Fort Lauderdale Florida is still hopping. Thousands of college kid's partying and dancing, beach parties, and girls, and more girls. Jonathan hasn't said a word; all he's doing is smiling. He's never been here. It's just what Carlton needed to do to get his mind off of his dad. (God rest his soul).

It was an incredible time in Florida. A vacation was long overdue especially the chance to be together again. Carlton and Jonathan reminisced about their school days and childhood dreams, how some of them just dissipated and how some are still developing today Carlton explained his invention the freeze wave and John told him about his adventures in the Philippine Islands. Jonathan and Carlton laughing the whole week, he explained how the people were relentless hustlers. It's so hot there so you are always in shorts and T-shirts and the women selling big goods would say;"hey chicken legs" "by something" two dollar nice watch. Carlton was cracking up with laughter. So one day at the beach John got up from his beach chair to get some drinks and Carlton said to him; hey chicken legs, buy something for me, I got two dolla! Jonathan laughed and said; okay mama son.

Carlton arrived home from his pleasurable vacation with mixed emotions. He's feeling much better mentally and at the same time he's a little saddened over his friend having to go back to the Marine Corps. They had such a great time together and Jonathan was an absolute steppingstone in my time of need. My best friend's tenacious demeanor and his compassion overwhelmed me. His attention to detail was flawless and I knew right then and there I had a good friend for life.

Carlton finds himself isolating in his father's study. Day after day he refused to answer the telephone; he doesn't want to be bothered by the outside world. He doesn't get the door and doesn't even open the mail. He's possessed, a man on a mission. He reads his father's memories tirelessly and he finally finishes all the scientific research and now has a much better understanding about his father. In a small way we are kind of similar. We both are relentless in our pursuit for completing whatever agenda we set out to accomplish. Finally Carlton comes across his father's last will and testament and places it aside to take it to an attorney.

Carlton discovers through his persistence and relentless nights of insomnia due to reading his father's life story, he himself was not only a miracle of modern-day science(his dad's greatest achievement) but his father's intentions for his son were, for him to become the next Albert Einstein, a genius. He pauses to reflect back and abruptly realizes this must have been why my father pushed me so hard and then helplessly gave up when I rebelled and acted out against him, especially when I intentionally sabotaged my SAT scores. My father must have been devastated; maybe he thought even a failure. It would be understandable for why he locked himself up in his laboratory and shut out the world as he knew it.

As a result of Carlton's findings he slowly realized his father wanted nothing but the best for his son (the test tube baby). Another sad discovery was when he read on to find out that Charles could not have children of his own because he was born sterile. For this personal dilemma he had pioneered Vitro fertilization, henceforth the birth of" test tube babies" of the 80s decade.

Carlton only now realized how his father could be perceived as the so-called mad scientists, as he duly noted in his journal. His colleagues started regarding him in this aspect. It explains quite a bit about his father's solitude and how and why he always locked himself in his private laboratory in his own home.

Carlton just can't seem to cope with all the memories that keep flooding his mind as he stays in his father's house. It's extremely agitating and very depressing. He did have many good memories here to go along with some memories that weren't so good.

Carlton made a decision pack up all of his personal belongings and moving to his great great grandfather's estate, Michael Van Helsangs country home. A decision not made in haste, he's been contemplating this move for some time. His number one priority is partially disassembling his transport machine so he can discreetly remove it from his house and set it up at his new residence. He'll do this alone before even calling a movement company.

Carlton does however called the lake view real estate company in the next town over from him on them of his intentions. They made an appointment with him one day next week for an employee to stop by and perform an appraisal of the home so it could be placed on the market.

Carlton inherited this old house. It was in the reading of his father's" will". Besides this beautiful home there was also a sizable amount of money. The Van Helsangs were very frugal with their assets, there was enough money left to Carlton to last an entire lifetime, never mind what cash that he had already had gotten from the safe. He would never have to rely on finding a job of any kind for the rest of his life.

Carlton's intense studying of his father's cloning research intrigued him immensely, in a dreadful sort of way, mind you. Carlton examines every single page of his father's closest Secrets, including every single scientific research document. There were numerous medicinal discoveries and cures in his early days, and associated with these revelations came the impressive documentations of achievements and honors. It's too bad we couldn't share each other's secrets before he passed, he mused. It's the only thing we did have in common the thought. Carlton was also mystified by his father's research and in his experiments on crossbreeding; his own endeavors were more of a technical nature unlike his dads. He now realizes completely where his two basement friends came from; they had escaped from his father's laboratory.

Carlton's favorite room in his new home once frequented by Michael Van Helsang his great great grandfather is without question, the massive elaborate library. Hundreds upon hundreds of books and encyclopedias lined the walls of this once impressive room. In my own opinion the most beautiful feature is the large solid mahogany Henry VIII desk. It was a magnificent antique piece of furniture.

The house itself was of simple construction externally but internally it exuded elegance. The library was the largest of all the rooms and the master bedroom was a close second. In the timeframe this house was built, it wasn't privy to include luxurious bathrooms connected with bedrooms. Carlton thought to himself his great great grandfather must been ahead of his time also as was the thought of his dad and maybe even of himself.

The house had an impeccable solid oak wood floor laid throughout the entire home, and one foot away from each wall surrounding the perimeter of each and every room was a 2 inch wide strip of slightly different shades of Oak wood which were inlaid, an elaborate theme for the times. Every fireplace on the main floor was constructed of marble, specially imported from Italy. The library had the most beautiful brass screen of all the rooms. It was built directly into the marble keeping in any exploding embers of wood or coal from escaping and crackling on to the highly polished floor. The constructions of shelves were meticulously done with cedar wood and still emitted that wonderful woodsy smell. The kitchen was rather small but very practical; it had every modern convenience known to man. The main dining room was sheer elegance from ceiling to floor. A 14th century antique oriental rug gloriously sat on top of the polished oak wood floor. Heavy dining table for 12 with 12 handcrafted tall back chairs were proudly standing in the center of the room. The Square room itself had four columns 2 feet in diameter in each corner and to top it all off there was a 16 tier chandelier above the dining table.

The living room was used the most and it was a much more rugged decor with three lounge chairs of the leather, a large couch up against the wall and a teardrop coffee table in front of the couch. The West wall has a comfortable patio. The builder didn't leave anything out of his designs for this house, what I was also impressed with was the fact that the patio was also connected to the kitchen by a third door. There was one acre of fine green grass off the deck and a densely thick forest of trees beyond the picturesque scenery. The second floor held the living/sleeping quarters, along with one room furnished as yet another Van Helsang laboratory.

Aunt Peggy said that this house holds many secrets. She said it on more than one occasion; but now I wonder what she referred to since it's my new home. She said she had raised Charles in this house. I must make it a point to drive out to see her again and soon. She still doesn't know dad passed away. I wanted to tell her myself in person and make sure she was okay what had transpired. I'll need to think of something significant tell her so as not to hurt the old woman's feelings of not telling her earlier. Now I'm feeling sad and a little uncomfortable about the future visit with her.

Carlton's first night in this strange and unfamiliar house wasn't a very pleasant one. He could not for the life of him get to sleep. He was listening to the sounds of the house the noises it was making, the creaking and the whistling were all new to him and he wasn't use to it. Anyway he got up to make himself a scotch and soda and decided to read a few more pages of his father's memoirs. He's been very busy lately and it's already been a couple of months since Charles made it to the Promised Land. Finally Carlton drifts off to a deep peaceful sleep on a reclining chair in the library. The room is warm from the crackling fire and all is well three hours and 15 minutes later Carlton is overcome with horror. He awakens by a scream, momentarily disoriented from the new house he soon realizes, it was he himself who had screamed. It was so vividly real. The colors and smells were still dangling on the edge of his mind. He just witnessed himself brutally stabbing a young woman to death, blood had gushed from her deep neck wound splashing his face and clothing. He could taste the iron had a coppery taste. It's so eerie because he looked to be enjoying himself. He worked quickly. It was a precise laceration to the main neck artery, the jugular vein. Then he proceeded to remove chunks of skin, he put his hands inside Of her body and removes what he believes to be a bodily organ, yes! It's a kidney. (Oh my God) he wakes up at this point so with perspiration and his heart was being frantically. At first he was paralyzed with fear, not realizing he was in his new house. Now Carlton is genuinely mad at himself. I can't escape these nightmares even in my new house. What an opening-night, he muses.

Dr. Jonathan Fischer, Carlton's psychiatrist comes to a depressing overdue conclusion. The older Carlton gets the more acutely vivid his nightmares become and with more frequency. I'll make it a point to consider it. It is an unusual case. He's waking up with even more despicable horror shows than ever before. It's been going on for almost 22 years and still I cannot decipher a reasonable explanation, and the Lord above knows I've tried to suppress them. Nothing seems to work at least at this point in time.

Serious consideration must be taken in the immediate future to bring in another professional opinion. Carlton's last statement before he left the office today was painfully disturbing to me only because I've grown fond of him. I've watched him grow up from a small child to a respectful intelligent young menthe said; this is not me! I don't know these women; I've never ever laid eyes on any of them in my entire life. Please! Help me. I couldn't help but feel his pain. Last entry today; Carlton Van Helsang is still young man. He's surprisingly gotten used to his strangely bizarre dreams. But lately he's been more agitated outwardly as a result of them. It could be a direct culmination of all the stress he's been subjected to recently. He was not brought up witnessing any kind of terrors such as the murders and killings in his dreams. So it's been a difficult journey for the both of us through the years. In fact, Carlton was brought up quite the opposite and what his nightmares might dictate. He didn't exactly have a loving family and his stepmother was a bad influence, but there was respect and Carlton was disciplined when it was called for. He was expected by his father's account to grow up into distinguished, knowledgeable, worldly gentlemen. I do believe his father fantasized his son to become a genius of some sort, he expected nothing less than excellence and at a very young age. His expectations were unreasonable and the child protested and misbehaved at times, then he learned complaining wasn't the answers but doing poorly in school from time to time had given him more space. His father ultimately realized that his son was just another kid, wanting to do kid things and eventually gave up the notion that he could have been great scientists and possibly revered throughout the world. Charles had gotten depressed, it was a huge setback, so he slowly isolated himself from everyone then Carlton practically raised himself after about age 11 or 12.

On one exhausting and quiet night; Carlton's favorite pen his dad had given him for graduating from Yale University, a solid gold pen and pencil set from Tiffany's engraved with his name had fallen off the Henry VIII mahogany desk while he was shuffling some of his dad's files papers. It landed underneath the desk and Carlton couldn't see it at first, so he moved back the leather armchair, the wheels squeaked then he got off of the chair and crouched down on his hands and knees to look for it. Finally after clicking on a cigar lighter he spotted something shiny. Carlton soon realized that he could retrieve the pen so easily as he assumed he could, it had rolled into a crack in between the floorboards. He doesn't want to forget it, it's the only gift his father had ever given him and it means a great deal to him. His father told him that he had made a special trip to New York City to purchase it personally from the world's famous department store Tiffany's. It was solid gold with the name Carlton van Helsang inlaid in silver. It also had a matching mechanical pencil. His father had an overwhelming feeling of pride he was finally beaming with boastful love for his son. So Carlton immediately went into the kitchen to find something in order to help him get his pen dislodged from the crack in the floor, maybe a butter knife from within the sink will work.

Carlton heads back to the library down the dimly lit hallway almost knocking over a vase that sat perched atop of a narrow antique stand. He enters the library and bends down under the big desk, enduring the pain in his joints from sleeping awkwardly at this very desk the night before. He proceeds very carefully to try and dislodge his precious pan and painstakingly discovers it fell deeper into the floor. Now he's visibly puzzled and aggravated. He tries to get a better look and something slightly shifted unexpectedly. The floorboards under the massive mahogany desk seem to be loose. Carlton quickly surmised that he must move the large desk before you can retrieve his favorite pen. The desk won't budge, he even took out every single drawer and still it wouldn't move. I need some help, but whom?

Carlton remembers seeing a construction site nearby a few days ago when he had to stop at pharmacy for some hygiene items. How could he not remember this, he could almost hear the noise from home with all their groundbreaking equipment. I have an idea?

Carlton ventures outside of his new home. It's early spring now and although there's still a slight chill in the air when the breeze kicks up you can see that the oak trees are starting to bud and the grass is getting greener and greener. It was a Victorian set way back off the street; it was impressive with at least 13 gables painted dark Brown with a cream trim. I couldn't help but wonder who lives there. Down the street and around the corner he heads for the busy section of town, he assumes it's the downtown section, there is a mass of plaza's and restaurants and gas stations. He walks past an insurance company glancing up enormous is it was closed on Tuesdays and today's Tuesday. There is a huge cloud of dust not too much further in the distance. A new Plaza is being constructed. There is a big sign off the side of the road explaining a grand opening soon. The buildings look to be of a California theme. They are one floor buildings very long painted to hand on a stucco surface for its exterior eye appeal I guess. It sure is different for this area.

Just his luck, most of the construction workers were on their lunch break. They were sitting around with very large lunch pails and coolers; it looks like they were having a grand time at the expense of the new man on the job. Probably some type of initiation practice that's not written any company procedures, kind of like my early days at Yale when I was trying to be accepted into the frat house. It's funny how some things never change.

Carlton walked over among some of them and asked if he could talk to the boss, sure he's the dirtiest one out of those three standing over there; he's the one wearing the black work boots caked with mud, thank you. Carlton explained his dilemma about moving his heavy desk to the foreman. He offered to buy the entire work crew pizzas from the local pizzeria in return for them helping him move his great-great-grandfather's antique desk, the Henry VIII mahogany desk. He assured the boss it would only take 10 to 15 minutes tops because he only lives around the corner. Bob? The foreman yells; sure. It'll be my pleasure, that he asked three of his crew including the new man and they followed Carlton back to the house.

The men trailed Carlton into his home, one of them asked if he'd been living here long and Carlton said no as a matter of fact. I just moved in recently this was my great great grandfather's house and now it's mine. They all said it was a beautiful home. They all when into the library and said; is that the desk, yes sir, okay guys ready. Where do you want it and Carlton pointed over there against the

Wall. I had cleared it earlier today, that's it, thank you gentlemen.

Carlton kept his word and the entire construction crew took an unexpected extended lunch break when 16 assorted pizzas from the local Domino's pizza shop rolled into the dusty parking lot. All the men roared and were all very pleased when Bob said, let's eat. After the men had left, Carlton looked around the library for the butter knife that he had left behind; when he found it he returned it back to the kitchen. He was meticulous that way.

Were the huge desk had recently sat he noticed that there were dark stains left behind on the oak wood floor, proving that this desk has never moved an inch in all the years that it had rested here. The original stain was a great deal darker than the rest of the floor. No longer was his pen visible so he had to pry up the loose board and hope it didn't fall too deep into a hole or something. He also noticed that there was something else in the hole, but he really couldn't see what and then realized three more boards came loose. Now thinking quietly to himself he must get someone to fix this for before it gets too bad and also before you move's the desk back. When he got a closer look down in the hole in the floor, he again realizes there's nothing wrong whatsoever with the floor in the library and consequently he feels like a treasure hunter. Besides finding his pen he discovers something else. Now he knows for a fact that these boards were loose for a reason. Carlton's favorite pan is back in place without a scratch on top of its equally beautiful desk Carlton now gets down on his knees and attempts to pick up whatever it is that's in the hole in the floor.

It's really heavy and it's wrapped up in some kind of a cloth sack and now there is dust all over him. It's now placed beside him away from the whole and Carlton is tearing away the material with these. Now no longer held under the floorboards were a unique antique wooden box. Carlton is now anxious with anticipation to see what's in it if there indeed is something in it at all. There is an old-fashioned lock built right into it in the front of the box. The frame of the box looks to be a black type of metal; it could very well be made of cast iron. After quickly wiping off some dust he thinks to himself. Incredibly, this box is in mint condition and it's extremely heavy. He feels like Aladdin waiting to let out a magical genie.

Curiosity is hitting Carlton in epic proportions. It's a totally different feeling now than before when he was standing in front of his father's safe Holden the piece of paper his dad gave him staring at his birthday written on it. Carlton was told to go to his father's safe and his bedroom by his dying father. This was an altogether different type of sensation, a stumble on discovery, his heart was beaten at an accelerated pace. His eyes were wide in surprise as a young child's when he/ she notices all the presents surrounding the tree on Christmas morning. I got to get it open he says aloud; with the enthusiasm of a child.

Carlton rushes towards the kitchen not knowing what to look for in the first place, just hoping to find something, anything that can aid him in opening this box. As he looks for something he thinks that this discovery in this old house could very well be monumental. For some peculiar reason his aunt Peggy instantly pops into his head. He remembers that she said something about this house, yes, he recollects his thoughts and she said this house holds many secrets, if only the walls could talk. Now Carlton is mesmerized, he's daydreaming. I wonder if there is a secret or to in here. I wonder if and Peggy ever seen this box. The box looks much older than his dad would have been had he not passed away.

Carlton heads back to the library with the same butter knife he had earlier, maybe it'll work this time he thought. It did fit into the keyhole but wouldn't turn. It was a lock that required an old-fashioned skeleton key. Still, Carlton wasn't ready to give up yet. He felt like an excited big kid.

He went back into the kitchen because the closest door to the garage was in there and that garage held a multitude of tools. as he looked around for something he found an iron coat hanger, the one you get from the drycleaners. He grabbed a pair of pliers and started to make a couple of bends in the hangar. Carlton then went back into the library with so little pep in his step and tried again. This time the coat hanger did indeed turn but still nothing happened. He was relentless in his attempts to open the old box, but the box winning. Finally after two hours of frustration he gracefully conceded to the box.

The first thing the very next morning, Carlton grabbed the phone book and opened it to the Yellow Pages and found the local locksmith listed and made a note of the telephone number. He called the locksmith after breakfast and inquired if the man who answered the phone made house calls. Who is this? Alan the locksmith inquired. I'm sorry; I was a little excited about something I found. My name is Carlton and yours sir; my name is Alan Barbosa, I am the proprietor. Can I help you sir? Carlton said yes I hope so. Can you come to my house today, I have a lockbox that is too heavy to be moving around and I lost the key, it's a very old box. I think it's a skeleton type key that opens it. Alan said; I'm very busy today. I won't be free until after one in the afternoon. Carlton said very well then. I'll be expecting you sometime this afternoon and gave Alan his phone number and his street address. Alan said I will see you around 2 PM then and hung up the telephone.

Carlton's curiosity turned quickly to fantasy during the next few wait and hours that it would take for the locksmith Alan, to arrive. Carlton decided to take a break and lay back down for a while, he hasn't been sleeping properly lately and this was a good opportunity to get some well-deserved rest. He walked upstairs to his bedroom and pulled the shades closed and set the alarm clock four 1:45 PM. As he stood there silently in the dark his mind was transfixed on that old box. Surprisingly Carlton didn't have to endure another outlandishly dreadful nightmare. It's a rare and pleasant welcomed change. Carlton found himself relaxing on a tropical island may be in the Bahamas with dazzling's suntanned beauties all around him. The sky was bright blue the sun was shining brilliantly and a soft ocean breeze found its way onto the beautiful white sand beach. The girls were pretty with flowers in their hair and wearing enticing bikinis. Money was no object and it was flowing like water and Carlton knew for some strange reason that anything he wanted he could have. Carlton is subconsciously in a state of euphoria. He's momentarily rich beyond his wildest dreams, he even had his wooden box with cast iron frame gold plated, to commemorate his newly found impressive lifestyle since it was the box in which all of this is possible in the first place.

Carlton awakens from his brief fantasy, he is dazed and confused. It's extremely rare that he has a wonderful dream; he usually has unexplained nightmares and now he's a little disappointed that it couldn't continue. He thought he heard a noise maybe it's just an old house talk to him again. Carlton is still not use to every creak and whistle. He glances over at the alarm clock and notices that it's 2:05 PM. Now he hears a loud bang and it's not the house creaking again, he forgot to switch the alarm button on from time to arm and now someone is at the front door banging impatiently. Realizing it must be Alan the locksmith, he runs down the stairs and opens the door a little out of breath. Yes hello, Mr. Van Helsang, yes that's me, I my name is Alan Barbosa, I'm the locksmith you called earlier today, oh yes Carlton said; Won't you please come on in. I apologize for not hearing you knock sooner I just moved into this house a few months ago and I'm still not used to the noises it makes. It's a beautiful house Alan replies. It was my great great grandfather's home, Dr. Michael Van Helsang. I do believe I heard that name before when I was a young boy. Really Carlton says. Would you like a cup of coffee, no thank you Mr. Van Helsang, please call me Carlton okay, okay Carlton. Okay then follow me it's in here, the library.

Alan's instantly impressed with the condition of the box, it was remarkable. His eyes lit right up with the youthful excitement. For an old man and presumably at this trade for some time Carlton appreciated the try tremor of admiration that Alan showed towards his treasure. He distinctly had known that this box is very old; he recognized the lock to be one of the first of its kind. Did you know this boxes from overseas, England to be precise and it's very old Allen said. No, I don't really know how old it is.

Alan Barbosa has been in this business all of his life, he started when he was a child. He's a third-generation locksmith and became intrigued with this trade because of his own grandfather. One day long ago when he was about 10 years old he and his grandfather went fishing down at the lake about half mile from the home and when they got to their favorite spot the tackle box was locked. How are we going to open it grandpa? He looked at me and smiled, I said we don't have the key. And he said; not to worry son. Come over here and now show you a trick. I inched myself a little closer to my grandfather and watched him take the fishing hook off of the fishing pole and bend it a little bit.

Then he grabbed the tackle box and he put the bent fishing hook into the lock and wiggled it a few times and the lock popped open. I was instantly impressed and surprised beyond words. After we went home that day mom cooked the freshwater bass we caught and I tried and tried to open every lock I could find. I was hooked (no pun intended) this is how I became a locksmith and now I'm about six years passed my retirement age.

Alan, now trying to seize the moment says to Carlton please call me Al, he's trying to throw off a little tension and curiosity that's been engulfing him in the last few minutes. Alan now says, after I open it if by chance you have no use for this box itself I would like to have it, of course I would pay you for it. It would be a very unique business display in my shop window, not to mention the fond memories I've long forgotten of my own grandfather.

Inside the box held a number of manuscripts and journals. There's one in particular that was kind of eerie looking. There were hand-painted gargoyles on all four corners. It was a hard cover with a leather jacket. Also on the cover centered was Carlton's great great grandfathers name, this too was hand painted Michael Van Helsang. I knew it was from England said Alan. Carlton looked further into the box and noticed a cloth sack. It was very heavy as he attempted to lift it. He had to remove some of the journals to get himself a better grip. Finally he grasps hold of the sac and heaves it out-of-the-box, it must be one of the reasons the boxes so heavy he said. Carlton unties the sack quickly, his anticipation is physically expressed across his face even Alan is curious. It looks like some type of knives, solid silver. Very interesting treasure you have their Alan said. There is a puzzled look on Carlton's face, he says aloud; could they be some kind of tools, they sure look medieval to me. That's right, I remember my aunt saying to me that my grandfather was a surgeon. There ancient surgical tools. They must be worth a small fortune Al says. Yes indeed! Carlton is astonished at this incredible find. He's actually taken aback and off guard. His response is nothing short of or stricken. Carlton now asks Alan; how much do I owe you for your services Al? Both senses a local call and it's an easy say let's call it $25, okay. Okay Carlton gave him $40 and said thank you very much, you don't know how much I appreciate this please keep the change and have lunch on me. Thank you very much Carlton. I promise to get back to you about purchasing the box, but right now I've got something personal a must attend to Carlton said. All right then, Al said it was a pleasure to meet you son, likewise said Carlton if you don't hear from me in a weeks' time be sure to give me a call Alan. Have a pleasant afternoon. Carlton watched Al walked out to his work van and leave the property.

With all the excitement Carlton almost forgot his appointment with the manager and kids at the sacred hearts children's home. He only remembered because the mailman at the new house arrived earlier this morning then usual with all his diverted mail from his father's house. Some of the letters were from a couple of kids from the children's home which is exactly what reminded him of the appointment.

It was a very windy cool day. The sun was asleep and the sky was gray. Looks like rain too. Tree branches were bending and shaking. In Boston the weather didn't stop merchants from selling their products out on the streets. Carlton stopped at a hot dog vendor, he had a very bright umbrella above his cart and you couldn't help but notice how shrewd a businessman, so he bought a chili dog and a Coke with a small bag of potato chips and ate his lunch under the protection of the big umbrella.

The sacred hearts children's home was around the corner on Massachusetts Avenue. Carlton entered the building and in doing so went out of his way to make a little noise. He adored the children. They came running, three of them. Hi Carlton all at once hi Carlton can we go to the park, I want ice cream, I want McDonald's. One of them even said; I miss you Mr. Van Helsang. It hit a soft spot in Carlton's heart. He smiled at them and said; okay, okay, but first I have to talk to Mr. Jenkins. Awe, awe etc...

Carlton and Bob Jenkins having a pleasant conversation explaining that he wanted to do something special for the kids when all of a sudden the young boy who looked shaken up was abruptly brought into the building. Hello the stranger said, my name is Carl Frates and this here is my son's friend Joshua. He's a neighbor of mine. I live a few houses down the street from him and his family if you want to call it a family. Excuse me; I shouldn't have said that, it's just that I'm furious right now. What's the problem Bob said? Carlton sat in silence. Joshua looks very frightened; he wasn't making a sound he was just looking from side to side with wide eyes. I found him in my son's tree house in our backyard bleeding and crying. I went out back to empty some trash and I heard a noise in the direction of the tree house. I was going to surprise my son so I quietly climbed the ladder and looked in and saw Joshua in there huddled in the corner, his knees were bent up to his chest and his arms wrapped around them and his head was buried. He was shaking and crying. Hey what's wrong I said; at first I thought he might have fallen out of the tree or something? He didn't answer me so I went back to the house and got my son to see him and see if he's okay.

My son came back into the house about 20 minutes later. Joshua told him what happened and said to me: don't say anything. My son is a good kid and knows our family doesn't condone physical abuse so he told me anyway. I went back outside with Timmy my son, and told Josh to come into the house.

Joshua reluctantly told me that his stepfather Danny Evans was drunk and beat him. I heard about this abuse before through my son, but I really didn't pay any attention to it until now. Kids do have interesting imaginations Carl said. Well, since Joshua was scared and visibly hurt and my son's best friend, I felt an overwhelming obligation to do something, especially since the poor kid came to my house. I was furious and wanted to hurt that S O B for hurting Josh. Carlton was also suddenly written with anger; you can see it all over his face. He listened to Carl intently even though it was none of his business.

You came to the Right place Mr. Frates. The police were called from the children's home, it was standard procedure, actually it wasn't unusual at all most of the children here are from abusive and broken families.

Carlton's heart went out to the young boy. He could relate to a certain extent because he too had an abusive drunk and drug-induced step parent, she also beat him too from time to time. The police came and took statements from Mr. Carl Frates and Bob Jenkins. Carlton told Bob that he'll see him soon and left. Carl left with his son and Joshua, with police following them home. The police knocked on the door of Joshua's house as Timmy and Timmy's dad watched from their own house. Mr. Danny Evans was escorted handcuffed to the police car in outside. When Joshua's mom came home from work he went home.

Back that very night, Carlton was having a very hard time trying his damnedest not to think of that poor unfortunate child. He wants to do something but it's out of his hands now. Police made an arrest, he was told by Bob. But still he feels the wheels of justice turned too slowly. He should be punished Carlton thought. Today's past now and Carlton gets a phone call from Bob Jenkins. Hi Carlton, it's Bob from the kids home, hello Bob how are you? You told me to call you when the tickets arrived. Well buddy they hear, all 25 of them. The children will sure be excited to go to Fenway Park. The Red Sox are taken on the Baltimore Orioles. Looks like good seats to, I wish I could go. There for this Saturday afternoon's game at 1 PM. Terrific Carlton said, you sure you can't go? I'm afraid I have to stay and look over the rest of the children, a responsible job indeed and I commend you for it. I'll be there at 10 AM. I already have a bus arranged and the drive is a fan too, he'll be watching the game with us.

Carlton continues reading night after night until he passes out every night from mental exhaustion. He finally finishes reading the last of his late father's journals, and he can't help but be greatly impressed with all his dads' accomplishments. He's not sure if he can really call him his father anymore though, after all I was cloned with DNA from my great great grandfather, and could he in fact be my dad? It's a little confusing when my mind is tired.

Carlton straightens out his father's journals and files and makes room in the new safe he had installed in the basement. He vows never to make these files public. It would be foolish to be on public display, plus the world is definitely not ready for any of this!

Now his attention turns to his great great grandfather's journals. Michael Van Helsang. All he knows about him was bits and pieces that he has heard throughout the years. He was supposedly a very discreet and an ardently private man. Aunt Peggy said; once, the good Doc Michael Van Helsang never received visitors, he was strange in that regard. so now more than ever Carlton was extremely intrigued. He has these ancient journals ready to expel the mystery of none other than whom? Why himself of course. (I need a drink) the journals can wait a little longer after all, it's been a couple hundred years, I think. Carlton is off to the Boston Red Sox game with 24 smiling faces. It was the best medicine he can think of to relieve his mind of his great great grandfather.

It was an awesome game and the first six and is the lead changed four times. The Red Sox took the lead in the bottom of the sixth and never looked back after that. All the smiling faces and all the kids were screaming and having a fantastic time, and one of them even came pretty close to catching a foul ball. All in all they were extremely well behaved; even Joe the bus driver had a terrific time.

Now, back at home. Life proceeded as usual, it's Sunday afternoon and the sun is shining radiantly. There's a dry breeze rustling the leaves on the mighty Oak trees on the perimeter of the yard. Carlton opens up a window in the library and immediately was aware of the beautiful summer breeze. He can smell pine trees and wildflowers and an undeniable aroma of freshly cut grass. The smell of the first cut grass always made him feel exhilarated, for he knew summer is finally upon us. He loved summer more than any other season in New England.

Carlton sits back in a lazy boy recliner that he had purchased from the new store called country furnishings, a furniture store on the outskirts of town. He carefully places a tall glass of cold lemonade on the table lamp by the chair, making sure to use a coaster. Now he's ready, ready to abandon all distractions and concentrate on every page of Dr. Van Helsangs private journals. He doesn't stop reading until late into the night. It's 11:30 in the evening when he finally gets up from his still comfortable position. The recliner is like a soft puffy cloud, he thought to himself. If he didn't have to use the bathroom he'd still be reading in that big beautiful chair. He had made himself a sandwich and decided to watch some television. The twilight zone was about to come on. He always found himself fascinated with some of its bizarre episodes.

For the next few days Carlton's concentration changed directions to his laboratory. He finished his work on his microchip transmitter. He purposely made it into pieces so as not to accidentally set it in motion. It would be very hard to explain to someone if he accidentally disappeared from a public place without a trace, especially if he was in someone's company. The final procedure now was to surgically implant the two microchip sensors under the skin of his hand maybe the wrist area. They'll be virtually invisible to the naked eye, and to activate the transport machines home and device all he has to do is be pressed the two microchip sensors simultaneously and presto, he finds himself at home safe and sound on the transporter's platform. He briefly thinks to himself, another family secret.

After Carlton comes home from a terrific home-cooked meal at the country house kitchen he steps into the now familiar library with a scotch on the rocks in his hand. He opens up another one of his great great grandfathers journals and reads on.

Carlton comes across something and his granddad's Journal that absolutely without a doubt knocks him on the floor. His entire body, mind and soul is dramatically overcome with panic and fear. His emotions are painfully chaotic; a murky wave of dread falls over him completely. It can't be, he says. His breathing is irregular, and all of the sudden the room is frantically spinning, he can't stop it. He's fallen and can't breathe, his heart is beating expeditiously for, he screams, no! Lost all control over his body, he feels he's suspended in midair, he can only see a faint flicker of light, it's getting smaller and further away. Then all the lights went out.

Carlton wakes up a couple hours later on the floor confused, not exactly sure how he got there, because he's still a little groggy. He stays still as he momentarily contemplates if it was a mild heart attack he might have suffered. A million thoughts danced through his mind. Maybe it's hereditary, his father now in his thoughts, no wait, not hereditary, it couldn't be, I was formed in a test tube. Another thought runs across his agitated mind. He remembers a bad dream. I was reading my great-great-grandfather's journal. I must've passed out and fell on the floor from that awful nightmare. He temporarily speculated as he slowly rises to a sitting position, it might have just been a panic attack. And he sees his grandfather's Journal opened up on the floor approximately 2 feet from the reclining chair that he was sitting in last night.

Now Carlton is feeling beyond scared, he's actually distraught. His short-term memory is flooding his mind. He's trying to get a grip on his breathing as he humbly stares down at the old journal. He's overcome with an agonizing horrifying sense of distress. He slowly becomes utterly mortified now that is. As a back

What am I to do? I must tell someone, but whom? I wish my father was still here. Damn! Why this? Maybe I could talk with a doctor. Doctor-patient relationships are strictly confidential. He's laughing now. They'll lock me up and throw away the key. This is too much! It's way too much to keep to myself. If I don't get some kind of help am afraid I might go mad.

Carlton at this point despairingly succumbs to the scientific fact of what and who he really is. His origins initially shocked him, but after thinking about it a while now submissively concedes to it all, he has to. All my life!

Years of tormenting visions, and brutal, hellish nightmares, wondering where they came from. Now I know! They all belonged to my great great grandfather, Michael Van Hellsang. Dr. Fisher will be delighted to know that it wasn't anything he did wrong in his pursuit to free my mind of all those bad dreams and holistic visions. Carlton makes an appointment to see Dr. Fischer.

Carlton leaves the library the way it is and decides to get away from his father's mess. He walks into the kitchen and opens the basement door, which leads him to his transport machine. He wants to get away! Go to someplace sunny, but first he needs to take care of the final details of his own secret. He surgically implants 2 finished micro-transmitters under the skin of his left hand. The surgical procedure only took a mere 45 minutes from start to finish. Each incision was only 1 cm long. He delicately set one transmitter on top of his forearm, right below his wrist and the other transmitter exactly below the first on the underside of his forearm. It was done this way so as to avoid accidental activation. You have to depress both transmitters simultaneously to activate the transporters homing device in the computer. He thought this was a good idea because we all bump ourselves from time to time, and it's very unlikely that both transmitters will be bumped at exactly the same time. Perfect safeguard Carlton for.

Carlton packs a light duffel bag. One pair of shorts a pair of jeans. Two T-shirts underwear and a toothbrush. He grabs a vacation guide so he can choose a retreat. He decides any small island in the Caribbean and without hesitation, computes the coordinates into the transporter's computer and leaves. No driving or crowded airports this time! He's taken full advantage of his incredible invention. Now he's at peace finally. Beautiful gold sanded each with crystal clear turquoise water and palm trees looming all about. The air is clean and sweet and there's a perfect light breeze coming from the vast ocean. I can stay here a long time, he thinks.

The sunset is spectacular. I've never seen a more breathtaking sight. There is even an ocean liner off to the right in the distance. It's a masterpiece, even then go would envy. As Carlton strolls toward the hotel suddenly he drifts back in his memory to the recent visit with Dr. Fischer, right before he came to his peaceful paradise. Now, down on himself, feeling a little more vulnerable for talent Dr. Fischer what he had discovered. He now wishes he hadn't said anything at all. He has an awkward predicament now. He has to be absolutely positive that Dr. Fischer doesn't reveal anything he had said to him. The more Carlton thinks about it, the more uncomfortable he gets. It could ruin and expose him. The media would have themselves a field day.

Carlton is now obsessed in planning an elaborate covert scheme. I Dr. Jekyll and Mr. Hyde feeling overtakes his devious mind. I want the world to know! I have risen! Carlton's adrenaline is now pumping furiously. That vehemently tormented by his now accepted, recognizable demons bellowing to his subconscious mind. Now as he is feeling somehow nostalgic, he's determined to devise an intricate, foolhardy, cynical itinerary that he alone will be aware of. In order to achieve this shocking goal! Carlton has to inspire geographical changes in research real estate for sale. All for certain old associates! A few sites don't need changing, they're already purely coincidental. Some lucky people will inherit new homes, complete with title. Carlton will no doubt pay for some of these homes under a unanimous name. It's to ensure no paper trails leading back to him. Truly a gift from just a plain old Good Samaritan wishing to be anonymous. Furthermore, he'll use cash. Everybody knows that money talks.

Carlton uses Dr. Jekyll's charm and charisma and his worldly knowledge to easily manipulate certain real estate companies and their agents, in order to successfully set his invention use plan into motion...I'll be known as the alphabet man, then quietly chuckles to himself. Who wouldn't want to a free home?

Carlton is now well over the fact of who he is and what he must do. Death and destruction are aggressive inescapable sustaining thoughts. It's like night and day Dr. Jekyll; calm, collective and thoughtful during the day in the public eye. Then Mr. Hyde when daybreak ends and the devil himself blankets the earth with the mystical dark cape. There must be a way to control it. As he methodically moves into the future, he undeniably never forgets the outlandish and mental abuse intentionally exhibited on himself or his friends and colleagues.

Her heart was beaten frantically. Someone grabbed her from behind squeezing her throat tightly. Her anxiety skyrocketed as her windpipe was being crushed. She couldn't even let out the tiniest of whimpers. It was completely overpowering. No longer could she combat the sudden darkness that's slowly falling upon her. Her landlady screams as she discovered that decomposing body. The police arrive at the grisly crime scene. A young officer in Plain Street clothes, No doubt a cheap suit from Anderson Little. He's got very short blonde hair, blue expressive eyes and is clean shaven. He yells, hey gunny, it doesn't look like any foul play here. Is that a fact? Looks like it could be a hot attack. The gunny grunted, there is no forced entry on the door or windows and the landlady said she opened the locked door with her extra key because she was concerned. She said her tenant has been he is a very long time and not once did she ever miss a rent payment. The rent was due over a week ago. So she went against the grain, her rules of privacy and checked up on her tenant, she was old, so you see. When she opened the door there was an awful smell, and her attendant was right where she is now, sitting hunched over in a chair.

Harry Ferreira, a retired United States Marine gunnery Sgt. Gunny for short, is the lead detective in the small town of Johnston Rhode Island. By the looks of this old jarhead it was easy to assume that he probably could break you in pieces if he wants to, and enjoy doing. Nobody loves their job more than the gunny. He was a take charge, no-nonsense, gun ho leatherneck. Detective Harry Ferreira said to the young suit with an unnerving tone of voice. It's your job to determine a cause of death. Isn't it! No Sir.

The forensic team came in and proceeded to do what they do while the gunny spoke with the building's landlord. The landlord said the lady's name was Jerry; it was short for something else. Eventually the body was brought to the hospital morgue for autopsy. The young officer in training to become a detective was at this point significantly more subdued in his approach to gunny Ferreira. I'm finished here, he said.

Detective Harry Ferreira's mere presence demanded respect. He had an aura of power. He stood perfectly erect at 6 feet tall and tipped the scales at 225 pounds. He still sported a military crew cut high in tight, even the swagger in his walk exuded authority. He was a person not used to hearing criticism. He was terrific physical condition for a man approaching his 60s. Harry carried himself with graceful ease for a man of his large physical stature. He was a handsome man with rugged features and was still appealing to the ladies.

Carlton waits patiently in the plush waiting area at Dr. Fischer's office. He's watching the television that's bolted high up in the corner of the room. The local news channel is on. The doctor's secretary Susan, informs the doctor that has 3 o'clock appointment is here. There is be on the TV a newsflash, a woman was found last night murdered in her apartment on Whipple Street in Johnston Rhode Island. A name is being withheld; any information concerning her demise would be appreciated. Please call our hotline... Detective Harry Ferreira is the lead investigator.

Dr. Jonathon Fischer and Carlton exceeding the normal time allotment weren't very happy with each other this past hour. Carlton was adamant about getting some answers whether or not the good Dr., his friend, kept strict confidences or not regarding his patients, all of his patients. Especially himself, the doctor did momentarily slip up and told Carlton in an agitated state of mind that it's normal for most psychiatrists to sit in with another more prominent psychiatrist than themselves. it helps to keep a more positive perspective on our own personal lives. We do have our own problems too, nobody's perfect. Anyone can see Carlton and Dr. Fischer are really close, after all Carlton has been seeing him well over 15 years. After hearing this last attempt to make Carlton understand, the Dr. stopped talking. I wish I hadn't said that was the thought going through his mind. The last thing Carlton said was; so you to huh. You're seeing a shrink also. Then Carlton stormed out of the room furiously knocking over a chair in the process.

Back home now and still upset. Carlton hangs out with lassie and Felix. The rock band Boston is loudly pumping out of the 300 watt stereo system by Pioneer. More than a feeling, an appropriate song he thought.

Carlton takes an unexpected trip via his transport machine. He uses it more frequently now. He's developed the means of materializing unnoticed. At a supermarket near his hometown he has to purchase some groceries and pet food. It was a sunny day and most people wearing sunglasses and as he turned the corner he noticed the police car Parked at the curbside and both officers were eating hot dogs at a portable hot dog stand. Carlton always wondered about the health problems of police officers, as he watched them eat their hotdogs. It is always a picture of an obese cop in the news. Such bad diets with fast food on the go all the time. A very tough life he thought.

Barbara, Carlton's stepmother, used to whistle the catchy tune from an old Andy Griffith show, whenever she was high on drugs and booze. He had an overwhelming urge to see her and couldn't explain why. The Melody kept right on playing in his head. Maybe it was on TV one night this past week while he was channel surfing, he just doesn't know how to explain it. Then he caught himself whistling the same tune the other day and immediately stopped himself because of who it reminded him of.

Years of hidden anguish came flooding back. All the pent up physical and emotional abuse flashed across Carlton's overworked mind. When he again snuck up on her in her hospital room, she was no doubt comatose on medication for she was softly whistling that very same tune again. So pathetic Carlton thought...Mr. Hyde said, do it!... Do it! Dr. Jekyll said, no! Yes do it! I've got to go home. This is unnerving. 1.2 seconds later Carlton materialized in the living room and heard the Pioneer stereo pumping out an old song from foreigner, hot-blooded, another one of them mind confusing songs. He noticed the mice enjoying their food in the corners of the kitchen, as he saw something stir in that direction.

It's only been a couple of months since Carlton's father passed away, and once again Carlton is making funeral arrangements. The phone call came early this morning, it was still dark outside as Carlton looked towards the window and saw the silver moon casting a faint light down on the earth. The answering machine said it was 6:05 AM and to please call Dr. McGregor from the Andover Memorial Hospital. It's an important matter. That's all the machines said.

Carlton rose out of bed at approximately 8:30 AM. He made himself a pot of strong Columbian coffee and then looked up Dr. McGregor's phone number from his Rolodex. He dialed the phone number and got the hospitals switchboard. Can I speak to Dr. McGregor please he said, who's calling? This is Jack Van Helsang, one moment please while I connect you. Dr. McGregor here, can I help you sir. Yes Dr. this is Carlton Van Hellsang. I was told you need to speak with me, something urgent. Yes Mr. Van Helsang. I'm Afraid I have some disturbing news. Still half asleep he said what? What is it? I'm afraid your stepmother Barbara Van Helsang has passed away. What do you mean? How? What happened? Did she have a heart attack or a stroke like my father did? Mr. Van Helsang I would prefer to discuss it in private rather than over the telephone. It's somewhat complicated. I have an opening in my schedule tonight at 6 PM or if you prefer any time tomorrow, that would also be fine. Okay I'll be there at 1 PM tomorrow afternoon Carlton said. Very well then, tomorrow. Goodbye, goodbye.

The State Department would file the same paperwork that they usually did pertaining to someone whom has passed away at the hospital. A routine formality, people die all the time in hospitals, unless of course there were overwhelming circumstances contradicting death by natural causes.

Carlton had received an invitation in the mail for certain alumni of Yale University. It was a dinner benefit for future inventors. They stated that his invention the freeze wave had surpassed all other new inventions year to date. That year the entrepreneur magazine was holding this benefit. All proceeds and donations are to be given over to a new project at Yale University. Even the mayor was to be present for a speech.

Paula Robertson, lead detective in Cambridge Massachusetts. Precinct 354, she was enjoying a rare lunch at Marshall's pub when over the radio she heard her name. Detective Robertson please call dispatch. Damn, she said, always an interruption. She called in on her portable two-way radio. She's like a tiny two-way radio; it was new technology her department was using. Detective Robertson here, crackling sound then… be advised your assistance is needed at 824 Albany St., it's a condominium called Neptune condos. Roger, I know the place. I'm on my way. Hey Charlie can I get this to go; it's an emergency sure, thanks.

Paul is upset that once again she could not even come close to finishing her lunch this week. Today's Friday and not once did I sit through a lunch this week uninterrupted she said to Charlie? Charlie was the owner of the cozy little restaurant. He was an Irish Italian with a surprisingly upbeat and friendly attitude. Most Irish and Italians in this part of town where quick-tempered and leery toward not only customers, but everyone. Charlie was half and half and couldn't be a nicer guy. He paused at the restaurant's door with a smile and yelled with his hand in the air, don't work too hard Paula! She raised an eyebrow with a half-smile and drove off with her doggie bag, of her partially eaten lunch. She very much dislikes driving away from this part of town because she has to go through the rough neighborhood that was once called the combat zone. The name was conjured up many years ago. It's always been an infestation of drugs, prostitutes, pimps, and drug dealers. Most of life's unfortunate misfits. Leeches and cockroaches was a much more genuine description of these people. 95% of all those people were predestined for a lifetime of disappointment, Paula thought. They'll forever be looking in windows, and sometimes wishing, wondering and wanting something they could never have. Dreams of what if this, why not's, and how comes. Unattainable goals, because of the lifestyles that were handed down to them. Some of them were pitiful and most would downright despicable and dangerous.

People around Paula sometimes get extremely intimidated, not to mention very aggravated at times. She's cocky and straightforward. She is a downright perfectionist. When she's conducted high profile homicides, everything is blatantly unequivocal. Paula exudes an overwhelming radiant and copulate sexual quality whenever she's in this aggressive state of mind. Her classical good looks don't help to ease any kind of tension floating through a room. In fact, it's quite the opposite. Not too many people in this town like a beautiful woman in an authoritative power position.

Paula, Detective Paula Robertson makes her presence known immediately as she energetically makes her way towards the crowd of police officers in the room of the deceased. Hello George she says. Does anyone have the victim's name yet? Yes ma'am, a pretty young black female officer replied. Someone with answers and a woman to boot Paula thought. This could be the start of good professional relationship. His name is Eugene Banks, the young female officer said. What's your name asks Paula, and in turn the police officer said Sonia. Well Sonia is there anything else you can tell me? Now excited and visibly so she said, I think he's a teacher or something. What do you mean a teacher or something? Yes down the hall bears a room with a computer in it, looks like a small office or something. As she said this she nodded in the direction of the hallway.

He has plaques on the desk and college diplomas on the walls and one of them I noticed, said teacher or counselors. Paula then nodded and made her way through the small crowd of people all doing their job.

Paula assumes this role to be a small office as Sonia had guessed. A makeshift office. A Dell computer sat atop the desk along with the appropriate peripherals, a printer/fax machine, keyboard and a scanner. Everything was nice and neat. There was a telephone and answering machine and the message light was blinking. The desk's nameplate is engraved in bold lettering, his name no doubt, and in much smaller lettering on the back side it says, Mount St. Charles Academy. I heard of the school. Ed Bradley of the TV show 60 minutes went to that school. A high school Paula thought to herself as she inspected the tight surroundings of the office.

Who a forensics team already finished their preliminary inspections, and policed the area. The yellow police tape was attached to the outside door of the condo, even the patio was sealed off. Why I couldn't tell you, we are on the eighth floor. Maybe a rookie she thought.

Detective Paula Robertson is very good at her job. It took her only four years to become lead detective. Some people wondered if it had something to do with other than tactful work ethics. Every now and then she gets cold shoulder from a jealous colleague, nothing she can't handle.

Every crime scene is different as is this victims is. Once in a while an exceptionally grotesque body turns up. It never feels to amuse her when she witnesses grown men running to the latrine or an isolated Bush to vomit, not Paula. Besides being a 10 in the looks department, she is as tough as nails. She never had a problem with dead people or animals. Some people say her cast iron stomach rubs off on her personality. She has to be a hard ass, because it's a man's world, at least at her chosen profession. And being a beautiful woman made things even more awkward sometimes. Most first impressions she receives are rather uncomfortable. She always had to prove that there were brains beyond her good looks.

The forensics team determined that Eugene Banks had been deceased for at least 36 hours. He was a student guidance counselor at a boarding high school in Woonsocket Rhode Island called; Mount St. Charles Academy.

The forensics teams report was significantly graphic. It said Mr. Banks dies very slowly and there was a great deal of blood loss in the process. The coroner confirmed that he died due to the numerous lacerations and also looks like he was tied up. His wrists had rope burns. The coroner said it was a frightening way to die. He added, it's some sick twisted human being that can tie a person up and just watch him bleed to death. Another interesting note was that the instrument used to actually make the incisions and cuts were extremely sharp, and couldn't be just an ordinary knife. It had to be some type of a precision instrument or tool.

Detective Paula Robertson is somewhat puzzled, but that won't stop her, it's never stopped her before. She's solved every single case she's had and she'll solve this one too. Perhaps that's why she's the lead detective. Whenever she gets that excited look in her eyes, they shoot sparks. It looks as if she can see right through you, her whole persona becomes electrified. She seems to be onto something her colleagues express. He carefully watches her without trying to be too obvious making sure that to stay out of her way. Sometimes her beauty is more intimidating than her bite. There were immediate coworkers, the people who were close to her never cease in learning invaluable techniques from her. This case will be no different.

Capt. Adams called Paula into his office. He is her commanding officer and has a great deal of respect for her. He pulls no punches as some people do just because she's female. He's always straight with her and treats her like one of the guys. She wouldn't have it any other way. The chief was just on the phone with me and has informed me that the governor of Massachusetts expressed that he wants to bring in the FBI on the Eugene Banks case. What! The forensic scientists believe that the same lethal instruments were used in another murder case, as they were used in this one. Are they sure? There is a case in Andover Massachusetts that is undeniably similar. There is something else too. What? What is it? They found some type of foreign substance in the your autopsy, it appears to be a chemical of some sort in the late woman's blood and I already informed the doctors to check our latest victim to see if there's a chance of the same substance in his blood. I'm hoping there is nothing there but if there is there could be someone out there who's a serial killer. We don't need that kind of publicity again. So, do you remember the highway killings over 15 years ago? There was a widespread panic. I do remember, I was in college and I was only 19. Everyone was terrified and people were staying home, there was even a small recession because of it. It was a really bad time. Yes it was, the captain said.

At first detective Paula Robertson was furious, but after the in depth explanation she believed that he had made sense, still she said; I've never let you down Capt. Do we really need the FBI. Capt. Adams, a hard ass himself, made it a point to quickly standup shove his desk chair careening into the wall behind him while raising his voice. The governor wants it! The governor gets it! And you'll just have to live with it. Do I make myself clear! Yes sir but, no butts! You're dismissed. As she turned and opened the office door looking defeated, he said; by the way, his name is Bob Davis, who? Your new partner! Agent Bob Davis. So you'll might as well get used to it because you will be working together for a while and both of you will be reporting directly to me. She didn't look at him; she just paused and looked down at the floor. When he stopped talking, she left without a comeback. She knew after years of working together with her captain that a serene approach was more effective on his mind rather than a verbal confrontation.

Detective Paula Robertson is the lead detective on an unsolved murder case. There is just an autopsy report indicating the possibility of a matching weapon in another case halfway across the state. The autopsy isn't even finished yet! And now I'm getting a new partner she muses, a stranger, and a suit of all people. He's probably a pencil neck dork for all she knew. He better not slow me down if he knows what's good for him. Damn! I can't believe this shit!

This morning Carlton accidentally walked into a robbery in progress. The counter person was a middle aged lady; Asian with long dark hair graying at the temples was acting somewhat strangely. She was rolling her eyes and then Carlton noticed someone lying on the floor. It was 2 people. He can see them through a reflection from a glass shelf behind the cash register where another nervous counter person was standing. Carlton's mind started racing, he wanted to help so he had to act fast. He paid for the gallon of milk and the newspaper and made off in a hurry saying, have a nice day and keep the change.

Carlton now thinking to himself, I feel like a comic strip character, Batman, Spiderman, maybe even Superman. He throws the milk and newspaper into the trunk of his car and simultaneously grabs the crowbar. Then he uses his transport machine as the key element of surprise. The unsuspecting thief never knew what or how the next events happened. Carlton seizes the moment. He knew there were two of them and when he materialized on top of one of them out of thin air, there was a shriek! Carlton quickly swung the crowbar and hit the other thief right across the back of the head, it was a phone crushing blow and the perpetrator went down quickly. The Asian man that was underneath him sprung up with astonishing speed and both he and Carlton jumped at the other thief who was at the counter trying to pass himself off as a store clerk.

There was a slight struggle as the Asian man tried to sub do the other stranger that was watching his wife. Everything happened so fast. Then Carlton seizes the moment again, when the other thief saw Carlton brandishing a crowbar and shouting for him to stop moving or I will crack your skull, he stopped. He told the Asian man's wife to go and get some rope or twine so weak tie them up for the police. She understood because she came back in less than 20 seconds with some nylon twine or string, whatever it was it worked. The police were called and showed up on the scene 10 minutes later and arrested the man who was per train himself to be work and as the store clerk without incident, but his partner wasn't so lucky. He was taken away by ambulance. He did indeed have an escort, courtesy of the local police department. The Asian woman was holding on to her husband with tears rolling down her cheeks, they Point towards Carlton nodding their heads. When Carlton looked at them they smile. The police took statements from the couple that owned and worked at the small variety store and then approached Carlton. One of them said; according to the storeowners it seems that you're a hero today. The husband was being held down on the floor by knifepoint when you came into the store. What I don't understand is that you left they said, and only moments later you were on top of one of them who is now on his way to hospital. She said she didn't see you come back but they you were, plain as day helping her husband. I saw a reflection in the window case behind the counter and acted fast he said. I left quickly without my change and went to my car for something to protect myself with and snuck back into the store, and that's when I quietly immobilize the person on top of the owner. Then I guess being afraid for his wife he lunged at the other one and I quickly caught up and helped him. 10 minutes later you guys arrived. Well that about sums it up the policeman said. They took Carlton's name and address and told him that the Mayor appreciates this kind of help every now and then; it's a big city you know. Just don't make it a habit okay! The cop said with a smile. Okay! Job security you know! The policeman said as he walked away still smiling.

Feeling good about himself, now Carlton visits the kids the next day at the Sacred Heart's children's home. He quickly walks in and as he does he notices a bunch of them huddled around the television set in their dayroom, watching cartoons. The TV was tuned to the cartoon network channel Nickelodeon, I believe this is the station that ran old-time cartoon reruns, and at this particular moment one of my own childhood favorites was playing, it was Yosemite Sam. It brought a smile to my face. Carlton paused briefly and smiled wider reminiscing of when he had watched the same exact cartoons when he was a small boy. Life was so simple back then he thought.

One of the kids spots Carlton as he's eating a piece of toast. Carlton is talking to Bob and he excitedly relays this top-secret information to the other kids. Then the next thing you know all hell breaks loose. Asking and hoping to go to the ballpark again. One of them yells out; the Yankees are in town and we want to see the Red Sox pound them. A couple of smaller children were now crying because they couldn't get to the office door, and they wanted to see Carlton too. Only one of them stood in the TV room watching the cartoons, and was so slick enough to slip into the best seat in the room. It was obvious and how much the children loved Carlton, and he reciprocated the same enthusiasm and love.

Television made an awful sound. A high pitched squeal that vibrates right through you, like on a chalkboard and everyone winced. I thought they were getting ready to announce something on the television and I was right they are getting ready to a no something from the FCC. The FCC is conducting a test, this is only a test from the emergency broadcast system, something like that anyway but instead the television screen showed police vehicles and an ambulance, and a couple of news vans with reporters standing around. Men and women in police jackets, with large bold white lettering. A bald headed man in a blue pinstripe suit filled the TV screen next and said; there has been a ruthless murder last night in this once peaceful skiing town of Killington Vermont. Only 1 mile from the Mount Killington ski resort in Massachusetts. It's the first murder in more than 40 years in this town and the neighbors, especially the older folks are dramatically concerned. Some of them remembered the terror that the town endured for months over 40 years ago, that was until the ax murderer was captured. Back then a prisoner escaped from a southern chain gang and killed three people in this very same town with one of the victim's ax's that he was using to split word for his very own fireplace. We don't want to be frightened like that again an elderly man said.

A woman in her late 20s was a loan at her place of business tending to some paperwork. She owned the part-time health and fitness spa and from information gathered she usually was the last person to leave and always the first one to get there. She always went through the figures of the day, and checks the schedule for the next day to make sure of who's coming in as a client and who is coming in to work. Some clients had personal trainers, but most of them didn't. She didn't like it when an employee couldn't make it into work. It's not that she's a slave driver; no not that at all, everyone that worked for her did genuinely like her. What it meant was; she had to stay late and make a telephone call to the client and scheduled the appointment using as much charm as she can muster. The customer always comes first! Her parents had taught her that at a very young age, and it stuck. They've been business owners since before they married and knew exactly what a happy customer and.

Glenda Walker's parents gave her this fitness spa business as a gift for graduating top of her class at yield University, they were so proud of her and tried their best to keep her close to home. The FBI agent in charge, talked with her grieving parents. As agent Bob Davis tried to be as brief as he possibly could for now. Her parents were understandably in agony and disheartened in a way that they never thought possible. They obviously were not told to the extent of how brutal and grizzly the actual murder scene really was. She was ceremoniously disfigured beyond recognition. The blunt of the mutilations were on your sexual organs. She was lacerated from her stomach downward and under and up to her lower back. Both her breasts were carved right off her chest. The entire room was blood-soaked.

Her parents, while Crying said; Glenda was a very nice girl. She was beautiful inside and out. She worked very hard all the time, that's how we taught her growing up, her father said. I didn't like her work and so much her mother said. She had no life outside of work, not even a boyfriend. Did I tell you she paid most of your own way through college? By modeling, her father said. She was very independent. Why would someone do this to her as her mother started crying again. I'll do everything I can to get the answer to that question ma'am, said agent Anderson.

Carlton listened to the television intently. Although the name of the woman wasn't mentioned, he knew who it was. Mount Killington has a very small population and there was only one spot fair in that town. His ex-girlfriend from his old college days owns the only fitness Spa in Killington Vermont. Carlton was now staring at the TV. He seemed to be lost in a moment of time, a tear rolled down his cheek. Hey! Are you okay, Bob said? He thought to himself as his face turned red with that fired below. Glenda's demons finally caught up with her. Yes! Yes some I'm fine it's just, just that I once knew that girl. What, that woman that got killed in Vermont? Yes. I'm pretty sure we dated in college.

Bob Davis's own thoughts provoked a furious anger with him. The sheer perfection of these hideous murders imitated him beyond reason or words. I won't stop until I catch him. He wondered as he drove in silence if this murder was also related to the other murders that he was soon to be involved in.

Agent Bob Davis was now heading in the direction of Boston Massachusetts. This happened to be a quick and unplanned detour. His boss had phoned him when he was at the airport on his way to meet his new temporary partner, Paula Roberts, the lead detective in the Cambridge Massachusetts Police Department.

He boarded a plane for Vermont instead of Logan and report in Boston and now after his brief investigation he has to drive all the way to Cambridge Massachusetts Tonight, because there are no flights into Boston for at least 24 hours. Someone at the car rental agency said that Boston is a five hour ride from here and that only made him angrier.

It's been a couple of hours since agent Davis left the crime scene. He found himself lost in thought. Is it fact or myth that police love coffee and doughnuts as he pulls into a Dunkin' Donuts drive-through with his brand-new crown Victoria rental car. As he sits patiently waiting his turn he scans the outside menu and determines that it's the convenience of fast food in which attracts so many people, especially up here in New England where it's always nice to get a steaming hot cup of coffee when it's cold outside. It just so happens that most coffee shops sell donuts also as she smiles when the counter girl said; can I help you sir, through the mounted speaker in the menu sign.

Bob Davis parks his car overlooking the busy lunch traffic and calls his boss. The ADIC. (Assistant director in charge) at FBI headquarters in New York, N.Y. Bill Maurer answered the phone. He's the ADIC's male secretary. I'll never understand why a man would choose to be a secretary. Hey Bill its Bob Davis, hello Bob. What can I do for you? Maybe he's gay? Agent Davis thought. Can I speak to Mr. Villamere? Hold on a moment while I see if he's still available. As he waits he looks on over at the drive thru with donuts and muffins on the dashboards of cars, as they pay for their indulgence of cholesterol. He immediately felt embarrassed at this thought because of the blueberry muffin on his own cars dashboard, ah what the hell.

Carlton says to the manager of the Sacred Heart children's home, while at the same time about 12 screaming and crying kids are pulling at his hand and his coat. I have reserved 20 seats for the Yankees/Red Sox game this Saturday afternoon. Actually, they were a gift from the mayor; did you know he was a big fan of the Boston Red Sox? No I didn't know that and how did you come about this minor feat. Red Sox tickets are hard to come by these days.

I spoiled a robbery the other day at a small convenience store, what? What you mean by spoil, what did you do? Bob said. Yeah, I walked right in on it and the guy was trying to portray himself as the clerk and I saw someone on the floor through a reflection from a window behind the fake clerk. I knocked over the guy on the floor then the owner and I jumped on top of the other guy. He didn't know what hit him. They both got arrested and I guess the police told the mayor, because now the mayor is proclaiming me to be a hero. While! That took a lot of guts. I guess I was at the right place at the right time. Weren't you scared? Huh? Carlton's attention was momentarily drawn to one of the children. Are you kidding? I thought I was going to wet my pants, then both men laughed. So can you make it to this Saturday's game Bob? I think this Saturday is doable. Bob's now shaking his head, wonders never cease he says.

Agent Davis's boss has informed him to keep him abreast of everything, and especially of any progress pertaining to this particular case. It took the ADIC, Vincent Villamere about six minutes to picked up the telephone. Hello! Hello Mr. Villamere, agent Davis here... It was a yes sir no sir one-sided conversation. He insisted on the utmost discrete nests and said this could very well be the work of some new demented serial killer, yes sir. Report back to me in two days. Yes sir. Have any problems yet? No Sir. Good. I've got work to do here. Two days Davis! Yes sir, the next thing agent Davis heard was a dial tone, not even a goodbye. No wonder they call him a Dick. (ADIC).

As agent Davis made his way into Boston he double parked to ask directions to the Cambridge police station from a gentleman walking by. You're not far off my friend the stranger said. Take this left and go through three lights then take that left and you'll see it. Thank you sir, any time, you can't miss it.

Agent Bob Davis parks his Crown Victoria automobile in a visitors parking slot and heads into the building. Agent Davis inquires about seeing Capt. Adams and studies the face of the heavyset desk Sgt. He neglected to tell the Sgt. He was FBI. He just used his birth name without his title. He's done this before and has been conducting a personal observational test ever since he became an agent of the

FBI. It amazes him. The weight isn't funny but you got to give a little to get a little. After 5 to 10 minutes he asks again. The desk sergeant's reaction is what Bob is looking for. Sorry sir were very busy right now, you'll just have to wait your turn. Agent Davis sits and tries to calculate how much time it will take him to tell you overweight desk sergeant that he's FBI or he just might sit until the captain shows up and then he could tell them that he's FBI. He wonders whether or not the captain will reprimand the Sgt. Or not. It's a personal game he plays. It's not very nice to manipulate people but it's a kind of practice he learned in classes at the Academy. Now the desk sergeant looks at him pensively and shrugs his shoulders and says, I'm sorry but I don't know if he's still here and then turns his attention to something probably trivial trying to look busy. Agent Davis makes up his mind after the last comment and gets up from his chair. He approaches the desk. Tell Capt. Adams that agent Bob Davis is here as he takes out his wallet and shows his ID. Tell him that I'm with the Federal Bureau of investigations. That usually gets people's attention. Bob quietly smiles to himself as the desk sergeant starts to sweat.

It was a good idea to be on the good side of the ADIC, his boss. After all he can be very helpful if I ever get into any tight situations out here in Boston. So, the first order of business is to not spread around the nickname of the boss, like the rest of the guys do at the Bureau. Every chance they get the guys at the Bureau call the boss a dick, it works for me.

Captain Adams appeared within two minutes after the last encounter with the desk sergeant he approached agent Davis with his hand outstretched eager to greet a stranger. Hello the captain said. Hi ya doing agent Davis said, with a New York accent. I hope you had a pleasant trip the captain said. It was interesting to say the least. As I was at the airport I got a call from my ADIC telling me to divert to Vermont on an urgent matter, and immediately after I finished there I was to proceed directly to Boston to meet with you. I had to drive here from Vermont because there were no more flights into Boston via Vermont for over 24 hours, and am totally exhausted now. Well now, we won't keep you here too long today then. We have a hotel efficiency room set up just for you at the South suites right outside of town. You can go there if you like to get some rest and be here first thing in the morning, 8 AM sharp. I'll introduce you to my lead detective whom you will be working with. What's his name if I mask; it's detective Paula Robertson the captain said. Oh... A woman! Yes. Yeah, let me to you something about detective Paula Roberts. You don't have to worry about her. She's the best detective in Boston as far as I'm concerned, and you'll be hard-pressed to keep up with her and besides all that, I envy you. Why? Because you and her will be working very closely and she doesn't exactly hurt the eyes, if you know what I mean. Really? Have a nice night and get some rest. I'll introduce you to Paula Robinson in the morning. Thank you Capt.

Paula is supposed to be agent Bob Davis his partner during these investigations of all of these latest homicides. Agent Davis is now on his way to the hotel suite and is picturing in his mind some home we ugly broad with a crew cut and appears poor attitude to match. All man, why me? Capt. Adams said he envies me because she's easy on the eyes. I bet she's a dike and really ugly and he's just saying all of this just to throw me off because she's a woman. There aren't too many good-looking women who investigate gruesome murders. It's mostly a man's job because you need a strong stomach for it. I won't fret about it for now; I want a steak, a shower and a comfortable bed.

Carlton was as happy as he could be. All of his little friends were ecstatic. They were all yelling and screaming and so was he. They were chanting Go Red Sox and yelling each of the players' names. The Red Sox never trailed in this game. It couldn't be a better day. It was a total shellacking in of the New York Yankees. The Red Sox had no eras the Yankees made three eras. Sox had accumulated 18 hits and the Yankees were held to five hits. The final score was 13 to 3 Boston. The stadium was still packed at Fenway Park. People were trying to get autographs and fans were still calling out players' names. It was a merry frenzy whenever we'd beat the dreaded New York Yankees.

Agent Bob Davis awoke early after a restful night's sleep. He had gone to bed early and is ready to meet his new temporary partner. He's hoping it's not going to be a disastrous confrontation. He steps out onto the patio of his hotel room and takes in the warm rays of the morning sun. At least it's a beautiful day he thought.

Agent Davis is with the captain in his office, patiently waiting for her timely arrival. She's late the captain said. Bob just smirks and shrugs his shoulders. Here she is. Wow! Holy shit he says quietly to himself, Capt. Adams introduced Detective Paula Robertson to agent Bob Davis. They shook hands and both of them looked momentarily and simultaneously stunned. Even their handshake seemed to drag on. Capt. Adams had to intentionally clear his throat, uh-hum. Both of them turned towards the captain at the same time smiling weakly and a little embarrassed.

Paula immediately noticed the FBI agent's physical traits; he was in terrific shape physically. Bob Davis also realized how incredibly wrong his assumptions were. What happens when you assume dummy. She is a damn knockout! Why isn't she a model or something he thought to himself? She in turn couldn't believe what she saw. I hope he's as smart and witty as his good looks are she thought to herself.

Agent Bob Davis surmised she was a possessive woman and got what she wanted. I hope she'll grow to want me. Little did he know that was already an idea on her mind? She had a spectacular flair and poise and not to mention her elegantly stunning good looks could be a crime in itself.

She moved about the office with such effortless grace and ease, she looked like an angel he thought. The office was a maze of desks, filing cabinets, waste paper baskets, partitions, and people. As Bob watched her he mumbled under his breath. You do not learn presence, you are born with it! He felt embarrassed, for he couldn't keep his eyes off of her.

At the same time but trying really hard not to be noticed, Paula was breathing hard herself. I wonder if he's married or if he has a steady girlfriend. As she snuck a peek in his direction across the room, their eyes momentarily met.

Her heart skipped a beat. He smiled embarrassed. Agent Davis finally broke the awkward silence as the captain entered the room and sensed something uncomfortable between the new partners, then smirked. Capt. Adams is a very wise person and understood perfectly what was going on. He quietly summarized to himself that each one of them expected something totally different than what they got. A pleasant surprise for both of them he thought.

There's been a string of bizarre murders in the New England area with what looks to possibly be a serial killer agent Bob Davis said Now apparently aware of the captain, Paul's reply was late. Still mesmerized she blurted, Police stations, detectives, offices and even private detectives are looking for clues and are trying to solve these heinous crimes. It's my understanding that each of the forensics teams during their autopsies has discovered the same foreign substance in the examination of the blood. Yes that's right captain Adams said. How many separate people are there Paula asked? The captain had a folder in his hand and opened it and said; let's see. One in Johnston Rhode Island, one in Andover Mass., one in Cambridge Mass. That makes three so far, what you mean so far Paula asked, and then realized it was a dumb question. The captain said there is one I forgot, the paperwork is on my desk and I was about to go over it again before I came into this room but everyone showed up at the same time, so that makes four. We need to get some results, and fast! To answer you agent Davis, yes. It is some sort of crazed serial killer.

Carlton sat in his comfortable La-Z-Boy reclining chair and started to read more of his great great grandfather's private diary.

The setting was of London England. It was a foggy quiet night and a noisy laden horse driven coach was traveling south on the damp cobblestone road heading in the general direction of what looks to be Portsmouth point. Chatter of hooves and creaking of carriage wheels were the only sounds in the still of this moist and grim night... Those in power in England have no pity at all in their hearts. They absolutely love the guillotine. I despise them and their tools of devastation. Others with less power had more devious means of distinction. With some regards they were much more cruel and unusual.

The Kami typhus plague spread throughout London this past summer. It took nine weeks of painstaking and exhausting research and experimenting to finally find a vaccine. Once again I was hailed as a miracle worker. If they all only new I've selfishly indulged myself in much too my dismay already too many secret bestialities in which

I would undoubtedly have myself facing their favorite guillotine.

His Majesty's secret office had watchers everywhere. I must be ever more clever than any and all of them... I knew what it felt like to take a life from something delicate and tender and also from something not so delicate. To be mentally assaulted by my visions as I watch the flailing of the bodies. It was their panic stricken eyes that have bewitched. I make a valiant attempt to put on paper, remembering to recapture her last moments on this temporary planet we call Earth. My favorite goose quill pen was lightly dipped in a small flask of black ink as I shuddered at the obsession in which has suddenly overcome me. There was a hired carriage with too many horses shuffling their hooves on the wide cobblestone road. I heard no voice coming from the large cabbage but I did hear laughter in music from the busy brothel, which stood squeezed in between two taverns on the eccentric and Dean Street! A very well-known red light district. A large constable, fat would be more appropriate for this man appeared from within the tavern with a look of disgust on his face. I heard him yell at the redheaded young Doxy who was flirtatiously greeting a young French royalist soldier. The soldier is clearly interested in her as his arm is loosely around her shoulder, but he is secretly hoping not to catch a contract case of the parks from this eager wastrel. To schillings might be worth it the young soldier thought to himself. He hasn't been with a woman in more than nine months...

Michael Van Helsang uses, I so deeply despise this dirty city. I will leave it someday and someday soon. Back home I'm much more relaxed with my closest companion, a flat nosed long gray-haired Persian feline. I call her granny.

Ring ring ring Carlton looked up from the diary as he heard the telephone. He slowly rose from the chair and stiffly walked over to the phone in the hallway, hello. Hey weirdo did you watch the game yesterday? I not only watched it I threw out first pitch Carlton said. Wow! That's kind of why I called but I didn't know how to bring it up without sounding crazy. I could swear it was you on the television. How did you manage that? I thought I spoiled a robbery at a corner store, or yeah. I remember now. The mayor had a party in my honor and gave me tickets to the game. I didn't know I was going to throw out first pitch though, not until someone approached me in the stands and asked me to follow him to see the mayor. The Mayor was waiting on the field outside of the Red Sox's dugout. Cool huh Carlton said! So what's new with you Johnny? Do you have a girlfriend yet? As a matter of fact I do. Really! Yes she's in the Navy and works at the Navy hospital. It was strange how we first met though; it wasn't your typical fix up. I had a one night stand with a girl named Carol, we were at the enlisted club and both of us were feeling really good. We were dancing all night and ended up together and talked for hours. I never saw her again and that was a month ago. Then I was in the enlisted club again and I was playing some pool and a beautiful girl with blonde hair came up to me and she grabbed at the cue ball on the pool table. I just stood there just looking at her. My eyebrows were raised in curiosity. What the hell is she doing? Was going through her mind? What happen next Carlton asked? We'll let me see John said. Come on don't keep me in suspense. Okay, okay. I never met this girl before and it was obvious she was intent on getting something. She was a looker so I played along. She came up to me real close and touched my chest with her hand and said; I worked with Carol at the hospital, my name is Donna. I've been wanting to meet you! Why? Now I'm playing it cool. My friend told me about her night out with you. Where is she I said? I'm sorry but she got transferred two weeks ago. Anyway she said you are the best lover she ever had! I know she was leaving soon and I waited until she was gone to find you. Oh, I said. You'll never believe what she said next. I still don't believe it myself except for the fact that it's now a wonderful memory. Okay what happened next, you piqued my curiosity Carlton and said?

The next thing she said and she was really intoxicating when she said it. Carol told me how you were an awesome lover and I want to find out for myself. Then she looked at me with the sexiest eyes you ever seen. I was speechless. She knew she had my complete attention and didn't say a word; she just grabs my hand and pulled me out of the club. Of course, the gentleman that I am, I followed her without hesitation. Need I say more? Sounds like a good time Carlton said. It was incredible! I've been seeing her from time to time.

It been over three months now, no kidding Carlton said. Well good for you. So far it's just the physical attraction; we really do not discuss any intimate problems' guess some okay with it for now, after all neither one of us hasn't got a clue if or when the next transfer will come in. We each have someone to hold onto and have a little fun together every now and then. I think she's happy with the situation, I know I am. Only time will tell Carlton said. You're right about that buddy. So how's your love life? Don't ask!

United States Marine Corps retired gunnery Sgt. Michael Cote was investigating one of Rhode Island's biggest drug cartels in the history of the small ocean state. The main suspect was none other than soupy Stephen Santana. They call him soupy because he's always eaten soup. Would it be any other reason? When a person would get a cup of coffee, soupy would get a cup of soup instead. When he was in his early 20s he graduated from a vocational technical high school, majoring in culinary arts. He was a very bright student and he even marketed a new soup for a small town, a company started on the other side of the country. That's how he really got his nickname' soupy'. His closest friends call him triple S. Short for soupy Stephen Santana.

Triple S works for an undisclosed Scituate-based warehouse, which sits on the waterfront of Narragansett Bay in Rhode Island. Gunny Cote has been investigating triple S in connection with numerous drug deals that are being accessed through vending machines. A very slick character to say the least. You wouldn't think so to look at him; he weighs over 300 pounds and gets around pretty easily for a person of his massive size. At first glance at him, a person would assume he has a hard time with his mobility. After watching him for so long, we now know for a fact that that's simply not the case with him.

We are real close to nailing this creep. Nine months of monotonous and exhausting work when into this case so far. It's such a classified and completely confidential case, that not even the regular beat cops know about it.

Soupy Stephen Santana is a twice convicted drug dealer. He's done small time in New Bedford Massachusetts Ash Street jail for minor offenses, and this is where we think he's learned about his latest scheme with the vending Machines. There is an electronic technician who repairs these machines that actually spent a few months in the ash Street jail for drunk driving. It just so happens that triple S was there at the same time, So we think this is who and where he got his education when it comes to the vending machines.

The same person works for the situate Rhode Island's Narragansett Bay's warehouse. The warehouse supplies various products ranging in all types of junk food's for vending machines such as; assorted candies, small bags of chips, soda, gum, Rolaids, etc…

Stephen Santana was born and raised the low income projects of Fall River, Massachusetts. It's a well-known established community known for its ruthlessness! There are well known and feared dangerous drug dealers, loan sharks, prostitution, strong arming and felons all living harmoniously in fear of each other. The dark maple tree Gardens is located in the South end of Fall River Massachusetts. Only a 15 minute car ride to Scituate Rhode Island.

Gunny Michael Cote, the lead narcotics detective of Scituate R.I. gets an unexpected promotion to homicide, a newly appointed office at the Scituate Police Department in Rhode Island. A newly appointed office at the situate Police Department. When Detective Cote finds out about his new promotion, he's furious, especially at his captain for the sudden change of departments. He didn't ask this and he knows from experience that all cases must be handed over for reassignment when changing departments. Even though it's a promotion, he bellows; we don't even have a homicide department! We do now! The chief said with blazon authority. (The room got very quiet). Now already hot under the collar from witnessing this ungrateful and disrespectful conduct exhibited towards a superior Officer, he aggressively steps into the captain's office with the same attitude.

The narcotics case involving the vending machines, no longer belongs to you Detective Cote. Do I make myself clear! The chief said. But chief it's a very complicated case. It's gotten reassigned to your protégé the captain said. I just don't get it detected Cote said, I've worked on this case day and night for almost a year. There are many suspected suspects such as; route drivers, warehouse managers, district managers, and warehouse supervisors. The list goes on and on... There are the owners of the vending machines and the technicians who service the machines etc. hundreds and hundreds of man-hours went into this investigation, I just don't understand how at the snap of a finger is being taken away from me. Was it something I did or didn't do? Of course it was something you did, said the chief. Huh! I was damn close to nailing that sleazebag son of a bitch Santana, and now you're telling me, actually ordering me off the case. I spent most of all my free time consumed by stake outs and exhausting research, we understand how you feel detective and we know it's just a matter of weeks before the entire trafficking network crumbles, said the chief. Is the reason why you were the perfect choice for promotion? I don't understand? What! Do I really have to spell it out for you Cote? Look you done a terrific job on this case and were going to arrest a slew of people behind the scenes not to mention some of the craftiness truck dealers New England has ever seen. The chief looked from Detective Cote to Capt. Logan, rolled his eyes and left the room.

I like to be kissed before I get fucked Detective Cote said as he attempted to leave the captain's office. Get back in here and simmer down. Now! Detective Cote was balancing on a fine line and he suddenly realized it. He turned around with a grunt and sat back down. Look here the captain said we all know how hard you work and not only on this particular case, but every single case you've been assigned to. The government is creating a new division to our Police Department. All the higher ups from the chief, the mayor, and the governor himself recommended you to be in charge of this new department. Do you realize the magnitude of this opportunity? Got to admit, it does sound a little more interesting now that you put it that way. You didn't give us a chance to explain said the captain. You immediately started ranting and raven. Your partner is taken over your case and you'll be expected to help in whatever and whenever you can... They both just looked at each other in silence, and then captain Adams said with a smile; look at the bright side, if you're not happy being promoted to lieutenant and running the new homicide division, think of the extra time you'll be spending with your jar-head buddy from the Johnston precinct. What's his name again? Oh yeah it's Harry, gunny Harry Ferreira Oh yeah. Thats right the captain said.

Here is the memo from City Hall. The Mayors quote; we need our best man for this job! Here's the case. The deceased man's name is Jimmy Welch. All we know about him so far is that he was a football star from Yale University when he was enrolled there. He graduated top of his class and now he works, I mean he did work at the government center. Do you understand now why the mayor is interested? This is an election year and this could affect his reelection campaign. The murder took place two floors below the mayor's office. The Providence Rhode Island's Police department is letting us borrow a team of people to help out with this investigation. A forensics team and to investigators are already on the scene, and they are waiting to hear from you Lieutenant Oh! By the way a graduation's is in order, gunny Cote looks at the captain as he stands nearby. Capt. Logan is smiling with his hand outstretched, after the gunny grunted he shook the captain's hand and said thank you sir. Now get out of here and get over to the mayor's office. Yes sir! Said Lieutenant Cote! As he turned to leave he heard wait! You'll need this I think, what is it? A surprised look came over his appearance, it's my new ID, Lieutenant Cote, has a nice ring to it don't you think so said the Captain. Gunny Ferreira is at the crime scene waiting to brief you. Why? I took the initiative to ask him for a favor, him being a friend of yours and not to mention how the Marines are family. Thank you Capt.

These two Devil dogs' were old friends. They met each other years ago. They were both trying to get with the same girl at the enlisted man's club and instantly became friends. They were stationed together at the Marine Corps air station called; Cherry point. They were both young and were both from New England with heavy Boston and New York accents. They spent a great deal of time together and were always surrounded by lots of women. The women couldn't resist their northern accents. They used to ask them to say; quarter (quarta),(pock) the car. Their accents made it sound funny. The girls couldn't get enough. They were a team, when one of them struck out at a nightclub; the other always came through with two girls. It was really uncanny. Both of them had black hair and strong jawbones, they could have passed for brothers. It was hard separating them, they both craved excitement and adventures and where ever they went all the local ladies loved listening to them talk. They were both deployed at the same time overseas, it was generally called Westpac. Although they were in separate squadrons all the Marines were stationed on the same base at Subic Bay outside of Olongapo city, the Philippine Islands. It was a six-month deployment, their first deployment overseas. It was a somewhat nervous time for the island and also. It was an election year and there was fighting from time to time, mostly the natives. It didn't stop Harry and Mike from getting quickly acquainted with all the pretty girls. They had the time of their lives. There were practically five girls to every guy and money was no object because the American dollar was worth much more than the islands peso'. You can actually have a terrific night out with a measly $10 bill, and still have enough money left over for breakfast the next morning.

Detective Paula Robertson and agent Bob Davis are getting absolutely nowhere with their impersonal relationship towards each other. The press is over dramatizing the killer as a ruthless assassin. Personal injury attorneys whom are representing the victims' families are causing waves of confusion and chaos, not to mention a stunning public hysteria. The Mayor and the chief of police from Cambridge Massachusetts as well as the governor of Rhode Island want answers! Agent Davis has been getting an earful from the FBI's ADIC as well.

As the old saying goes; all work and no play make people dull. Well then maybe that's another reason why Bob and Paula are actually aware of each other's attraction to one another. Despite what despicable scenes are unfolding around them, with people being bludgeoned to death. Bob and Paula are quietly fantasizing about each other. As a matter of fact, tonight is a night away from the office; Bob and Paula are going out to play. No one is going to call any one of them dull. Not tonight anyway.

Paula suggested that she picked up Bob tonight since she's familiar with Boston. It's 8 o'clock in the evening and a warm breeze is blowing the leaves of the trees and the sun is setting so perfectly. Bob is waiting patiently outside of his health. She's late, he's thinking. In Hornby's from an unfamiliar car, he bends down to look into the vehicle and can't see because of the darkness of the car's interior. Then the interior light comes on and there she was Paula waving with a smile. Bob quickly gets in. Hi handsome, high yourself hot stuff he said. You look beautiful. Now I know why she's late he thought. We'll go to one of my favorite spots for dinner okay, it's quaint and clean, I like the owners and I'm sure you'll be pleased also. I'm sure he says. They pulled up to the restaurant/pub went inside and sat down. A waitress with the thick fire red hair and lipstick to match approached us smacking some gum. Hello can I help you tonight, sure two coffees and for now give us a minute to look over your menu. Sure thing lovey she said, and left us.

As we were mulling over the menu glad to be together away from the office, an old man came into the restaurant. We both just stared in wonder. He must've been at least, 70 years old. He was standing erect, he had impeccable posture. He was handsome with thick silver hair and had a half assed grin. Smiling, probably because of the young attractive woman hanging tightly on his arm. He was wearing a light blue Italian sports jacket and a buttoned white shirt; the two top buttons were undone sure and off a couple curls of silver chest hair. He looked to be really enjoying life. Bob and Paula looked back to each other and smiled. Bob said, I wish I knew his secret. Suddenly a hum of sexual tension had begun between them. She said softly, and not too bad yourself as he blushed. Are you ready yet? The waitress asked. Yes, I believe we are Paula said. I will have the house specialty and my date will have the same. Be sure to tell Jimmy it's for Paula. Whose Jimmy Bob asked? She was smiling now. Jimmy is the owner. So you know him well I take it. Well yeah he's my uncle. 10 minutes later an older man with a thin gray mustache brought out their meals. Hello sweetheart he said he gave her a light kiss on the cheek. He was a jovial kind of guy and looked at me and said to his knees; who is this handsome stranger. He must be someone special because you never come to my restaurant with anyone. I like this guy Bob said; now Paula is blushing.

Jimmy Welch's office walls were ceremoniously decorated with what looks like every trophy, commemorative plaque, and achievements he was ever awarded from the Yale University's athletic department. Now he's unexpectedly dead, and there's no doubt about it that it was murder, premeditated murder. It was an absolute horrible scene. Blood covered the entire office. It was streaked across his desk, and walls were sprayed with blood covering his achievements. The forensics Dr. on the scene almost vomited as she tried to explain to Lieut. Cote that it looks as if he struggled. The victim's arm was lacerated right off of his body; it was on the floor 10 feet away from the victim.

The first person on the scene apparently fainted of shock and is being tended to as we speak. She was revived after the police discovered that she still had a strong pulse. She wasn't hurt at all, she just happened to walk in unexpectedly onto this grisly scene. Her name is Susan McKay. The police say she's a suspect and accompanied her to the hospital. She was handcuffed while they read her her rights.

Forensics Burst onto the gruesome scene over and hour ago. They were trying with precisioned exaggeration not to disturb the large amounts of blood soaked carpeting. They already took samples off the walls. The body is being moved along with its arm in a separate plastic bag. They'll be an autopsy as soon as the body is at the morgue and the entire floor of the building is being sealed off immediately.

Newly appointed homicide detective, Michael Cote gathers up as much information as possible. Two police officers ask him why he's here with arrogant attitudes. I asked myself the same question. Gunny Cote said to himself. I'm the lead detective here! What! This isn't a narcotics case, get lost and go find some drug dealers like you're supposed to. Be careful officer Kolinsky, gunny Cote says. I'm no longer in the narcotics department. I'm in homicide now, no thanks to the chief and the bloody mayor. Furthermore I'll forget about the arrogant attitudes towards a superior officer since you didn't know yet. Know what? Officer kolinsky says. I recently got promoted to Lieut. To go along with the new homicide office, as he said this he showed his bars on his shirt and his new ID. Both offices looked at each other with a puzzled look on their faces. You look exactly how I feel the gunny said. The other offices said; congratulations and officer kolinsky just stared at the gunny. Now if you have any evidence or information pertaining to this case I would like to see it, otherwise it seems everything is about to wrap up here for now. You do know of course you will be sending your reports into my office. Maybe even ask for you to forward them to me by fax. Have a good day gentlemen. I'll look forward to hearing from you. Lieut. Cote then turned and left.

Jonathon hunt, Sgt. Hunt US MC. Takes leave to visit his family and his best friend. Jonathon can't wait to see his buddy Carlton. It's a surprise visit and no one was expecting him, he even rang the doorbell at his parents' house and then he hid behind a rose bush. His mother opened the door and didn't see anyone and frowned not sure now if she even did hear the doorbell. John watched her turn and go back inside and then he rang the bell again. He stood there this time and yelled "surprise". She yelled his name Johnny and then gave him a great bear hug and a kiss on the cheek. What are you doing here, you didn't even call us. I wanted this visit to be a surprise. I was feeling kind of spontaneous. Is anyone home?

Jonathon's feeling really good about this particular visit. It's a happy occasion. His last visit was a bit gloomy and he had to be mentally strong for his best friend at the time. It was his best friend's dad's funeral and John was a pallbearer and also a strong emotional support for his friend Carlton. Since then, John has thought about the many times that Carlton was his support, especially when they were in high school together. They don't know it but both of them have made a subconscious commitment to each other, friends for life.

Getting himself all worked up this morning, John can't wait to drive over to see his friend. He's planning on pulling the same prank as he did with his mother. Although he's feeling mischievous he still wants to ask him about his invention, how is everything going with it? So many questions?

Ring, ring, and Carlton opens his front door and no one was there. Jonathan heard him curse lightly, Damn kids.

He turns around walks back in the house closes the door. ring, ring, Carlton opened the door again seen nothing again but this time Jonathan jumped from the bushes and yells halt, who goes there? Hey jar head Carlton said great with excitement and a wide grin. What the hell you doing here? I just figured I'd come out to see you buddy. Wow! What a nice surprise, come on in. I was feeling homesick and so here I am.

So what's happening? How's the freeze wave doing? You still making money? Of course, but it leveled off a little. I think I told you that Yale University gets a percentage since the invention was conceived on school property. Yeah I remember. So what's in store for your future? I'm not sure Carlton replied. Well you know buddy, the Marines are still looking for a few good men! You would surely go to OCS (officer's candidate school). Oh yeah, I can see it now, you and me officer and a gentleman. Carlton Says smiling. At least we would know who the officer would be. Very funny civilian ha ha. Hey wait a minute that might not be a bad idea. You really think so John said. Yeah! Isn't it true that you would have to salute me and call me sir, hey now wait a minute Jonathan said! Now you think it's a good idea. Carlton couldn't help but crack a smile and say okay, go ahead and do it, now he's talking and laughing at the same time. Try it he says, you think that's funny huh Sir, and they both cracked up like a couple of school kids.

Agent Bob Davis and Detective Paula Robertson are on another anticipated date. There is no work involved whatsoever this time, no shop talk tonight. Tonight is their lucky night. Their sitting in the lounge on bar stools at the bar having Cocktails as they wait patiently for a table to open the restaurant. The four season's restaurant is very busy this time of year. They don't mind waiting for a table because both of them have something else on their minds. They are priming each other up with drinks. The television is on at the end of the bar where they are sitting. Its reporter Dan Ackerman in front of a local news Van, which in turn is parked outside the steps of the Rhode Island government center. He's reporting the latest news about the string of unsolved murders. People are being tortured to death and there's no way of knowing whether or not some of these victims were conscious or not. He pauses a few seconds as he looks directly into the camera. Tell me folks? What are the police hidings from us? People are questioning the mayor's office, is anything being done? One angry relative of the latest victim is saying; the person is obviously some kind of demented psychopath. He's causing and uproar with the public. People want answers and they want answers now!

Finally the waiter calls for table 2, the Davis party please. Bob and Paula were relieved to get away from the bar hoping that they are not profiled on the television. They were graciously seated and the maître d' apologized for the delay, don't worry about it Bob said. Tom thought Paula had the most infectious laugh and he loved listening to her. so the wait was just finding his mind.

She thinks to herself, enough of this passiveness. I definitely have to be more assertive. Paula is wasted no time finding out what makes Bob tick. The sexual tension is driving them both mad, a blind person can see it. They talk about their spouses how each one of them was married to a civilian and how each one is now divorced with similar stories. Bob divorced with 2 ½ years and Paula for three years. Amazingly each one of them has been celibate all this time, not one date. Again something in common, they both put all their efforts and concentration in their own work. This is how each one of them mourned the separations of their old partners.

Tonight they're both ready to unleash all those pent-up desires and frustrations. After dinner they took a drive along the River and then went back to Tom's hotel and ravished each other. She was hungry for him and she was acting selfish tonight. She took from him what she's been craving ever since they first met. She told him; your mine tonight and don't move or I'll handcuff you, laughter ensues. Her soft hot lips kissed his neck and she made her way down his chest ever so slowly, she reminded him not to move. He strained against her as she lightly bit his nipples, it was extremely difficult keeping still but he knew his turn would come. She was feeling good from the drinks they shared as she makes a beeline straight to his manliness. He felt himself going mad. She kissed him, caressed him and licked him and slowly took him whole. His lips were warm and wet. She looked up at him and she smiled as their eyes met. She was caressing his inner thighs and the strong muscles on his legs, she is incredible, just simply amazing he thought.

The room turned red in his mind as he finally exploded. She didn't stop and his whole world was slipping out of focus. He tried to push her away as he was feeling the peak of pleasure and pain simultaneously. She moaned and slowed her rhythm not once letting her lose control. They found themselves sweating heavily, and breathing irregularly. She finally let up when she heard him say; it's my turn now baby.

As he hugged her he could feel her taut nipples against his chest. Her responsiveness overwhelmed him. She gasped in pleasure as his experience mouth lavished her best Treasure feverishly. She twitched and convulsed as his strong hands squeezed her soft round ass. Now he looked up at her, as she caught his eye, he smiled and told her to keep still, this is payback. She rolled her eyes and moaned. She tried pushing his head away from her as she violently reached climax, he was too strong and firmly held her in place as his tongue rhythmically danced all about her. His salacious appetite in giving oral sex to his lover was unmatched. He was utterly the best lover she ever had. I want to lock them him up and throw away the key. He's incredible she thought. He reluctantly took a breath of air as she lay limp, totally spent of every ounce of energy. Feeling herself tingling and marveled at the way he made her feel. With a husky raspy voice in between deep breaths of air, she managed to say; you're amazing. He smiled and gently pulled her into his strong arms and kissed her ever so gently, then whispered; I love you... It was simply meant to be. Bob and Paula fall in love.

Carlton and Jonathon went out on the town. The local hotspot called The Golden Cage. This nightclub has come a long way since the days that Carlton used come here. If Carlton only knew his father use to come here, even worse was if he ever found out this is where his father met his wicked stepmother, he would probably stop in his tracks and never step in here again. Well, ancient history.

It was a night of drinking and raising a little hell. We were watching exotic dancers, drinking, dancing, more drinking and laughing. John and Bob decided to play a whole game they used to play years ago, back in high school. They both had on a good buzz by now so it was a hilarious time. While sitting at their table looking at everyone that passes by, they take turns guessing what famous person that the person passing by them might resemble. Was kind of fun. Neither one of them can remember who initiated that old name game, nor they didn't care they were having a good time. John even recalled the time when they thought this one girl looked like Elvis Presley. And the next thing you know, John started day in her. They both laughed so hard Bob fell off his chair. Anyone who glanced in their way instantly knew they had a special relationship. They were best friends for life.

Capt. Logan had given newly appointed Lieut. Cote an idea. He called his old friend. The two old Marines got to catching up on old times. Hey! You old goat gunny Cote exulted. Semper Fi Devil dog, exclaimed gunny Ferreirai. Obviously a true Marines exact reply would be what gunny Cote had said; do or die buddy.

The two jar heads met up at a Starbucks coffee house somewhere halfway between Scituate Rhode Island and Johnston Rhode Island. Some small talk ensued and then they got down to business. Gunny Ferreira said we keep a file of MO's at the office. I'll be glad to have a copy made and sent over to you. It would be helpful to your new office and staff. So what have you got on the Gertrude Steele case? I hope it's more than I have on the Jimmy Welch case. Both agreed that familiar behaviors and patterns only mean that we are looking for a psychotic serial killer. Yes, a very intelligent one! None of the perpetrators tools or instruments used have ever been discovered, and there's not one single shred of evidence, except. Except what gunny Cote said with a raised eyebrow. So far there are five victims, five! I didn't know there were five. Did you know each one of them has an unknown substance that's been injected into their bloodstream? The straight scoop I got from three different examiners was that this foreign substance was no doubt injected after each one of them had already died. They all concurred this was the case. Unusual as it sounds, the person responsible for these atrocities wants it to be known that it's he himself, who is accountable. No one else! Yes it is strange. Sound like its right out of the X-Files or something like that, gunny Cote said.

While gunny Ferreira was explaining his hunch, he managed to drop some Apple turnover pastry flakes on his jersey. I've never been here before gunny Cote said. It's quite comfortable. It's a far cry from our old hangouts back at Cherry point eh Harry? You must be joking. What, don't you remember a table similar to this one back at the bar off base? What was the name and Place, all yeah! Burtons! That's it, Burton's restaurant lounge. Don't you remember the game I thought you? Of course I remember it was the first time we met. Game called smiles. Yeah there were five of us at that table with our pants down, and the first guy that smiled had to buy a round for the whole table. No one told me that there was a girl under the table. It was an experience I'll never forget and with that they both cracked up laughing again. Here is to the old days and they clicked coffee cups.

Mr. Van Helsang, a graduate from Yale University, Recently recognized by the city of Boston Massachusetts some three months ago as a modern day hero. He stopped a potentially dangerous robbery in progress at a convenience store. Now he is being given a well-deserved Good Samaritan award.

On the front page of Boston's most popular newspaper, the Globe was a picture of Carlton Van Helsang. A very happy and grateful woman was smiling with her arm wrapped around his waist. The headlines read "one more time". Authorities say he was in the right place at the right time and once again didn't hesitate to do what was right.

A homeless man was attacking a woman in an alley one block away from the sacred hearts children's home. It was broad daylight. Mr. Van Helsang said; he was on his way to meet a friend for dinner at Luciano's Italian restaurant and after leaving Bob Jenkins and the kids, sure enough that's when he heard a woman desperately crying rape. She was screaming and making a lot of noise. It surprised me that no one else heard anything so I assumed I must have been the first person to hear her cries.

Carlton said anyone would have done the same. All I did was yell HEY! What are you doing! I guess the man got scared and ran off before he could actually commit the rape or assault. The woman's clothes were half torn off her and she was severely shaken. I helped a terrified young woman to her feet and then we both called the police.

The police arrived 10 minutes later and then met us at a corner diner. They wrote down a description of the pervert from the still badly shaken up girl. She told the police that I saved her life; I think she was a little dramatic. You know, with what she just went through. After the police finished with all their questions they volunteer to bring her home. Carlton said he still had business to attend to hear in the city... Once again the help of his transport machine, he was able to surprise attack the crazy pervert. Who knows maybe she was right and Carlton did save her life.

Carlton Van Helsang was again invited to the governor's mansion as the guest of honor. A party with high officials! The upper-class society of Boston! Wall-to-wall politicians trying to get a leg up on everyone else to further advance all their own careers and enhance their reelection campaigns. Nosy reporters everywhere! I wish I didn't have to go. After the first half hour the main attraction always seems to fade off into the crowd. I guess I'll just mingle a while and then leave.

Carlton's been very busy lately with the surprise visit from his friend Jonathon hunt, with rescuing storeowners, his invention the freeze wave being marketed, saving damsels in distress etc... It's all just plain exhausted. I need another vacation he thought to himself. Carlton decides to visit a favorite college spot. Five days of sun and skimpy bikinis at the wet and wild Myrtle Beach South Carolina. As he starts packing a suitcase for his trip he takes a minute to load an Elvis tape into his Pioneer stereo system. Elvis always cheered him up. While Carlton sings along to I'm all shook up". His thoughts start to wander. Carlton is usually a reclusive character by nature, but at Party, at the governor's mansion, he had gotten a little tipsy and couldn't help eavesdrop and on certain conversations. He sometimes wondered what went on behind the curtains of these elaborate political gatherings. He did hear a surprising number of family secrets, and then slowly realized it's just normal every day gossip, no different from any other family having problems. Just a different class of people that's all. All in all he thought, every class of people have the same similar problems. The continuous cycle of the human race

Detective Paula Robertson an agent Bob Davis are presently in their shared office of the Cambridge Massachusetts police station. They just can't seem to spend enough time together. Bob especially, he fell really hard for her.

There both working on the same case but are following up on different victims. They are trying to find similarities other than the known toxic substance that is already associated with these specific victims. Something, anything at this point would be most welcome. It's tedious work at this junction of the investigation because now they are concentrating on their pasts. In a nutshell, they're gathering as much history as possible from relatives. Information such as what schools they went to starting as far back as seventh and eighth grades, and everything else into the future right up to their untimely demise. It's very frustrating work

A young pimple faced redheaded rookie officer approaches Detective Robertson and tells her there's a woman on the phone that wants to speak with someone in charge of the latest murders plaguing New England. She says she can see into the future and claims to have seen the latest murder, she even mentioned an office is where it happened. She's claiming to be a psychic. Paula said to the young rookie with the bad complexion; just get her name and phone number and where she can be reached... It's probably another weirdo looking for some attention, PR, publicity Paula said. Yeah you're probably right he replies. As she looked at Bob he gives her his best Hollywood smile and a wink making absolutely sure no one is watching, Paula blows him a kiss.

I received a phone call from the Andover police station said Cheryl, a female officer. It's another unsolved murder and their people seem to think it could be related to the other homicides that took place at the Andover Memorial mental hospital. It was almost 2 months ago Officer Cheryl said. Capt. Adams trailed behind Officer Cheryl and said; it looks similar there are no prints or any tangible evidence except for a photograph that the forensics team took. A photograph said Bob.

The victim Barbara Helsang, bled to death from a laceration to a vulnerable artery, and as she was bleeding it looks like she was trying to spell something with their own blood and abruptly stopped. I want you to check this out, it could be a break somehow or a clue. Well! Said the captain! They both were just staring at him. Get outta here and get on over to the hospital. Yes sir said Paula. Bob and Paula immediately got up from their desks and left the office.

Paula and Bob exited the station and drove through Main Street. It was tree-lined each side and we seen some of the unusual stores here. Meat market's, a hardware store, and an ice cream Parlor and even a small pool hall. The highway exit is right around the corner from the pool hall Paula said. Bob was driving because he wanted to learn the area. Paula noticed a man standing in a doorway dressed in a dark blue blazer, a beige shirt and a pair of designer jeans. He looked like came right out of a Gucci magazine and was out of place standing in the doorway of a pool hall. She wanted to stop and question him but conceded it'll have to wait because they had more pressing matters at hand to deal with. How long until we reach Andover asked Bob? Huh? What? Sorry someone caught my attention on the street. It's about an hour's ride from here.

It doesn't seem that this freak has any kind of preference in his victims, does it Bob asked. They range in class from high society to very low income. Let's get a cup of coffee for the ride, so Bob pulled over and exited the highway right outside of Boston. They both walked into an old Diner and asked for 2 cups of coffee regular, that's two sugars and cream for both of them.

The diner has a large round clock right smack in the middle of the wall. Bob looks at the time on the big clock which in turn resembles an old clock from his youthful school days. Bob Cocks an eyebrow as he looks at Paula. How about dinner tonight? Where? My place! There is someone I want you to meet. Paula gladly accepts. Who? She asks. It's a surprise. A surprise, surprises make me nervous. Don't worry honey it's a good surprise. Okay…if you say so, I do trust you. I know.

While watching beautiful girls parading up and down the white sandy beach, Carlton thinks back to his days in college. How every student lived for these beaches? Carlton relaxes and soaks up a little sun today. This was long overdue he thinks. He lies down on his beach blanket alongside a small RCA radio and a six-pack cooler full of beers. All I need at the beach is right here he thought. Number one refreshment at the beach associated with spring break is in fact beer. So he knows for sure he's satisfied and happy. Carlton Props up his head and gets ready to crack open a beer when suddenly a gorgeous young college girl struts by without her top on. Carlton spilled the beer all over himself and she saw him and giggled. You did that on purpose Carlton said to the girl! She boldly looked at him and said with a smile as she shook her perfectly round booty. I know! And she proceeded to walk away slowly, teasing him with every step. is she flirting with me he thought? Wow! Now surprised at himself for not realizing it sooner! I'm so out of touch the scene.

Carlton wipes himself off with his beach towel and notices he still has a good physique. Maybe she was for, and he smiles as he reaches for his great-great-grandfather's Journal. Now he proceeds to finish reading it. Carlton smiles to himself as he smells saltwater in the air. Breathing in the clean-air he surmises that he can't help but feel wonderful. It's smoggy back in New England, its noisy dark and gloomy and it's way too fast-paced. Someday soon I think I'll be moving out of the New England. How I despise gloomy days. His thoughts drift to a memory when he and Glenda are right here on this very beach. It was their first spring break together. They were making love under the moonlight by a small crackling fire. How time flies he thought.

A small man in a tan colored suit was exiting the hotel. His face was rugged and sunburned and his skin looked like leather, most likely from too much sun exposure. He had extremely small beady eyes and he rarely blinked. His hair was fiery red and curly, he needed a haircut. His voice was deep and he was deliberately slow to the point when he spoke. He was eerie. I wouldn't want to meet up with a character like him in a dark alley.

Mr. Van Helsang, he asked. Yes, your appointment for your full body massage is in 15 minutes down by the sauna room. The sauna room and the gym are located on level II Sir. Thank you.

There were soldiers with dark-colored bonnets and large muskets by their side's way off into the distance. They were the kings Honor guards. They are always at the ready to defend their king.

As I strolled through the damp city, a large constable was flogging a pickpocket. I never powder my hair like all these others do; I do tie it in a ponytail and always with a black ribbon. This night will be my last night of ridding London of its worst. But first I will dine at the lamplighter Tavern Downtown.

The waitress approached, can I help you sir? With an over exaggerated smile. Yes indeed, a canter of wine to start out with and then I'll have the rib-eye steak medium for my entrée. As I looked out the French windows of the restaurant I noticed the lamp lighters start to commence with their work as daylight starts to dissipate. After dinner I exited the restaurant stepping down the twisted staircase. I decided to walk past the Haymarket. I surely do hate this damp dark country, one day I will definitely leave. The dry Datura is a favorite of mine. It never fails to stimulate the senses. My patients sometimes hallucinate. I momentarily and carefully observe them before ministering some of the medicine, always being careful.

I alone advocate death. Although no one knows me I'm regarded as the most renowned serial killer London has ever bear witness to. Someone in the hierarchy of his majesties Court has given me a peculiar nickname I don't quite fancy.

After the twitching flames of the streetlamps have been extinguished, only then is when I can make my clever escape.

Finally at last I'm home in my favorite room with my favorite companion. Who now is lying peacefully on the bear rug before the hearth soaking up the heat of the fire? I love my loyal finicky friend. Like me, cats needed no one to care for them. We both simply demanded our do.

A doorbell rings. Ding dong, ding dong. Paula can hear someone in the background inside of Bob's new condo. Ding dong ding dong ding dong. Okay okay I'll get it, Dale don't bother. Come in Miss Paula who now has a confused look on her face. Bob looks her over. Wow! You look absolutely gorgeous Bob said. She smiled and said thank you very much handsome as she's already forgot about what she just heard through the door.

Something smells great as she followed the scent into the kitchen. I bet you didn't know that I knew my way around the kitchen huh and playfully nudged her in the ribs. Paul was smiling again as she exclaims, boy oh boy you are full of surprises aren't you. She steps very close to him wraps her arms around his thick neck and kisses him hard.

She has this heated boiling passion beneath her hard exterior. A steamy, provocative, sexuality and if you got close enough to her you could actually sense it. An irresistible ache crept up into me. I've never felt anything like this not even when I was married to my ex-wife. This woman was driving mad. I have to have her. One day she'll be mine and mine only. His eyes were steel gray and deadly serious as he looked at her. She noticed something different. What's wrong? Nothing he said. Are you sure? You look like something's wrong. No no, not at all. I was just thinking how great I've been feeling since I've met you. Okay now what you want, nothing really. I'm just happy that's all.

There's someone I want you to meet Ms. Robertson. If you will accompany me into the living room I will introduce you. Now he's very shy so don't be offended if he doesn't acknowledge you. What you mean? What's going on Bob? You'll see, trust me it's okay.

There is a man sitting down on the floor in the living room watching TV. Hey Dale! I want you to meet a really nice lady. Paula and Bob noticed Dale's body stiffened up. This is Paula. Paula this is Dale. Say hello Dale. He's scared; he doesn't move an inch, not even to turn his head. Dale stands totally still and looks directly at his brother Bob. Paula smiles and says hello Dale. His eyes are the only part of him moving. His eyes moved from Bob to Paula and then to the kitchen where Bob is now pouring drinks for them, All the while carefully tending to his dinner. He checks the oven and the pots on the stove.

Paula isn't saying a word; she's just watching Bob Cooking in the kitchen. Finally the curiosity is overwhelming, she says quietly. Who is he? Bob walks away from the hot stove with oven mitts still in his hand and looks her directly in the eyes with a concerned and very serious look in his own eyes. He's my only brother. He's waiting for a response and not sure what kind of response, but hoping it would be something positive. She smiles, really she said. Bob goes on to explain that his brother is autistic. My parents didn't know he was born that way at first; he was eventually diagnosed at a very young age. Dale is very shy with strangers. He's never mean to anyone he's kind of a big sweet kid and at times is very bright... There is one thing I want you to know though. There is one thing he hates. What's that? Dale hates to be touched, in any way. Research shows usually there's only one family member that is usually chosen subconsciously who eventually is allowed to come close enough, this is what the doctors say. This is the case with 89% of these special people. It takes a lifetime usually for them to trust just one person.

Dale stays at an institution in the state of Connecticut. It's private; I always got a kick out of the name of the place.

What's the name Paula said? It's called mind over matter Bob said. This is kind of unique set. I pick him up once a month and keep in for a weekend. On his only family and he trusts me. Our parents passed away together in a car accident a long time ago so I do whatever I can to stay in touch with him. We both come a long way. In a lot of ways Dale is like that movie character they call Raymond, did you ever see that movie, ah, I think it's called Rain man. Yes, oh I love that movie Paula said. Seen it over and over when it first came out but sometimes it was disturbing. Most of the times it was quite funny... Paula asks Bob with a mischievous grin. Does Dale think Kmart sucks to? Ha ha. Bob smiled as some pressure was released he thought, he wasn't sure how Paula would react and now he's relieved.

He looks healthy and in good spirits Paula said. He is healthy and happy. He doesn't need anything when he is. He even as a couple of friends he hangs out with at the hospital. Is it a nice place where he is looked after, or where he lives Paula asks? Oh yeah, it's actually very old. It's a very impressive complex indeed. It's an extremely well groomed sanitarium. An old mansion converted into an elaborate hospital type facility. There is a wing specifically designed for people with autism. It's an incredible place and some of the patients, ah, people there, are absolutely brilliant. But each and every one of them is lacking in some sort of chromosome or something that in turn holds them back from being functional in mainstream society. It's too bad; I like some of these people here.

Dale is even allowed to have his own pet. Really she said? People like that are allowed to have pets. Can they take care of them properly she asks? Sure, sometimes better than most people. Let me explain. There are allowed to have certain pet birds like parakeets, finches or canaries. Nothing too major like a dog. Gail has a pet cockatiel. You wouldn't believe what this bird can say and do. My brother Dale trained this bird to say over 15 different words. The doctors and nurses tell me that the bird goes everywhere Dale goes. He even insisted on bringing it over to my place a few times. One of the nurses told me that they have an unbreakable bond, Dale and the bird that is. She said it's like he can actually communicate with it and the damnedest thing happens. What's that? The bird talks back to him. Laughter ensues. One time Dale put the bird out on the patio in its cage so that it can get some fresh air and maybe smell of flowers and surround the deck dancing in the summer breeze. While she said, Dale got up to use the bathroom and while he was gone another patient accidentally knocked over the cage and the bird escaped. We all panicked! We know what to do? We all thought he was going to freak out or something. When he came back we told him what happened and everyone pointed to a large oak tree. Those who were sitting on the patio that is. Dale looked scared; he was pacing the floor back and forth. As he walked over to the same tree he called out to the bird. He just said the birds name about three times and just like magic it flew right to him and perched itself right on Dales shoulder. Gail turned his face towards pretty boy, that's the bird's name and I swear to you the bird kissed him and Dale smiled as he walked back to the patio. Everyone was so happy for him and started clapping their hands in appreciation and joy. There's only one place is not allowed to take it next to the dining room. The doctor says you never know it'll just up and fly to a rafter or something like that and drop a few presents along its flight path. So I don't allow him to bring it into the dining room or anywhere near the dinner table.

Sometimes Dale's repetitiveness can get under people's skin Bob said while refilling Paula's glass. I heard him while I was in the hall waiting for you to answer the door. I don't know who or what it was, I heard him saying, dingdong, dingdong. Bob smiled and in turn made Paula smile... Shush Bob said as he motioned his index finger to his lips, listen! Clap on clap off clap on clap off. He gets a lot of this kind of stuff from TV. He must have just seen that television commercial with the little old lady in bed Paula said, you know which one I'm talking about she asks Bob as she quietly chuckles to herself. You think it's funny huh and laughs himself, yeah me too sometimes.

I can hardly wait to eat Paula said. I'm absolutely famished. I haven't had anything to eat except for a salad at noon today. What are you cooking any way it smells wonderful. It's my specialty Bob replies as he gave her a seductive sideways glance. It's for when I want to win over someone's heart. Seems like you've done this before? Paula sneaks over to the oven with Bobs standing; she wraps her slender arms around him, hugs him hard and kisses his neck. I did tell you that I was married once, just like you. So I learned a few things around the kitchen. She pinches his butt, so that's it! She teased. Go put on some music and I'll take care of this. Dinner will be served by the time you get back.

Lisa Cates is frustrated as hell; the police won't take her seriously. They're given her the runaround. They're assuming she's a crackpot or she's just seeking some particular kind of attention for personal gain. Like so many of those other homeless people claiming to be the person committing these hideous crimes.

Lisa Cates was raised in the suburbs of Atlanta Georgia. She was the epitome of what you would call a southern belle. Lisa grew up with three brothers, she was the baby of the family and since being the only girl she was showered with attention. Her favorite brother was Mike, he's the oldest. The two other brothers were closer to her in age and teased her a lot. Mike had a few years in between her and was much more mature, he always treated her like a young lady and she liked that about him.

Lisa grew up to be a very beautiful, intelligent and extremely independent woman, despite wrestling and fighting with her brothers when she was younger. Without her ever realizing it, independence was introduced to her and practically branded into her at a very young age. Call it luck of the draw. Being that she's the only girl her independence started with her having to have their own bedroom. The young lady couldn't possibly share a bedroom with a boy especially in a practicing Catholic family. She had three brothers who shared a big bedroom, one of them on a single twin bed and the other two on bunk beds. She longed for a sister but her parents weren't getting any younger. Her and her mom became best friends as she grew up.

Independence was branded in her long time ago. She had to compete with her 2 younger of brothers and they always teamed up together which wasn't fair, but all in all she still won her fair share of contests and tricks. She vowed, never to have to count on a man for anything like her mom did. She saw the things her mom went through and she didn't want to go through the same.

Lisa made her own way in the world. She was optimistic and persistent. She was a college graduate and ranked in the top of her class. She worked and less hours as a waitress to support yourself while going through college. She worked very hard, and it paid off.

Lisa succeeded at everything she set her mind to. Everything was a challenge for her so to cope she associated these things with how she grew up with her brothers. It was her against the world. When she got older she rarely ever failed at any task she took on. She learned at a young age when you want something, whether you set a goal or not, if you go the extra mile at any task only good things come from hard work. Maybe it's because she carefully picked and chose her projects with the wisdom of someone way beyond her years. Maybe it was the gift she possessed, a special gift from her higher power that enabled her to see things no one else could.

Clairvoyants see beyond, Lisa Cates most intimate and special secret. Secrecy held for years until she understood it completely. This is how she was always a step ahead of her brothers as children. She could always find them whenever they went outside to play hide and seek, whether it was at the neighborhood Park or in the schoolyard. Whenever they played kick the can it was the same thing, she always found them. Everyone used to want Lisa on the team because she had wisdom they thought. Most people in school looked up to her whenever there was some type of competition or a debate in something.

One day it was all clear to her. The time was finally right. She became suddenly em- powered by a strange and bizarre feeling to reveal its well hidden existence. Lisa had this gift (sometimes she viewed it as a curse) since she could remember. Relationships with boys were the worst because she always knew what they thought, sometimes before they knew themselves. Most of her childhood premonitions confused her and tormented her thinking. And then again on certain occasions they were outlandishly confident and exhilarating, not to mention extremely useful. Once she understood it all and was in control of it she decided to get into the law enforcement field. She helped the police and certain other authorities to find missing children. She became well known in this area and the police asked her for assistance many times even to catch certain dangerous and notorious criminals that were still at large. Eluding all efforts by the authorities to apprehend these subjects, sometimes they just needed a little extra help.

Paula was acting frisky as she gives Bob a seductive look and says; don't you think the snow falling is so romantically enchanting? Bob you know the way the ground gets covered with the fresh beautiful untouched luster. Bob and Paula both can't stand the pressure any longer. The Sexual tension is so thick that you can cut it with a knife, my brother has been asleep for over two hours now, and he's a very sound sleeper, Bob was smiling at her while he was telling her this. He leads her (both of them with excruciating anticipation) towards his bedroom. As they both entered the bedroom he abruptly turns to her startling her, while breathing heavily he whispers in her ear. I just got to have you. From the moment I first laid eyes on you, I knew you were for me he said.

I have a confession to make officer as she stands on her tippy toes and looks up into his dark eyes. I've been in a trance ever since we've met. I want you too honey, with all my heart.

Both of them had chills run up and down their spines. They immediately embraced in a tender hug and kissed each other slowly in anticipation of the next few moments together. The way Bob undressed her with his eyes was so provocative she could hardly contain herself. He was a great lover as she quivered with ecstasy. His hot sensuous lips delightfully ravaged her most private treasures. She was absolutely ravishing with great curves, he thought he can do it is forever. She cried out desperately as he kept up a torturous easy rhythm. He climbed above her entering her slowly. Now they were one, and he methodically drove her crazy. Feeling her tremble beneath him, it made him increasingly more excited and hard. He loved to please her. She couldn't hold back much longer, the heat and weight of his muscular body, and his sexy musky smell. Her body spasmed beneath him and her legs tightened around him like a vise grip she thought. He plunged even deeper into her as if their bodies would meld together. It was a body sweeping rush that crept all over her as her vision went momentarily blank. Oh yes she loudly moaned and then they both held their breath for a fraction of a second as if it was a timed reflex, and climaxed together.

I feel fantastic Paula said as she lay beside Bob panting for air. He turns on his side and looks at her. She's beautiful he thought and he told her so. You're so beautiful, he's rubbing her belly. Thank you, I think you're beautiful too. She looks at him with serious puppy dog eyes. I don't want to lose you she said. He said it's been such a long long time since I felt this way, me too. I love you, I love you too.

Carlton is having a swell time. He's being pampered like a spoiled rich kid at his birthday party. He fell asleep on the beach after having two strong Manhattan Ice-T's then he woke up couple hours later looking like a well done lobster. His sunscreen had faded off and now he'll pay for it later. He smartly decides to pack up his belongings and grabs his keys, his towel, his Walkman radio and his suntan lotion and hastily bundles all of it in the center of his beach blanket, then he balls it up and heads back to his hotel. Wincing in pain from every step he took because of his sunburn. Carlton remembers a similar situation when he and his friend Jonathan when young teenagers. He remembers when he and his friend went to the beach back home together on one hot summer day. Carlton had just gotten his driver's license the day before, and they skipped school that day. Summer vacation was still two weeks away but they didn't care, they were too excited about Carlton's new driver's license. It was a new feeling for them. It was freedom; they could go where ever they wanted so they went to the beach.

After Carlton got into the hotel room he looked at himself in a tall full-bodied mirror then remembered something and said to himself; I look just like John did when we were kids and I don't even have his fair skin. As Carlton showers off sand from the beach he is making sure to be gentle, he really is in a lot of pain. He starts thinking about Dr. Fischer, his psychiatrist. I think I said too much to the good doctor. I don't know for sure if I can trust him anymore. I really shouldn't put trust in him or anybody for that matter. What's going on in my life is just too bizarre and important right now. Carlton steps out of the shower, and from past experiences knows his sunburn will be even worse because of the shower. He looks at himself again shakes his head in disbelief at his bright red reflection. He remembers something he forgot back home. He uses his transport invention and goes back home in an instant. Grabs the solar caine spray for sunburns out from the medicine cabinet and he also grabs the skin lotion with aloe that was lying on his bed. He retrieves what he forgot and instantly transports back to his hotel room. He didn't even realize he was still only wearing a bath towel until he steps back into the bathroom and looks into the mirror to apply some of the soothing lotion. He smirks at his image, the greatest invention on earth he whispers as he's smiling.

It's early in the morning and agent Bob Davis is making good use of the stations gym. It's probably got something to do with his new girl; he's feeling fantastic but himself lately. Many of the police department's personnel work out in the gym at work. It's safer for them and more convenient. Not too many people like cops. There are many frustrations and disappointments that go along with being a police officer. It's the perfect place to get rid of some tension. Other officers take very different approaches which are consequently frowned upon such as; drinking, clubbing and, and gambling. Some of them are just plain hermits. Once they get home they stay-at-home and rarely leave the house.

While Bob is working out getting and all buff, Paula is playing psychiatrist as one of her friends and fellow offices was dumping her marital problems all over her at once. Paula was overwhelmed. She just had one of the best nights of her life with Bob, her new boyfriend. Although neither one of them actually said it, they both knew in their hearts they were together and it was going to be a lasting relationship. She listened to her friend talking and complaining about her husband. She was crying and didn't know how to reconnect with her husband. He was a civilian, so Paula understood what her friend was going through. Paula was divorced from her civilian husband and there is no way she can tell her friend it wasn't going to work, so she just listened to her with an understanding and caring ear. It was really awkward for Paula at the moment because of her newly found excitement for another man. After 20 minutes her friend regained her composure, she thanked Paula for listening to her bitch and moan and said she was a good friend, then went back to work. Everything will work out, you'll see. Paula said to her friend walking out of her office.

The United States Marine Corps has many sayings. They were handed down from certain battles they had fought in the past especially that early history. For instance the term devil dog was a name given to the Marines from one of their bloodiest battles in history. I could be mistaken but I do believe it was the battle of Tarawa. History says, they fought furiously and ferocious just like devil dog's.

One saying all the Marines were very fond of is Band of Brothers. Every Marine no matter what race, color, creed, he or she is, and will forever be, one big family.

These two old jar heads rekindled an old friendship quickly. They shared so many adventures when they were younger. Ups as well as downs. They were inseparable for a long time. These two warhorses had it made. They were indeed 2 true leathernecks from the short crew cuts they still sported right down to the military swagger they still have in their step today.

Gunny Cote said as he sat down in his friend's office. What are you thinking about this fine morning? I for one can't stand those damn reporters, you know. The way they make things look. I saw it on TV. Yeah, I hear ya. They're frustrated as hell like the rest of us but now there trying to say all of us, meaning the police aren't doing our jobs. They're saying it looks as if the mysterious New England serial killer might've struck again. So what are the police doing about this? Is there actually someone working on this? What do we all have to do, lock our doors and never go out…? It doesn't make things any easier for us that's for sure replies gunny Ferreira. It's been on every channel I turn to. CNN has been profiling the case 24 seven.

No one knows any facts yet. There's not one shred of concrete evidence. Although I did hear that there is an FBI agent working on the case. His office is that the Cambridge precinct. He's working with local authorities, a team effort.

The president of the United States has been briefed about this case. I don't have to tell you but you know as well as I that shit rolls downhill. Both of us are involved in this case whether we like it or not so get ready my friend for when the fan gets turned on. I did manage to gather some information as of last night. There are now six bodies. I have dates in approximate time's deaths. I also have cities where the murders happened. Let's see what else we can come up with as far as possible motives. We'll need to go way back, maybe as far back as childhood experiences.

Yeah, we can check out family, friends and associates as well as any business colleagues. We don't want to be asked any questions that we can't possibly answer. I hear you loud and clear jar head.

I'll start with my case gunny Ferreira said, and you can start with your case. Remember, the FBI is eventually going to be invading us, recon style. So, as career Marines, we'll be ready for them. Semper Fi brother, do or die! What'd you say get back together at the end of the week to compare notes and maybe a little rehashing of days gone by? Sounds great gunning Cote said.

Bob Jenkins finally got to sit down and relax. His ritual was to read his newspaper he had bought from the vendor down the street right after the kids were put to bed and the lights were turned off. Tonight was a little different. Little Peaty and Josh had gotten into a fist fight sometime after dinner. It was about the TV, they both wanted to watch different programs. Most of the trouble that goes on here with kids is over which programs were on TV. There are a lot of children here and there is only one TV. Josh had banged his head on a small chair that one of the smaller kids use any got himself a nasty cut on his left cheek. He needed medical attention. So to further disrupt the natural flow of things here at the children's home, Bob had to call one of the weekend employees to come down and watched the children, while he brought the scared child to the hospital. On the way Josh was crying, I'm going to jail he said, no of course you're not. We're going to fix you up at the hospital. I'm not getting the needle am I? I really don't know? I do know you'll be okay, so don't worry about a thing.

When Bob and Josh got back to the children's home, he put Josh to bed himself. Josh was sleeping already and Bob didn't want to wake him. They only took two hours from the time they left until the time they came back, so Bob's replacement was pleasantly surprised. Wow! Debra said. Back so soon? Yeah, can you believe it! You can go home now if you like and thank you very much for coming in Debra. Don't mention it. You know I would do anything for these kids. I know I can always count on you. Well, have a pleasant evening then she said good night and left.

Bob turned on the TV in his office and made sure the volume was real low. He poured himself a cup of coffee and opened a package of chocolate chip cookies. What you know, he says a little too loudly. Bob reads the caption on the front page. On the top was a small picture, it was his friend Carlton Van Helsang.

Modern-day hero does it again! Police and authorities are now regarding Carlton Van Helsang, a modern day hero. He's got and uncanny Knack for being in the right place at the right time. The report goes on to say that the governor of Massachusetts invited once again to another social gathering at the beautiful governor's mansion. There is a picture of Carlton shaking the hand of the Massachusetts governor. Bob Jenkins muses as the Governor is trying to improve his image no doubt, and he's exploiting Carlton. Everyone knows that his popularity has drastically dwindled since the outbreak of these horrendous murders.

Bob heard a noise coming from the dorms where the children sleep. He listens intently hoping it's not another fight. He yells from his office, its lights out! This means, be quiet, and go to sleep. He continues to read the article in silence.

Paul and Bob get bombarded with reporters as they exit from their own cars in front of the Cambridge Police Department. A reporter sticks a microphone in their face and says; is it true the New England serial killer struck again last night right next door in Brookline? What! Another said, is it true there is an unidentified substance found in the bodies of the victims by the forensic scientists. Could it also be true that the reason why this awful case is dragging along is because you're not spending enough time on the case, and you're spending a little too much time doing other things? Another said; Aren't you agent Davis and you are detective Paula Robertson, is it true you both are falling love? That one did it; Paula lashed out and quickly stopped herself. She turned around and walks swiftly away. As she did so the reporters followed asking outrageously personal questions. She ducks low, heading towards the building's entrance. Most of the reporters were following detective Robertson, they are like a school of piranha.

Once they noticed the first hesitation or a jerky look of the eyes, they were on her. Paula was furious, she had to get away from them or something publicly embarrassing most likely would've taken place. It was a decision that in all likelihood was good for her, as well as good for some unsuspecting reporter.

Agent Davis, excuse me, is a true about you and Paula Robertson? What do you mean? Are you a couple? Actually that is not of your business! My personal life, her personal life, and anyone else's personal life has absolutely nothing to do with this serious case were all working on. Now after saying that, I'll answer a few questions if you like.

A large man in a black suit, it looked like an Anderson little, stepped forward. A surprised look of amusement came over Bob's face. This man look like a skunk he thought. He has black figure 2 weeks white stripe of hair rights back in the middle of his head start from his forehead and faded back with, it almost looked fake but it's real all right.

I took it upon myself to check you out he said, what you mean agent Davis said? Nothing illegal I assure you, it was just a few clicks of a mouse accessing certain databases. What did you find Bob said with confidence. I found your credentials were impeccable, a most distinguishing career so far. Bob looks at him with a cocked eyebrow wondering what his angle was, so far. He's smarter than he looks Bob thought.

Agent Bob Davis nonchalantly looks over at the other reporters who were patiently scribbling in their notepads trying to make sense of what information they retrieved, in order to make the six o'clock news. Agent Davis! Agent Davis! Bob turned. What can you tell me about Dr. Jonathan Fischer skunk had asked? I'm sorry I have no comment right now, excuse me! Wait a minute Bob said, come back at 5 o'clock and come alone, maybe we'll talk. Skunk head the say anything, he just nodded and slowly walked away.

Capt. Adams greets Paula and Bob. He's looking out his window and he says hello agent Davis, welcome to the Boston media. What a madhouse Bob said, what'd you know about skunk head? Who? The tall reporter with the white stripe in his hair! OH, that's Dennis, he's a winner. Really knows his stuff the captain said. Keep him on your good side if you can. He's the kind of guy that can make you a break you, so to speak. He kind of does this work more or less as a hobby. Comes from a very wealthy family and doesn't need the money. He's a computer whiz. Be careful of what you say around him.

Well, back to the business at hand. I am being hounded not only by the mayor of Boston, but also the governor of Massachusetts. And now I'm hearing a bunch of crap from your ADIC Bob. Have you two made any progress yet? What the hell is going on with you too? I'm hearing all kinds of bull shit except what I want to hear. Not much yet Captain Paula said. We've been going over all the medical examiner's reports. We found the autopsy reports indicating dramatically similar results. It's the same weapon used on all the victims. This person is extremely intelligent agent Davis interjected, or he could be just plain lucky Paula said. We believe after talking with a number of scientists that he could possibly have some knowledge of medicine. One of the researchers told us that the killer was leaving his calling card. Pathologists call it artistic touches; it's more or less his personal signature. What'd you talking about Captain Adams said, there is a substance in each of the last five victims that has yet to be identified. One of the forensic scientists told me it'll only be a matter of a couple more days and that was yesterday. I'm willing to bet the same stuff is in the latest victim, I only just heard about. How do those damn reporters know so much, asked agent Davis? I want you to go check it out said Captain Adams with a little agitation on the face. The body is at the Brookline medical center. They're supposed to be examining the body as we speak. See what you can find out. Hopefully it's not the same maniac responsible.

Carlton takes care of his personal business and instantly returns to his hotel room smiling to himself. I can't wait to see all of their faces, especially those people in my father's journals who publicly ousted him from their scientific ranks of society. They will be dying from envy, not only because of me the actual living proof that human cloning is successful, but also my own invention. I can't be too hasty, so it will have to be one monumental unveiling at the time, he ponders. I will reestablish my father's good name. He'll go down in history as one of the greatest scientists of our generation. Maybe then it'll be the right time to unveil my own invention" the transporter", making sure to add to my father's already great name. I can envision it, a speech in front of millions. It wouldn't be possible if it weren't for my father's painstaking research and making it conceivable to actually bring me into this world. I had a dream like he did.

The killer is taunting the police. He has special plans for one of them. He doesn't like all the attention they're getting. Need to show them who the boss really is. Paula and Bob were on their way to Brookline, Paula was driving again as they cruised out of the city of Cambridge, Bob noticed how impressive all the homes were in this neighborhood. Every yard was meticulously manicured. There were large pine trees and Oak tree's everywhere and there was a bunch of small oh white birch trees skewed in between. The cause Windows rolled down because of the beautiful day and the smell of flowers drifted into the car. It was intoxicating. I can't believe how peaceful and beautiful it is out here and how crazy it is just around the next block agent Davis said to Paula as she's driving the car. It is beautiful in this area.

The Brookline police were at the coroner's office as agent Davis and Detective Paula Robertson flash their identification upon their arrival. Agent Davis asked one of the uniformed policemen, who is the doctor in charge here. The officer said, I don't know his name but he's in the office right over there pointing in the direction of his eyes. He is a tall man with white hair and is most likely holding a tobacco pipe. Thank you Paula said, and they both approached the office. They knocked as they entered and immediately noticed the scent of old leather polish mixed with the strong cherry pipe tobacco.

Hello Dr. How did I know you two would show up here the Dr. said. Looks like we're all going to be working closely together until we nail this basket case Paula said. Yes it does seem that way. Dr. LA fleur, can you tell me something differing about this one. I'm afraid I can't. The full autopsy hasn't been finished yet but I can tell you that it looks like the same instruments used here are one in the same for your last five murder victims. I'm still waiting on the blood tests from the lab to confirm whether or not the same substance exists in his blood as the other. I should have an answer in about two more hours.

I should tell you the doctor said, there was a phone call that disturbed me. It was a woman claiming to be a psychic; she said she saw the murder take place. What do you mean, I said? She said it was a vision. So I asked her, where are you? So someone can talk with you. She said she lives in Georgia and she's home. I wrote down her name and telephone number and then left to come here. What strange phone call. I have a relative who is into that sort of stuff. Our family always thought of her as somewhat eccentric. Detective Robertson said to Bob, I wonder if it's the same woman who called our office last week.

The leather faced officer from Brookline Massachusetts acted like he was glad that agent Davis and his partner Detective Robertson were taken over his case. He had on bifocals and was extremely overweight. He was close to retirement and didn't need or did he want any more complicated high profile cases. He was looking forward to a leisurely life and real soon too.

Paula and Bob gathered up everything they could from the soon to be retired officer and got back into their car to drive toward Rhode Island and me up with the Johnston Rhode Island police. They were both briefed by Capt. Adams earlier to meet up with the lead investigator Harry Ferreira.

On their way they briefly listen to the car radio. It was a news talk show. Paula quickly shut it off but not before they both heard the talk show host say, forensic doctors in law enforcement always have their hands in the investigations of murders. Postmortem testing and painstaking autopsies all play significantly and indicate positive conclusions. The whole process is time-consuming but in the end very conclusive.

I can't believe all the media attention this case is drawing, Paula said. I saw it printed somewhere that the economic status has dwindled. Yeah I saw the same thing Bob said. People are staying home, they're afraid to go out but what they don't understand is that not one of these tragedy's to place in public. The news media is really making a mess of things. Don't they realize what's happening in the bigger picture? Apparently not! I did catch a glimpse of a talk show last week pertaining to the economy. Someone had to mention the serial killer, when I heard that I changed channels, but not before someone else went on to say; police forensics photographers immortalize victims without family consent, with all their graphic pictures. Can something be done about this? So dead people have rights! Who authorizes the release of photographs? It did sound interesting but I had enough of it all lately. I know exactly how you feel Bob said.

Changing the subject slightly, so do you think we can subpoena Dr. Fischer's medical records? What do you mean his medical records Bob said? Yes his patients medical records, he is a shrink right? Maybe he's been treating some psychopath who's linked into this whole mess. It's a long shot Bob said. I understand that and I personally think a long shot is much more than nothing at all. Plus it'll give us another angle to investigate. Okay, you piqued my curiosity. I'll inform my boss, he has more influence when it comes to confidentiality's. Sometimes it's difficult to access personal records especially doctor-patient relationships.

Bob spent the night at Paula's condo. They helped each other prepare dinner. Paula prepared the T-bone steak while Bob was chopping up some fresh veggies for a salad. Before they started cooking they cleaned up sharing a shower. The teased each other and were quick wash. They were both famished and made their way back to the kitchen, she put the steak in the broiler and he set the salad on the table.

They briefly talked about work while they ate their dinner. They got along so well, it's like they were meant for each other. They talked about their future with each other. Does your brother Dale always speak in the third person context when he does speak, Paula asked? Bob laughed, ever since I can remember! You know I do really like him. The way the doctors had explained his condition hurt at first, they said it'll never change. It can't they said. What do they really know she said?

Dale has high energy impulses with a surplus amount of adrenaline and dopamine produced from his brain, pulsating directly into his immensely irregular central nervous system. It travels continuously to and from causing him to be intellectually imbalanced. It causes him to be seen as a freak by some people, or a mental case or as some other severely ignorant people on the East Coast of knowingly would say; a retard. He's still my brother and I love him. I love you too he said with conviction. So what do you want to do about it Paula said? I love you too and I like your brother.

Paula left a while after dinner. She had a few personal errands to run. Bob understood and left soon after her. I have some shopping to do, personal stuff you know. She was smiling as she was walking out the door. It's a girl thing! I'll call you when I get home, it should be early enough for night May be something else winked.

Capt. Adams wasn't sure if he should call agent Davis at this hour? He is absolutely mortified and even though he's already seen the body, he still can't comprehend the fact that this happened. The captain himself arrived at the accident scene the next town over. An old friend and colleague was at the scene and knew the person who suddenly perished in a car accident. The deceased worked for him and he wanted to inform his old friend personally.

I knew she worked for you! We met many times over the years, she was great at her job and I respected her tremendously. Captain Adams was stunned. It took him over two hours to decide to go ahead and make the unhappy phone call. He hated to be the one to have to make this call, but under the circumstances he knew it would be best if it was he who let Bob know what happened. The Captain wasn't as much of a stranger to Bob as everyone else in Boston was.

Capt. Adams grabs the phone on his desk at his office, he was crying softly in private. She was like a daughter to him and now she's gone. Agent Davis's phone rang at 3:35 AM, the answering machine came on. Dammit he said and hung up. He tried again! Who is it! Bob said with a touch of anger in his voice. It's me Capt. Adams, oh; I'm sorry Capt. What is it? And what the hell time is it? It's almost 3:45 in the morning. I'm afraid I have some bad news and there's no way to sugarcoat this. I found it hard to believe myself, so I'll just come right out and say it. Now you got me worried, what is it! There's been a tragic car accident, yeah! It happened sometime early last night, approximately 9 PM. What's that got to do with me at 4 o'clock in the morning as Bob groggily yawns? Agent Davis wipes his sleep from his eyes and sits up. The captain's next words absolutely crushed him. Bob was in complete shock! It was Paula in the car accident, she's... She's dead Bob. Silence... Hello, hello. Bob is still there? Hello, hello. A dial tone ensued.

Bob can't believe what he just heard. We just had dinner earlier tonight he thought. The Capt. Could be wrong, couldn't he? Oh my God, please! It can't be, it's that, that why she didn't call me later on after dinner like she said she would. Oh no. Bob jumped out of bed and put on a pair of old worn out jeans she had laid on the back of a chair for him. Then his running shoes Paula had bought him, a T-shirt, he grabbed his wallet and ID and ran out his crown Victoria. Then he broke all speed limits on his way to the precinct. Capt. Adams left five minutes earlier the overweight desk Sgt. told him.

The next day Capt. Adams was in earlier that morning, trying to prepare for Bob. Have you been here a while the captain asked? I got here 20 minutes after you called me last night and I haven't left his seat. Capt. Adams and agent Davis talked for at least an hour before all those damn news reporters, photographers and camera crews arrived. The news media was relentless; they wanted answers and wanted them now. The people of Boston are very angry and also demanded results from the police. City Hall is madhouse.

Capt. Adams said she was an outstanding officer. People admired her so did I? She was the daughter I never had; she gave Father's Day cards and presents. I can't explain what happened right now but I did know she craved action and adrenaline. She lived on the edge, maybe that's got some do with it.

Agent Davis didn't speak. He just stood still listening as a tear rolled down his pale cheek. Why don't you go home Bob, said the captain. Where is she, Bob said? She's at the mortuary in Brookline. Bob was still in shock, he moved like a robot. He got up from his seat and mechanically walked out the door. Someone came into the office and asked the captain if he'll be all right? I hope so. It looks like a zombie right now. I know exactly how he feels the Capt. Said.

Bob was absolutely positively sure that he and Paula were getting in engaged in the near future, and were going to get married. He never loved anyone the way he loved Paula Robertson. Not even his first wife had he felt such a strong bond. At home that night he kept thinking about her, whenever he put some music on it was worse. It seemed like every song was about her. With no music or television he sat in the dark. Looking up at the stars through a window that night then says to himself aloud; I'll never be with Paula again. Why did you take her from me, I've been a good man.

A deep unrelenting depression sets in. His eyes were trying to come into focus behind wanly tears. He touched her one last time and placed a photograph of himself beside her. I love her so much Bob told God, as he looked up towards the heavens kneeling down before her at her beautiful funeral. He stood there for a long time and then sat with her family in the front row of the flower filled funeral home.

The forensic scientists have finally figured out what the strange substance was which baffled them all for so long. The same common foreign substance which was found in six victims so far. Its clinical name is Datura. It's a very old drug. Its origins were derived from London England. It was used in surgery much like the way morphine is used today. It was also very popular amongst opium users back in the late 1700s and 1800s. Originally it was used as a stimulant, mostly for sicknesses. It has the same characteristics as morphine but it's much more expensive to develop. The side effects were; drowsiness, hallucinations and sometimes mild seizures with upset stomachs.

The doctor who performed Paula Robertson's autopsy was the same doctor who performed the autopsy of Dr. Jonathan Fischer a few days earlier.

This Dr. doesn't know about the similarities in the ongoing investigations of this serial killer. He found it hard that to total strangers could be injected with the same foreign substance, which incidentally hasn't been used for over 100 years.

When he did speak with Capt. Adams he hesitated a second, a little unsure of how to approach the Capt. Paula Robertson had enough Datura in her system to give a horse and overdose said the doctor. What you telling me Dr. said the captain? I'm afraid I'm saying that this woman didn't die from injuries she sustained in a car accident. She was already dead from an overdose of a very old and outdated hallucinogen. Frankly I don't understand it said the doctor. What you mean? Well, I did the autopsy on a psychiatrist a few days ago and found the same substance and him. So I looked it up in my computer files to read up on it and it looks very difficult to produce. A person has to be practically a genius to it put together. That's interesting said the distraught caption. Thank you very much Dr.

Williams, you've been a tremendous help. Now we have a somewhat idea, vague as it is in whom we are dealing with the captain thought. Capt. Adams got into his car noticed how hot it was outside and then dismissing it because of the cooler air-conditioned building he had just left. He's no dummy that's for sure he said himself as he pulled away from the curb.

Paula's family had a small reception. It was stricken with unbearable grief. Bob was no longer able to hold back his own tears. He left and went home without speaking a word to anyone.

Earlier that same morning he had said his final goodbyes. He did the old-fashioned manly thing at her funeral. He didn't cry there. He didn't shed one tear. He drove home like a zombie. He didn't even know how he got home while he was groping for his door keys. He dragged himself into his condo and proceeded to let out this gut wrenching soul shrieking cry. He was in his bathroom and his hands were a locked onto his sink, he was trying to look into the mirror and was yelling why! Why! Why her and not me?

Grief in this magnitude can either do two things to a person. It could turn them into a paralyzing zombie plunging them into a deeper state of despair or for some other people it could angrily turned them around 180 degrees, to take control with a vengeance. Becoming mad at the world just waiting for a fight, maybe even opening up a few doors and questions not asked yet!

After Paula's murder Bob Davis started making himself scarce. He was completely and utterly devastated. He was emotionally paralyzed. He had an undeniable resignation in his career he eyes. Bob Davis his heart and soul was dealt a smashing blow! He didn't even want to see his only brother this week. He barely was able to bring himself to phone the care home and let them know he couldn't pick his brother Dale up this month.

Bob's colleagues all said; there is no doubt about it, he's in a severe state of depression.

He is oversleeping and late for work and when he does show up, sometimes she sleeps all day. A couple of uniforms inquired about him at his condo. Some of the tenants said his car is always there, he rarely leaves the house. His lights are always off; you don't even hear a sound. Is he okay asked a concerned neighbor? The policeman said he's very hurt over the loss of his girlfriend. I think they were planning on getting married soon. The next door neighbor had a sad look come over her; she was very old and gray.

I heard about that but wasn't sure if it was my Bob next door here. My memory isn't what it used to be you know. I'll pray for him. When he first moved in here I baked him some chocolate chip cookies, maybe it's time I do it again for him. That would be a very thoughtful gesture ma'am, said the cop. He said to me the next day that he and his younger brother devoured them in five minutes and that they were delicious. What'd you think Sir? I think that would be sure to cheer him up ma'am. Please she said, call me Agnes. Well you have a pleasant day today Agnes, we need to get back to work. So long she said.

One of Paula's friends and coworkers said he's got a lack of interest in anything that might be happening around him. He lost his appetite too. Anyone can tell just by looking at him, his clothes are baggy and hanging off him, he's even neglected his personal hygiene habits. I seen him last week at the Stop & Shop on Bradford Avenue, he didn't see me. His hair was a mess as if he's just got out of bed and his face was unshaven. People were actually steering away from him as if his body odor was offensive. Another person in the office went as far as saying he's a damn bloody mess Capt. Maybe you could talk to him. You know, the worst thing in the world is not being able to help someone that you care about who is pain. I'm afraid he might have to mourn her in his own private way said the captain. I'll still pull him aside and try something, but I won't rush him. I've been in his shoes and I know exactly what he's going through.

Carlton Van Helsang has been back home from his wonderful vacation for a couple of weeks now. He's relaxed and has a nice golden brown to tan. He even met a nice woman his age that lives about an hour away from him. She was vacationing herself with some friends. After a couple of days down there it was nice to hear some New England accents.

Carlton did a lot of thinking while he enjoyed himself at the beach. He's ready to unveil his soon to become famous invention, his transport machine.

Now that the governor of Massachusetts and then Mayor of Boston are extremely impressed with him, he feels that it is an opportune time to seek out their professional advice on the future of his incredible invention.

Carlton had no problem and an appointment to see the governor. He was impressed beyond words. The governor expressed Carlton he had an idea that he would definitely get back to him as soon as it was possible. He thought it over for the rest of the morning and contemplated his next move carefully. Who would benefit the most besides the inventor?

The governor informed the secretary of defense of the United States of America. Without a doubt he assumes that the military of the United States could benefit most from this monumental achievement. Carlton was cordially invited to attend a private meeting and he could hardly believe it. It was being held at the White House 1600 Pennsylvania Ave. Washington DC… It read you have a limousine waiting for you at your convenience at the DC airport and also enclosed was a two way plane ticket.

It was a very private meeting, a ceremony of sorts. Carlton was given the Nobel Prize for his transportation device, that's what the government so adamantly wants to call it, in order to avoid any kind of suspicion. If any other country new what Carlton's invention was that the United States would no longer have a secret weapon. The secretary of defense said; the president himself attended and I must say he was a very impressive man. He ended the meeting by specifically expressing an absolute confidentiality about what took place here today. This was a meeting of monumental importance. I cannot express the importance of keeping this significant find under wraps. Does everyone here understand? Everyone agreed and was sworn to secrecy.

Somehow the press found out there was a meeting of the minds. Carlton's picture was on the front page of all the major newspapers throughout the entire country. Carlton's friend Sgt. Jonathon hunt USMC called him and congratulated him. I couldn't believe my eyes they you were on the front page, a nice picture of you, with the White House in the background. I suppose you think you can order me around now joked Jonathon... Why should things be any different from what they've always been laughed Carlton. Yeah okay ha ha. Both of them got a chuckle and Carlton was happy to hear from his good friend. A Very pleasant conversation ensued. Carlton didn't say anything about his invention because he was sworn to secrecy. He did talk about his latest vacation, alone at Fort Lauderdale Florida. Bikinis are skimpier than ever.

Carlton decides to pay a visit to the Sacred Heart's children's home to see the kids. He had ordered a bunch of toys and games from a novelty shop that he couldn't pass up. It wasn't the games that attracted him; it was the pretty blonde clerk sitting on a white wicker chair outside the shop. She was reading a book. She smiled at him as he walked on by and the next day he decided to stop in. Carlton was always cool with the ladies ever since his college days. He noticed she was reading a Stephen King novel the day before so he purchased King's latest novel and ended up having dinner with her this same night. He bought a whole bunch of stuff for the kids back home and also gave her the Stephen King book he had purchased.

Bob Jenkins was surprised to see Carlton. Hello buddy he said and congratulations. When the kids heard Carlton's voice as he was talking with his friend Bob all the kids in the dayroom came a running to greet him. They were all talking and yelling at the same time, they were pushing and shoving each other out of the way to get to him. One of them said we saw you on TV, you're famous another one said. Are you a movie star another one said? Bob was smiling with his arms folded across his chest listening to all the hoopla going on around him and Carlton. Carlton himself was blushing. Are you living in the White House now? Does the president of the United States live in the White House? Another one said.

Carlton was bombarded with 1 million questions from the kids, he looked at Bob and Bob smirked and shrugged his shoulders. You're on your own pal. Carlton sat back on a couch and smiled. He enjoyed all the attention and all the little smiles he was getting. The children were really behaved when he was with them. They always gave him their undivided attention. Carlton really loved these kids and after the initial excitement dies down it was Bob Jenkins turn. Bob has a few questions too but he patiently waited his turn. When the children got bored, which they always do, they all went back into their dayroom and watched some more television. So what's the White House really like Bob asked? Carlton used discretion as he was told and went on to explain what he saw and experienced.

Lisa Cate's shows up personally at the Cambridge Massachusetts police station. She's feeling a bit arrogant after being ignored repeatedly. She approached the information desk with a definite presumptuous attitude. She won't be ignored today she thought. A distinguished looking silver haired man with sharp delicate features, a curved nose and a full mouth who indeed looked like the ideal matrix of a CEO for a big firm and had an exceptionally shiny badge on his shirt. He looked out of place in a good way. Can I help you? He asked very politely I might add. Yes, I hope so. I traveled a long distance. I believe there's an FBI agent working here by the name of Davis, agent Bob Davis. May I speak with him please? I am not sure, the silver haired policeman said. I was informed he's the person in charge of these terrible murders throughout the New England area. Oh yes, yes indeed he is, officer Cromwell said.

I'm sorry Miss but he's out in the field at the moment and no one else is available to help you right now. His partner suffered a tragic accident most recently and these particular cases belong to them and them alone. Oh I I'm terribly sorry! Lisa immediately softened. Would you like to wait while I try to page him? Sure. Well then what's your name miss? It's Lisa, Lisa Cate's. I've called a few times and each time I've been brushed off. Tell him I drove nonstop all the way from my home town in Atlanta Georgia. Lisa looked around for someplace comfortable to sit while she decided to wait. The police station was a poverty-stricken dump on the ground floor she thought. Even the policemen who walked in and out of the building looked mean and angry. She could actually feel a great deal of hostility but was unsure of home it was emitting from.

There were wanted posters askew everywhere. It was very filthy indeed; something Lisa was very unaccustomed to back where she comes from. The police stations back home in the great state of Georgia were kept in immaculate condition at all times. It was a special program the government authorities put into effect for the minors who found themselves in trouble from time to time. Part of the community services in disciplining Atlanta's youngsters was that they have to clean up all government and city buildings. The kids were monitored and taught valuable lessons. It looks like Cambridge could benefit from a similar program she thought quietly to herself. Lisa was disgusted with the filth in the waiting area and God forbid if you had to use the bathroom facilities. There was a really foul smell working its stench all the way down the halls carving a pathway directly into the already vile visiting or waiting area she said under her breath.

Agent Bob Davis has rescheduled another appointment with the coroner who had taken care of Paula, and while Lisa Cate's waited patiently in the nasty waiting area of the Cambridge Police Department, Bob was going over a few more questions with the doctor he had missed the first time.

The doctor who performs the autopsy on Paula Robertson was a very large man. His face resembled that of a bird and he had a loud squeaky voice. Agent Davis noticed right away that the doctor had a nervous condition, he made morbid twitching movements. Quite frankly the man is eerie and Bob couldn't wait to get out of his office.

Agent Davis finally left the corners office after a painstaking hour realizing that the murderer was in fact intentionally toying with the police. He actually stormed out of the building angry as hell; he was somehow charged with a new vitality and could feel his adrenaline pumping throughout his body. He vowed right then and there to do everything in his power to solve the murder of his friend as well as the others. But secretly his friend takes precedence.

Agent Davis got into his car and drove around town in an oblivious state of mind, lost in his own rumination. He was lost in thought thinking about Paula. Why is it when a song or an aroma enters your mind, time and time again no matter what you might be doing at that particular moment? It always brings you back to that moment lost. You could be at work or just looking at the most innocent object. It must be love; it has to be he thought. Bob doesn't even know how he ended up at the precinct. Grandmother always told me, I think and analyze too much. She used to say; trust what you heart says an act accordingly. Now that I look back at her life I can see she was a very happy woman. There is much to be said for the free wisdom of a grandparent he thought. Bob shut off the engine of his car and discreetly entered through the side entrance avoiding those ruthless arrogant reporters, whom are intent on screwing up this entire investigation. Plus he almost forgot something.

Agent Bob Davis has been in denial too long and it's now finally caught up to him, and with a vengeance; his priorities were straightened out quickly. The first thing he did when he entered his office was call his brother's care home and let them know he'll be coming for Dale next weekend and that he's gonna be back on schedule.

Next thing was to address his boss back in New York. There was a message on his desk advising him to call the ADIC. After the phone call to New York one of the lights on his phone lit up, it was the desk sergeant on the first floor. Excuse me sir the Sgt. Said, there is a lady here wanting to see you. What lady Bob said? She said her name is Lisa Cate's and she drove all the way up here nonstop from Atlanta Georgia. She said something about being hung up on whenever she tried to phone someone pertaining to the New England murders... Silence ensued for a brief moment. She's been here almost 2 hours already the Sgt. Said. Okay, okay, tell her I'll be down in five minutes. One more thing the Sgt. Said, what's that asked Bob? She's a looker. She is very beautiful, just thought you might want to know. Thank you very much Sgt.

Capt. Adams came into the office at the same time that Bob did, how are you this morning the Capt. Said. Fine, never better as a matter of fact. There's someone I need to see downstairs Capt., excuse me agent Davis said.

Lisa Cate's noticed a very handsome man walking down the main hallway. He came from a stairway with a red exit sign above the door. He was wearing a dark Armani suit with light gray pinstripes, he almost looked gangster-ish, and he had on black Rock Port wing tip shoes nicely polished, and his hair was combed straight back. I noticed that he turned towards the desk sergeant then he looked directly at me. I felt butterflies in my stomach. I sensed something different about him. My heart skipped a beat as I noticed he was extremely handsome, his eyes caught my attention. He had a fiery look in his eyes like the look of a man on a mission. It made me nervous, I looked away. I'm sure that he noticed my uneasiness and in an instant he was right here standing in front of me and for the briefest of moments, I was dumbstruck.

Two hundred and sixty miles north in the town of Concord New Hampshire a man named Danny Evans is running for his life. What did I do? He thought. Danny Evans miraculously freed himself from the grips of the Grim Reaper. He was panting as he ran for cover and tried to hide his shaking body. He was scared confused it was raining harder. Thunder boomed and lightning flashed across the dismal sky. Danny was huddled down low beneath a trashcan as the lightning illuminated the attacker's silhouettes. It scared the hell out of him. He stood there frozen in time. Lightning struck again and the attacker was gone. It struck again quickly this time, then a large thunderous boom. The thunder shielded Danny's last screen.

Bob Davis introduced himself to the pretty Lisa Cates. He used his formal title. Hello, I'm agent Bob Davis; please accept my apology for making you wait for so long. Boston is a very busy city. I heard you drove all the way up here from Atlanta Georgia. Yes, that's right! My name is Lisa Cates. I'm concerned about all of these grisly murders up here in New England. Why is that? Agent Davis said. Excuse my managers please! I have a much more comfortable office we can use to discuss this. Please, as he motioned his left hand, palm open in the direction he wants to go in with his right hand he helps her to her feet. It was purely a gentleman's gesture. Her hand was soft and she smelled really nice Bob thought.

Would you like a cup of coffee he suggested after she sat comfortably? Yes please, two sugars and cream she said with a nervous smile. Agent Davis made himself a cup of coffee also. So, where do we start he asked? With a little more of an understandable attitude Lisa spoke. As I told more than one person on the telephone here, I am gifted with clairvoyance. I was born with it and have honed my abilities for years. I have seen visions of the people whom I believe were murdered here, at least four of them.

No one wants to talk with me over the telephone and I could see why. Y'all probably thought I was some kind of wacko something. It's nothing new, believe me. So now I'm here in person offering my services and help if you wanted. She's a tiny ball of fire Bob thought, and he loved her accent. He wanted her to keep on talking. Agent Davis's expression was of astonishment and amusement all-in-one.

How do you know what you say you saw in your visions were in fact the same people who were killed here in New England asked Agent Davis? I've been following these news clippings and CNN since these murders started. The faces of the victims in my dreams are the same faces that were on all the news channels. He had to admit to himself that he was pleasantly surprised with her straightforwardness, and just like that desk sergeant said. She didn't exactly hurt his eyes. She was a beautiful woman.

Agent Davis assessed the situation. I've got only one common piece of evidence that's related to every victim and nothing else. No one here seems to be able to help and she drove all the way over here from Atlanta Georgia, that's got to be over 1000 miles, so the least I could do was listen to her. God knows she can't do any worse than anyone else around here.

Miss Lisa Cates was a Spitfire for sure. She was full of energy. Her hair was thick, short and feathered back, and it had a lustrous shine to it. She's a natural strawberry blonde. Her high cheekbones were accentuated due to her short carefully styled hair. Another mesmerizing feature in which I noticed immediately was her huge deep set beautiful ice blue penetrating eyes. She is one of the most attractive women I've ever had the pleasure of being in the same company. She was about 5'7" in height with a knockout figure. No doubt she spends hours in the gym.

Yeah, what could it hurt agent Davis thought? He had someone checking out her identification at this time. Who knows, maybe she's for real. God only knows that I can sure use a helping hand in this case. No matter where it comes from at this point. I've heard of these things before, in how psychics use their extraordinary abilities to help find lost children and pets, but I've never been involved in any situation of its kind... This if anything, poses to be an interesting opportunity. Especially, if she's authentic!

She immediately wanted to start working on the case and when I hesitated for the briefest of moments, she realized she was jumping the gun. I'm sorry she said, I get ahead of myself sometimes. I realize you don't even know me. But rests assure I can give you references from some of the finest officers in the Atlanta crimes division. The Atlantic crimes division Bob said? Yes, I've worked on and off some of them for almost 3 years.

To prove she was real she asked agent Davis if there was something he managed to keep secret from the media and public. A clue she said? A medicine of a drug, something of that nature she said? How did you know, agent Davis asked her with an astonishing look on his face? It was a reaction she had grown accustomed to. It might be hard for you to believe, so first I'll have to ask you to have an open mind she said. Put it this way, there is been a string of murders and no one has the first inclination of who is responsible for them. So... She said with a cute tilt of her blonde head, you'll have nothing to lose, would you. It was at that precise moment that agent Davis knew he was going to spend more time with this stunning woman. Agent Davis's life took a complete turnaround in the last

24 hours. It was a good sign. Let's go upstairs agent Davis said. The detectives unit is on the third floor and it's much more pleasant than here. Will you follow me please? I'll get you a refill of that terrific coffee. Then he smiled.

Capt. Adams called Bob over for a private chat. How you doing Bob? I'm okay today. I'm actually feeling much better, an overwhelming feeling just come over me I can't quite explain. Well, you do look much more with it… You know Bob; you can say it as much as you like that you're not thinking of her. I do know you dream of her when you're relaxed. The deepest part of the mind comes back to a person when they're in a state of relaxation. I think about her too. What I'm trying to say this if you ever feel the need to talk sometime I'm here okay son, Capt. Adam said. By the way who's the beautiful blonde sitting at your desk? She's a real looker.

She came in today and she drove all the way here alone from Atlanta Georgia. What? Why did she do that? She wants to be taken seriously. What do you mean? She's claiming to be a psychic, a what? A psychic? She called a few times and she said that she was given the runaround, so now she's here in person. I you sure you're all right Bob replies Capt. Adams. With a slight smile and a small shoulder shrug he said; I'm fine sir. The captain raised his eyebrows and listened, he was a skeptic indeed.

Miss Lisa Cates insisted on helping with this case. She said she's prided herself on solving unsolvable cases just like this one. I'm having her check out as we speak. She claims to have helped in a few cases back home in Georgia. Okay, you know if memory serves me, I remember something about a psychic helping to find a child a few years back not far from here. It's a faint memory but it seemed as if everyone was claiming the same abilities soon after. Well from what I can see Capt., I don't have anything to lose at this point. So why not give her a shot if she does in fact check out.

It was getting a late. Lisa had no place to go because she was insistent on getting here to the main precinct as soon as possible, regarding the New England murders. She drove nonstop and now she's tired and hungry. Agent Davis offered to take her to dinner so they could talk a little more. He admirably remembers Paula doing it for him. After dinner he drove her to a comfortable hotel, compliments of the Cambridge Police Department.

There wasn't much conversation at dinner. The sun was shining through the drapes and a robin was singing to its mate in the tree outside of balcony. She walked onto the balcony squinting her eyes, due to the bright summer's sun. She took in a breath of fresh morning air as she watched three squirrels scurrying along the grounds. Lisa was due at the precinct at 9 AM. It's 7:15 am right now, so she had adequate time to get ready. As she was dressing a few minutes later she said quietly to herself, he is a handsome man. She then decided to look extra special. It was a strange feeling that came over her and also something she wasn't accustomed to. Lisa can almost always sense another person's emotions and feelings but agent Bob Davis definitely did pose a challenge. She wasn't able to reach him and she did make the attempt more than once. She did get a strong impression of the fact that he really did care for Paula Robertson, but it was from his words and not what she tried to extract from his mind. He was able to block her from reading his thoughts somehow. It's a new experience to her and it both baffled and intrigued her. She couldn't wait to get back to the office.

It's now 8:30 AM and the desk clerk called Lisa's room to inform her that a gentleman in uniform was here to drive her to the Brookline Police Department. Lisa was dropped off directly in front of the precinct. She said to the officer that she can find her way up to the office. He was polite and said very well. Have a pleasant day ma'am.

Lisa Cates met Capt. Adams and agent Davis upstairs. They were sharing a box of donuts and have coffee when agent Davis waved her in. Good morning, have you had some coffee yet? Would you like the usual breakfast of our police station Bob had said with a smile? Powder had fallen from a cream donut he was holding out towards her, no thank you she said. I would have to work out an extra hour to get rid of it. Please sit down agent Davis said. Capt. Adams excused himself and agent Davis sat down at his desk. Where do we start he said? How about I start she said, okay.

Lisa went on to describe the nature of her situation. When I heard of these terrible murders up here in New England I wondered to myself if there was a way I can be of any help. So I started focusing my talents in this direction and one night I saw a female die, another night about three weeks after I saw someone else die and then I recognized the building. It was the state capital of Rhode Island. CNN had a story that day about the same building in which murder actually occurred.

She went on and said she saw a beautiful woman drive off a cliff. At that, comment agent Davis winced and fidgeted in his chair. She immediately took notice and quickly pointed out another murder that took place in a busy office building, with blood everywhere. I think the office building and the Statehouse was the same incident. I found it strange that the victim wasn't scared at first and it seemed as if he knew his attacker. Another man died at the hands of the same Killer I think. He was possibly someone who did things for people, someone who helps people. Agent Davis thought to himself, Dr. Jonathan Fischer from Brookline.

Lisa Cates talked for almost 2 hours trying to convince agent Davis to allow her to help him this unusually difficult case. Agent Davis said to her that all the people she mentioned had that fit all the profiles. He didn't admit it but he felt just a little shaken by her. He decided to confide in her and said, to your question earlier the answer is yes. Yes what? She said with a curious look, there is in fact something we found. I knew it! She said and sat up at the edge of his seat. So does this mean I can help she asked? The day was over in a hurry. Lisa Cates was sworn into the investigation. Agent Davis dropped her off at the same hotel as before and then he moved into his own condominium finally. He went straight home and fell instantly asleep in his newly refinished bedroom.

The good Captain Said to Bob! That redoing a room in your house is a sign of closure, or at the very least, it's a positive step in the right direction as far as moving on. Could it be possible that there is also a new woman in his life?

Lisa took a hot bubble bath once she checked back into her hotel room. She was going over in her mind what transpired over the last few hours as she soaked up the steamy bubbles. Explaining her experiences about her psychic abilities always seemed to drain her of her energy and she quickly fell asleep after her bath.

A couple of weeks go by. Agent Davis and Lisa Cates have been on first name basis. There's an obvious attraction emanating in the air. It's like an electric current passing through them no matter where they are.

Lisa had the pleasure of meeting Bob's brother last week. Bob had told her it was only special people who actually get to meet him. It would be my pleasure she said. She said he's cute and got along just superbly and he then felt a little awkward. His brother never talked to anyone like this. In a way it was nice because Bob really liked Lisa. There is no doubt that Dale liked Lisa the moment he saw her. There was no usual shyness. Bob was simply a maze. Dale has never taken to anyone this easily before Agent Davis took Capt. Adams up on his offer and they got together. Bob told the captain. One evening last week Lisa and I were having dinner at my place with my brother Dale. I was in my kitchen preparing a salad when I overheard Dale repeat the commercial on the television for the hamburger joint Burger King. He was saying have it your way, have it your way, have it your Way. That was okay because he's known for repeating popular slogans. The unusual thing that I didn't understand was when Lisa broke in and finished the slogan by saying: at Burger King. My brother's face lit right up, his eyebrows were raised and he actually smiled at her. I couldn't believe it. I was shocked. Why so ask Capt. Adams? Dale never responds to anyone. Even the doctors and nurses still have a difficult time interacting with him and he's known them for years. He immediately responded to Lisa. That's when I was absolutely positive that there's something special about her. It sounds almost like a fairytale the Capt. Said. Maybe she can help him in some positive way that his doctors are not aware of. Maybe?

Lisa Cates and Bob Davis were fallen in love and why not. They were extremely attracted to each other. They were both single with no children. He was in law enforcement and she loved working in the same field helping the police with her psychic abilities. It was practically a match made in heaven. He still had lingering feelings of Paula, but he was indeed trying to get on with his life.

Carlton Van Helsang leaves work early one day, if you want to call signing autographs work. He chooses not to drive home today because it was a 45 minute ride. He surmises it was a little too long a ride for him because he was absolutely exhausted and also feeling a bit queasy from a taco he had eaten at lunch time. Carlton uses his transport invention to get home. He's used to the tingling sensation his skin gets from transporting.

To Carlton's unexpected surprise, he catches a burglary in progress at his home. It's what he thinks is happening or maybe it's a dog somehow running around. Surely it wasn't Felix and Lassie making a ruckus like that upstairs. He listens quietly and hears a scuffling of footsteps. Carlton's reaction is nothing short of astonishment from this intrusion. He is angrily bewildered.

The burglar, Glenn Choi you heard sounds emanating from downstairs. Now he's unexpectedly puzzled. He stood perfectly still for a moment. I checked out the entire house in every room was empty he thought. I staked it out for three weeks; maybe it's a housekeeper or something as he looks out the window. That's weird he said to himself, there's no car in the driveway or on the street. What the hell is going on here?

This guy lived alone and left the house each morning precisely at 6:30 AM and not once returned before 7:30

PM. Even now his car is nowhere in sight. What the hell went wrong? He was trying to think as panic was starting to consume his mind. Am I stoned?

It's not as if Carlton has a real job with consistency. He was signing autographs and it was just a temporary thing, he felt sick and wanted to go home.

Carlton is a big man, he is not excessively tall at about 6 feet even but he does tip the scales upwards of 225 pounds. He in fact does look somewhat intimidate. After all he was a football star college.

In a brave attempt Carlton grabs hold of a fireplace poker; it's the nearest weapon he can find. He instantaneously appears directly in front of this stranger in his house by using his transport invention. Carlton feels he's armed adequately enough to fight off this crazy intruder. He was furious that someone even had the gumption to break into his house in the first place. He wasn't thinking clearly, he didn't know whether or not the burglar has a weapon, maybe a knife or worse a gun. In his haste he felt he was armed adequately enough. After all if things get too crazy and out of hand he could easily and quickly disappear with the use of his transporter machine.

The burglar, a Mr. Glenn Choi was caught completely off guard. He was actually frozen in time. If it were a movie clip it would have been deemed a comedy. It was kind of like someone taken a picture.

Carlton and Glenn Choi struggled for what seemed like an eternity but in actuality was only mere seconds. Glenn was also a large man and they traded blows. Carlton was healthier and much stronger than his opponent but Glenn had the element of excitement on his side. Glenn actually narrowly escapes with what looked to be minor bruises. It was a fierce struggle. Carlton painly bangs his head up against a frame of a door and was woozy for a moment. Glenn saw his chance to escape and ran for the back door and when she came. Carlton slowly picks up his fireplace poker and roughly plops down onto the soft leather couch Panton, with short gulps of air. Then he dozed off due to a blow to the side of his head. There was a small trickle of blood at his temple.

Carlton wakes up abruptly after 40 minutes of soundful sleep. He quickly jumps to his feet noticing a painful throb on the side of his head. Scared for a moment from recent events he realizes the noise that just awoke him was the newspaper hitting the front door to his home. He ran to a window and seeing the newspaper carrier driving towards the next home in his familiar Ford Taurus,

Carlton turns around from his window and quickly scans his immediate surroundings. He realized just how that he briefly fell asleep or passed out was more accurate, after his desperate encounter with some crazed stranger and his own home. Now I'm feeling a little sicker as his stomach started churning. He remembered the days he had in college when he last held a toilet. He got up and rinsed his mouth and looked himself over in the mirror. He looked okay except for the small pump at his temple and his ashen complexion from vomiting.

Carlton thought about calling the police as he left his bathroom. With the telephone in his hand he decided against getting anyone else involved. No reports or questions, even the neighbors won't be warned. He felt wrong about the neighbors but stood firm in his decision. They should be warned somehow that someone's breaking into homes in the neighborhood he thought.

As he walks back into the room where the fight took place he spots something on the floor by an overturned end table. Carlton picks up the strange looking wallet, not his of course. He proceeds to go through it, investigate it. He notices how cheaply made it is and thought to himself. I would never buy something so shabby, there seems to be only three items inside, a piece of paper with the name Poppy on it and a phone number beside it, a cheaply made latex condom and a foil packet and the third item was significantly more interesting. It was a picture identification card. A Connecticut liquor ID, complete with a home address. Carlton couldn't believe his good fortune considering his current circumstances. He immediately comes to a desperate conclusion.

What happens next only took a second Carlton thought, but in his mind's eye it seemed like an eternity... Dr. Jekyll appeared and put him in an hypnotic trance. Glenn Choi of Kempton Connecticut will pay for breaking into my home; he will pay dearly Carlton thought.

Carlton cleaned up his house and stood home for the rest of the day wondering if Mr. Choi would dare to come back. The next day seemed to take forever to come. It was Monday morning and he decided to call in a big favor to the mayor's office. After all he was well-liked by the governor. He said he had a request to make. Someone was inquiring about a job working for me at my home and I'm not sure who to turn to for some information on him. Would it be possible for you to help me? His name is Mr. Glenn Choi and he said he was from Kempton Connecticut. It was a small lie and no one would beg to differ. It was a young lady named Nancy Ward; he talked with her over the phone.

She had attended both parties held in Carlton's honor at the governor's mansion and was more than happy to be of assistance to him. She insisted on meeting him for lunch the next day, that way she would give him the information he requested. He smiled to himself and accepted her bold invitation. He can remember how pretty and stylish she was, and remembers having a pleasant conversation with her at both parties. He recalls that it did seem like she was interested in him and maybe even liked him and now it was evident he thought. Okay Nancy, I look forward to tomorrow, have a fine day and thank you. See you soon she said, and then hung up the telephone.

It was a dreary afternoon. The morning news reported rain in the forecast but that didn't stop Nancy from meeting up with Carlton for lunch. The truth was she did find him interesting and also thought he was attractive. They got together at a small café called the Back Bay bistro. Carlton was already seated and recognized her the moment she walked through the door. Now that he got a good look at her he noticed she was an extremely good-looking woman. She had long straight black hair and was wearing a designer business suit. She had great legs he thought. She smiled at him, as she approached closer like she owned the place.

Hello Carlton, have you been here long? Hello, no not at all. I just got here as a matter of fact. Well then shall we get the business out of the way first, I famished she said. Sounds swell to me Carlton said. Nancy gracefully sat down and said; I received a fax late yesterday afternoon from a friend who owed me a favor. It confirms Mr. Glenn Choi's address. I don't think he's a good candidate for higher, I might be so bold to add. Oh... My source tells me he's a petty thief and a drug addict. She picked up a buffalo wing from Carlton's plate and took a bite out of it. Carlton just looked at her and was amused. He decided right there on the spot that he liked her. As she chewed her chicken wing she went on to say that Glenn Choi supports his habit by hustling in the streets. Carlton is smiling now. She stops and asks him why a you smiling at me? I like the way you tell a story he said. What you mean? I'm enjoying watching you wave that Buffalo wing around with such enthusiasm and animation. She abruptly stopped, her shoulders slumped and she shrunk in her chair and embarrassment, then she smiled and said I like you too.

She went on to say he also does petty thefts such as shoplifting in supermarkets and department stores. He was no stranger to the inside of a jail. All in all it was a very pleasant lunch. Carlton and Nancy both had a wonderful time catching up despite the gloomy day outside. He made plans for lunch again the same date next week and this time it wasn't the business.

Glenn Choi like most unfortunate drug addicts was a product of his environment. He grew up in the slums of Boston Massachusetts in the infamous combat zone, and later on had moved to Connecticut. Glenn's parents were drug addicts and thieves themselves. Glenn was destined to become his parents and he did his very best in that quest. Glenn Choi had no other family; in fact he himself was a mistake and was told so more than once.

He did have many outside influences though. When he was from there were many gangs. Boston was no different from any other city in America. Chinatown was next door to the combat zone and they too had their own problems with gang bangers, and it was these kinds of people who had a major influence in Glenn Choi's life. Glenn mainly stayed in the E St. projects. Most good-natured people don't walk these streets at night.

Pimps are running prostitution rings; they have no conscious when it comes to their girls. They refer to them as mere merchandise. They are considered commodities, its business they say. Even though it's illegal, it is what it is! Certain pimps say most of the women and girls are just castaways. They are society's misfits and are treated according to their so-called status. Most of them are controlled by substance abuse and are ignorant in the ways of sobriety. Cross-dressers and transvestites all working the streets together when the sun goes down with reckless abandon. Next door Chinatown is a whole different world by itself, and a whole other story.

The C.J.I.S.(Criminal Justice information services) is now connected to every law enforcement computer in the country. Even the smallest hick towns are now available with instant access. All they need is a Social Security number and in many cases just a birthday is sufficient. This was a follow-up call from Nancy's assistant that Carlton had received on his answering machine at home. The police voice said to ask for a profile for a potential employee. Work related of course the voice said. Have a pleasant day Mr. Van Helsang.

In the Johnston Rhode Island Police Department, detective's gunny Ferreira and gunny Cote were still working diligently on their own murder cases. They are both trying to be a step of head of the FBI. It's now after 7 PM and newly appointed homicide detective Cote suggests dinner. I know a restaurant nearby where we can get a home-cooked meal. Is that so? A retired Navy chief owns it, it's got military memorabilia everywhere, and you might like it. The service sucks and the food reminds me of the mess hall back in Cherry point. The Chiefs always got a story to tell though. You could say he's kind of like us, an old goat with 26 into Uncle Sam.

Gunny Ferreira replied, oorah old buddy. Let's move out! Double-time leatherneck. Smiling now he says; Sir! Yes Sir, Gunny Ferreira said; hey! I work for a living Marine so don't you dare call me sir! They looked at each other, stood at attention, saluted sloppily and laughed. Boy oh boy, haven't done that in years, it was fun. Yeah the memories it brings back are great. Are you ready for some chow or what?

Agent Bob Davis and psychic Lisa Cates were enjoying the ocean breezes aboard the ferry out of Woods Hole in Massachusetts. Their plan was to spend the day at Martha's Vineyard. Lisa has read stories about the islands having dealings to do with the Kennedys and more recently the Clintons. The mystique surrounding the island with the fishermen disappearing from time to time intrigued her. Some old folklore of sea monsters when she was a youngster in school made her young imagination run wild and now as an adult she was finally getting a chance to experience the island for herself firsthand.

They got there early at the dock in Edgartown. There was an excitement in her eyes that exhilarated me, Bob thought. We both watched the ferry slowly come to a stop. Seemed like the whole new world, a totally different country. She turned to Bob and gave him a surprise light kiss on the cheek and said; shall we. Yes ma'am. They walked off the ferry onto the dock hand-in-hand eager to explore. Bob rented two mopeds from a small weather worn shack and they started their own tour of the island. Bob knew his way around the island from being there a few times for business and a few more times for pleasure, so it's natural for him to take the lead.

Lisa always wanted to sample everything especially New England's famous clam chowder. But first they cruised the island on their mopeds. They rolled past vineyard Haven and then oak bluffs. Bob pointed out where the Clintons stood when they came to the island. Their next stop was a beach outside of Edgartown. They pulled their mopeds up by the sand off the side of the road. There was a small gray weathered shack similar to the one where they rented their mopeds. It was surrounded by beautiful white sand. Seagulls were in the air begging for scraps and the ocean was splashing off the reefs. It was so mesmerizing and exhilarating both at the same time. I love the smell of the ocean Lisa said. So do I. I wonder what it's like to live here. So do I. They walked hand-in-hand towards the shack. They only sell four items, fried clams, clam cakes, French fries and the best New England clam chowder on the East Coast.

Bob was not about to deprive the new lady in his life her heart's desire. One clam chowder he barks from the takeout window and winks at Lisa, then orders fried clams and we might as well splurge Lisa says and looks at the girl in the window whose zestfully yells, French fries too please, why not Bob says.

Lisa awoke him out of his deep despair. He still misses Paula and wondered if he was doing the right thing now by seeing the lovely Miss Lisa Cates. Quickly he dismissed the thought. It just feels so right! He was watching her walk off towards the white sand; she was smiling as she laid out a blanket and got her taste buds ready. She's wonderful he thought. After he paid the bill he joined her on blanket. They sat opposite each other. Lisa had her cup of clam chowder and he had the fried clams and clam cakes. This is delicious she said, it's everything I thought it would be, and then she winced when she saw Bob splash some vinegar and salt on his own meal. What the world are you doing she said? He smiled and said this is how we do it in New England. She was silent a moment, just watching him. Don't knock it till you try it he said... Okay. I'm game she said.

She felt really good about being with Bob. She usually can read someone's intentions and getting into their minds, but he was different, and it was a delectable feeling. Lisa liked him very much and not being able to read his mind was an absolute bonus. It wasn't uncommon not to be able to read a person, it actually happens from time to time. But this time it was a person she really liked and cared for. There was an aura of spontaneity surrounding this relationship and she found it exhilarating.

Lisa tried Bob's fried clams and her eyes instantly lit up. She really never tasted anything so good. She wanted her own order. Bob was smiling while watching her eat. He was really enjoying her company. They hung around the beach a while walking together on the edge of the water. Their jeans rolled up and their shoes and socks off. They watched the sunset and then reluctantly drove back to the ferry; they were having a splendid time. They didn't want to leave but they had to pick up Dale that night because it was his weekend to stay over.

When all three of them finally got home to Bob's condo, Bob found himself feeling a little jealous of Lisa for a brief moment. He was sitting in his kitchen thinking about how Dale went straight over to Lisa as he was escorted into the lobby of his building. A frown came over him as he replayed it in his mind, quickly replaced by a genuine smile.

Dale has never taken to anybody the way he's taking to Lisa. Even his doctors were unexpectedly surprised. They all drove to Bob's home listening to some music on the car radio. Bob drove by a Plaza, a small used car lot and then when he rode past this huge Chevy dealership Dale started up. He was staring out the window repeating the famous slogan," like a rock", "like a rock".

Bob found out quite a bit more about Lisa that afternoon. She told him about her being an accomplished ballet dancer when she was younger and how she came close to almost doing it for a living, if it wasn't for a broken ankle Bob smiled. Bob had a feeling she worked out somehow because he could see it in her legs whenever she wore a skirt or a short dress. Lisa had dancer's muscles; he noticed long ago how shapely her legs were as she glided effortlessly when she walked.

Before they went home they pulled their car into a plaza and parked at the market. All three of them exited the vehicle and went into the store for some of their favorite snacks. Next door was a video store where they picked up a comedy movie to watch at home. When they got home Lisa and Dale made the popcorn, actually Lisa made the popcorn and Dale just watched with a childlike enthusiasm. Bob set the movie in the VCR and straightened out the living room. They all got comfortable and watched the movie.

The night was still relatively young. It was only 10 PM and the movie is now over. Dale has gone to bed long ago. Out of nowhere Lisa came over towards Bob on the couch and kissed him gently on the lips. Her heart longed for him but him mind wanted to object. He was different and she wanted him. She was so used to reading the minds of people, so when it came to relationships she got frustrated quickly; always know in what was next. Bob was mysterious and she knew he was the one. She was unaccustomed to this feeling, but she loved it just the same. Bob cocked and eyebrow and looked at her when she whispered into his ear, let's go to bed honey

They undressed each other in the bedroom. Bob took total control and she let him. He gently teased her nipples and she was instantly catapulted into a sensational feeling of deep passion. It's been such a long time since a man touched her. She quivered with excitement as he hugged her tightly. He could feel her taut nipples try to pierce through her delicate chemise. She wanted him right now. Her breasts were firm and sensitive. She trembled with excitement anticipating his next move wanting and needing more; he removed her chemise and tossed it onto the floor. His mouth was soft and moist as he explored her entire naked body. The inside of his hand caressed her inner thighs, he felt intense heat as his hand moved upward, she dug her nails into his muscular shoulders the closer he came to her brazen oven. She was aching for his mouth. As he kissed her hard she pushed him away with all her might and with as much power her arms could muster she guided his head slowly downward. He wasn't about to deny her or himself for that matter. He lavishly took her pleasure and she arched her back moaning. Her muscular legs were wrapped around his shoulders as his hands were squeezing her tight round behind. His mouth was masterfully working on her most Secret treasure.

She was floating, sinking into oblivion with his soft hot lips. She had heavy cat eyes and her voice was husky when she moaned reaching climax. Oh my God she said, I never felt so good in my entire life. She lay in his arms at the curve of his shoulder. I feel so wonderful and sighed.

I'm going to jump in the shower honey, you can join me if you like she said. No thanks, I'm not used to this kind of activity so I think I'll rest up a bit but I will definitely take a rain check. She walked to the bathroom naked and as he watched her he started to get aroused again. She's gorgeous he's said to himself. She smiled at him as she left the bedroom. As he lay there he contemplated what their future would be like and then he heard her singing in the shower. He was at such peace with himself and he knew he loved her.

While drying off from her a hot shower she suddenly had an unsettling vision. She hurried back into the bedroom. I need to tell you something Bob. What's that? He said unexpectedly. He sits up and puts on his boxer shorts and then gives her his undivided attention. She describes the nature of her vision to him, as she's talking to him she carefully watches his expressions. He looks sincerely interested she thought. You've actually seen an address he said; his voice was loud with excitement. Yes! She said. She went on to say that nothing has happened yet, I did see a clock on a table with blue electronic lettering and it read 12:01 PM.

The next day FBI agent Bob Davis and psychic Lisa Cates drove to Kempton Connecticut. They arrived at the same address that she seen in her dream. They anxiously knocked on the door and discovered it was already ajar, so they both entered cautiously.

Bob has his weapon drawn and told Lisa to stay behind him as they tiptoed through the doorway. A man in a dark cape was standing over another man ready to strike him with a shiny chrome or silver instrument, they were too far away for us to make it out but we also instinctively knew we had to act fast.

Bob not over a knickknack in his haste to stop the assault and in turn the culprit heard the loud noise and in the next instant the attacker fled the scene, and eat just disappeared around the corner. He vanished, just like that. While agent Davis went after the assailant, Lisa was helping the would-be victim. Agent Davis came back to the scene of the assault and met up with Lisa all out of breath, and just looked at her mesmerized for what seemed like eternity when in fact was only mere seconds. Don't ask me how he said as she looked up at him from a crouched position, he's gone without a trace! What! She said looking at him with her head tilted to one side, what you mean disappeared. Agent Davis and Lisa were both stunned and confused, never mind that the intended victim felt he was going insane. His name was going to and he was absolutely petrified. Who the hell are you he said to them?

Who are you the Ghostbusters is something? My name is agent Bob Davis and this is my partner Lisa Cates. What the hell do you want? Now take it easy Mr. Choi. I believe we just saved your life. What! Did you see what he looked like Lisa asked? No! I didn't, did you?

Not one of them could give a description except for the fact that he was wearing a ski mask and black gloves. Agent Davis then asked Mr. Choi if you want to make a report. Did you see someone? Glenn Choi asked! Yes I did. Did he just vanish into thin air he asked? I'm not sure agent Davis said. I think he did? Now! Do you want to make a damn report? Huh? Agent Davis and Lisa both looked at Mr. Choi in silence. The room went suddenly silent.

Glenn Choi asked again with some arrogance in his voice this time. What are you doing here in my home and who the hell are you again? He didn't get their names the first time, Understandable with all the commotion that just took place. What the hell is happening?

I'm FBI agent Davis and this lady is my ah...my partner, her name is detective Cate's. She is a bona fide psychic and she's the one you can thank. Thank you for what? Glenn said with astonishment as he was get an up off the floor. I'm actually her back up today and it looks like she was correct about the vision she just had recently. I do believe she just saved your life. Now Bob was mad. You need to thank her Mr.! What the Fu... Glenn Choi said.

Glenn Choi softened his attitude slightly as he realized agent Davis was getting hot under the collar, and besides he was much bigger than him. What you mean a vision Glenn said? Yes, Lisa said. I saw you and your home. I saw the street and the number on the mailbox you were looking at. She looked to her left and said, that's probably one of the bills over there on the floor. To prove her point she said, I one of those bills from red horse oil company. Suddenly Glenn's eyes grew wide and he just looked at her not answering. She walked over to him and asked him if he was okay. He's never been so scared in his entire life; he was pale and visibly shook. He backed away from Lisa then agent Davis picked up the white envelope and was beyond amazed. He was flabbergasted. How did you? He said and stopped himself.

Agent Davis read the envelope out loud. Red horse Oil Company. I told you so Lisa said. Thank your lucky stars Mr. Choi, he is proof she really did save your life. No report was made. No one would believe it anyway so agent Davis and Lisa Cates left Mr. Choi's house handed him a business card, call us if you have any more trouble. When they both got home that night, the sitter for Dale went home and they held each other tightly for the rest of the night, in silence.

Later on that same night it's 1:30 AM and Dale Davis is sitting up in bed yelling out loud mother-of-pearl repeatedly, he was rocking in place back and forth like a robot. Mother-of-pearl, mother-of-pearl, rocking, rocking, yelling.

Simultaneously Lisa happens to be leaving the bathroom. Suddenly she experiences another startling vision, a most startling revelation indeed. Knowing full well that she's safe in Bob's home! a murder flashes across her mind! She has to sit down because she was already very tired. She chose to sit on the floor outside the bathroom door as the vivid details of this vision played out in her mind. Her energy always gets drained from her body when her visions occur, she surmised this for years that she had to give something to get something, but right now she was already exhausted from a busy day and was half asleep sitting on the floor in an old buttoned down T-shirt from Bob. She knew she had to concentrate to keep the vision from dissipating. The culprit slashes his victim with what looks like a straight razor, the kind used in old barbershops. It could even be some type of surgical scalpel. She noticed it had a colored handle, it was white and it was a rather large instrument. Blood was gushing from the victim as she realized who it was; she was looking right into the face of Mr. Glenn Choi himself. It was as if the murderer's eyes and her eyes were one in the same. She proceeds to walk that to the bedroom where Bob was fast asleep and probably still smiling from tonight's lovemaking. As she's tiptoeing, she hesitantly looks into the guestroom when she heard something. She observes Dale rocking back and forth in bed obsessively. He was shaking and sweating, he looked terrified, and he was white as a ghost. My immediate thought was he must have had a bad dream. Then I heard him repeat, mother-of-pearl, mother-of-pearl etc...

It was at this split-second of time that I thought he had the gift also. It kind of made sense how we became friends almost instantly and now this. I think he seen the same vision that I just saw. I know from reading that people with autism are regarded with an unusually high intelligence but also are incapable of tying it altogether into specific understandable performances. This has to be the reason we clicked right away. She thought about waking up Bob but decided against it. I'll tell him first thing in the morning she thought. I might even be able to help Dale with his acute condition and his emotional paralysis.

The two Rhode Island detectives, those world war two hell hounds, gunny Ferreira and gunny Cote left the chief and his restaurant both amusingly satisfied. Gunny Ferreira said to his friend that the Globe and anchor rest rock has a new customer. I can't wait to take my wife here, she loves military memorabilia. I'm glad you liked it gunny Cote said. How about a game of pool at the hub pool room for old time sake? Why not. I'd love to kick your ass at a game of pool. Smiling, Cote replies; yeah okay ha ha. You must be suffering from long term memory loss then he guffawed. Gunny Ferreira didn't know his old friend turned into a professional billiards player years ago.

As the two Marines drove towards their favorite billiards room, gunny Cote says; I've been given it a lot of thought you know. What's that Harry says? I've been thinking about retiring and maybe even writing a book. Sounds like a plan gunny Ferreira said. In Fact I've been contemplating retirement myself. Both of us have about the same amount of time in, and besides the Marine Corps 20 years, I've got 16 years in the police force Cote said. I know exactly how you're feeling. I've got 15 years in the force. My wife's been hinting about warmer weather, either Florida or maybe Arizona. I'll be sure to let you know what happens. Gunny Ferreira found a parking place right in front of the entrance to the poolroom. He shuts the car off and said; are you ready chump? I mean champ. Oh yeah, you'll pay for that one jar head.

Before the police could further interrogate Mr. Glenn Choi, he had checked himself into the 'living clean" detox. He vowed never to use drugs and alcohol ever again. He was really shocked by the bizarre and unnerving events that had recently taken place. He was scared to death. He summarized his experience as a bloodcurdling and hair-raising event. It finally dawned on him that he absolutely must stop using drugs!

Drugs and the streets. It's a suppressed lifestyle and it's not so simple to be rid of it. Glenn Choi truly believed he was going crazy and attributed it to the many years of abusing his body and mind with drugs. All kinds of drugs, anything he could get his hands on. He didn't care what it was or what it did to him, even if it was something he never heard of before. He took it and suffered its wrath. He swore a ghost miraculously appeared right before his very eyes. He never did say anything about it to the FBI agent or to his female partner. If he did they would really think he was nuts and maybe even section him into a mental institution. If it wasn't for the FBI man and that lady psychic, I might be dead right now he thought.

Mr. Glenn Choi was in the steamy hot showers at the detox. He was trying to wash away his fears and get ready for a secure and peaceful night's sleep when all of a sudden his body went cold and rigid with an undeniable fear. His heart pounded like a trip hammer, he was oblivious to any other sound except his own intense heartbeat. His eyes were acutely focused and his expression was completely twisted. His mouth opened but no sound emitted. It's the same ghost. An identifiable blackness suddenly shrouded the entire room.

A third shift male nurse, his nickname was "flip" he had long wavy black hair, a pock marked face and a small scar next to the cleft on his chin found a man face down and naked in the shower room of the living clean detox. The man was lying in a pool of his own blood.

The head nurse on duty was in her office when flip entered. We got another one he said to her. What he you mean she said without looking up from her desk? Another one, he said again and gave her a sideways crooked glance. She stopped what she was doing, looked at flip and said; not again! That's the third one this month.

The police arrived and questioned Flip. Was there anyone up and about? Is all he said? It's been a routine occurrence here lately. The head nurse explained that suicide is the only option many of these people see. Their lives are so screwed up from drugs they can't bear all of life's problems when they finally get clean, because, it all hits them like a sledgehammer or a ton of bricks. This is a depressing result but it's also a clear reality. Sometimes it's worse, how can it be worse, one of the cops said? Sometimes they don't do it right and end up as invalids or vegetables. What you mean do it right? Yeah, you can overdose, or do some bad drugs, anything really. In all the years I've been working here, I have never seen anyone go out like this before. The male nurse Flip Pauli Culhane worked at the living clean detox for over seven years. He himself was a recovering drug addict who's been clean and sober now for more than eight years.

The morning newspapers headlined; another spine chilling murder. It looks to be the work of the New England serial killer again, or maybe it's a copycat. A team of scientists is working out the details and confirmation should be made sometime this afternoon.

Glenn Choi of Kempton Connecticut was found in the bathroom of a medical treatment center called; The Living Clean detox. It's a facility for people to learn how to live a life without the use of drugs and alcohol. It has a 50% success rate, which is actually a high percentage compared to most treatment facilities like this one.

The captain of the Cambridge Police Department showed the USA today newspaper article to FBI agent Bob Davis. He was visibly shocked. He immediately told the captain about his visit the other day with the psychic woman (now his girlfriend) Lisa Cates.

This isn't good the captain said. I hope we're making progress. Everyone from the mayor's office to the governor's office is extremely concerned, and the media is causing a panic among the public. Even the sales from restaurants and department stores have drastically declined as a direct result of this serial killer. He must be stopped! The captain shouted simultaneously banging the desk in front of him with his fist.

Did you all get the report of the other victim Danny Evans? This man died in New Hampshire only the day before the last one. The killer seems to be able to get around with supersonic speed. And to top it all off he never leaves a trace of tangible evidence. Again, I say; he must be stopped! And stopped now!

The second-floor office of the Cambridge Police Department had an entire wall covered with information of each and every victim and location. There were pictures on top of pictures. Although the department was fully modernized with computers at all types of electronic devices and equipment, agent Davis wanted to be able to see everything all at once on a larger scale than a computer monitor.

So far the only clue that tied all these people together was the fact that every one of them was injected with a very old hallucinogen, the drug called "Datura".

This particular drug is no longer manufactured and hasn't been for over a century. The laboratories are doing everything they can to minimize and identify the particular ingredients in which is used to produce this distinguished drug. Once all the ingredients are isolated, a follow up investigation will take place on all manufacturers of these individual ingredients, particularly pharmaceutical companies that normally associate with these particular elements. Once this is done, we might be able to find who's purchasing this stuff and with a little luck maybe, just maybe it'll produce a lead.

As Special Agent Davis is explaining what's happening and what he wants done, a young pimple faced rookie police officer enters the room with a smile on his face. Happy to be a part of the new investigation team. He's holding a box of assorted. doughnuts and another box of assorted cold pizza. He rudely interrupts everyone by yelling out loud" anyone hungry"? He then looks at the victim's wall for the briefest of moments as he places the snacks on a table and says; well, would just look at that! Everyone in the office is speechless and surprisingly shocked at the gual of this young kid. Policeman or not. They've all looked up at the victim's wall as they've done 100s of times before, wondering what's up with this rookie. The acne ridden police officer says; aloud "Jack's back! Immediately as he enters the room, then he quietly pauses and dismisses it as probably just a coincidence.

- Gertrude Steele, Johnston RI.
- Barbara Helsang, Andover Ma.
- Eugene Banks, Cambridge Ma.
- Glenda Walker, Killington VT.
- James Welch, Situate RI. JACK'SBACK
- Johnathon Fischer, Brookline MA.
- Paula Robertson, Augusta ME
- Danny Evans, Concord NH.
- Glenn Choi, Kempton Ct.

A coincidence agent Davis repeated! What? What did you say? Yells agent Davis! The kids visibly scared now, not knowing if he did something wrong. I didn't say anything, what you want, some pizza or doughnuts? No I don't want pizza or doughnuts. You! What did you just say? Jack's back? What you mean by that agent Davis said? Now the rookie isn't feeling so scared. He said; look here. I'll circle all the letters you have on your board. It's kind of like one of those paintings were if you focus your eyes you can see a hidden message.

Is it just a coincidence or is it a real clue Lisa asks. The first letter of every city when combined in order of each murder spells out two words; (Jack's back) the room actually got deathly quiet. It was an eerie feeling. Everyone just looked at one another with twisted looks of surprise on their faces and mouths agape.

Then everyone started talking all at once. What does this mean one person blurted? Another said; Jack's back huh. Another said yeah, maybe Jack the Ripper? Another person said that Jack the Ripper does sound appropriate. Isn't the drug Daturagen the same drug the notorious Jack the Ripper used in London England? I do think I read that somewhere or maybe watched something about it on the Discovery Channel. I think I might have seen the same show agent Davis said. He told everyone in the office to check it out including the rookie responsible for discovering this possible development. One of the officers in the room was something of a history buff. Officer Joe Pavao added that, legend says that the notorious Jack the Ripper might have had an extensive knowledge of medicine, specializing in surgery. Didn't a few of his victims have missing organs? Yes they did someone blurted out with astonishment! In fact, one of them was missing an arm. Okay, okay let's not get too carried away with this said agent Davis. Like I said earlier, let's check it out a little more closely and maybe we can find something and maybe we won't. There was a low rumble of voices as agent Davis left the room. That's all we need he mumbled to himself, a copycat killer portraying Jack the Ripper.

Over six months have passed and all is well. There hasn't been another murder associated with this same killer since. That's the good news, the bad news is that he's still out there somewhere lurking about. He could even be in your own peaceful neighborhood. A prominent member of society? Someone children look up to. It's an unsolved case soon to be stored away like so many others. All we can do is hope he doesn't surface again.

The goodness in Carlton prevails. He was born and raised as the good son of the late renowned scientist Dr. Charles Van Helsang. Despite the fact only known to him, that he was cloned from the DNA of the late Jack the ripper. He did his best to turn his life around. Carlton packed up some of his belongings and moved out West. He wanted to get away from New England and start fresh in sunny California. A slew of classified information leaked out into the media over the past few months. It was an awful time in New England. Headlines in the newspapers read: Jack the Ripper, has he eerily resurfaced? It took months for it all to stop. It was a slow process but the public was time to resume their normal activities.

Carlton is absolutely 100% content these days. He made all the people in his past that hurt him pay the ultimate price. Through the help of his invention he was able to sneak up on his victims without a trace of evidence. Now, like his great great grandfather he must stop and preserve his legacy. Another 100 years will pass he thought, and still no one will solve the Van Helsang Secrets.

the end